Game
Set
Match

A DI Jack Allan Mystery

Book 2

By C G Penne

'Game, Set, Match'

Copyright © C G Penne 2025 –

All rights reserved

The right of C G Penne to be identified as

the author of this work has been asserted in accordance with

Section 77 and 78 of the

Copyright Designs and Patents Act 1988

All the characters in this book are fictitious

and any resemblance to

actual persons, living or dead,

is purely coincidental

Other books by C G Penne:

<u>Novels:</u>

Raw Heritage

Climatic Crisis

<u>DI Jack Allan series:</u>

Deadly Decision (Book 1)

<u>Short Stories:</u>

Never Assume and Other Stories

It Started with the Milk

Hidden Intent

For Adrian

Prologue

It was Thursday 18th February 2021 and the British Airways flight to Heathrow became a harrowing experience for many of the passengers as the plane came into land. With winds gusting at fifty-five miles per hour, the pilot needed all his skills to meet the challenge. The wings of the aircraft were tilting alarmingly first one way and then the other. Some passengers were screaming, others were staring in front of them with terrified expressions, gripping the arms of their seats so hard that the whites of their knuckles were showing. A couple of passengers had been hyperventilating and were now using oxygen masks. Even the cabin crew's faces were strained and drained of colour.

Sitting in the front row of the aircraft was a man in his early thirties. He had a shock of blonde hair and would have been deemed good looking by most if it hadn't been for the cold, supercilious expression on his face. He seemed totally unconcerned by what was going on around him or indeed by the prospect of a crash landing and possible death. He was looking out of the window but his mind was obviously focussed on his thoughts.

The wheels crashed onto the tarmac; one wing lower than the other but the plane righted itself sufficiently at the last moment. The pilot managed to line up the plane enough to land, if not smoothly, safely, and the big steel bird finally came to a stop.

Some of the passengers burst into tears with the sheer relief, others clapped and cheered. When the seatbelt signs had been switched off and the announcement made that passengers could disembark shortly, there was a round of applause for the captain and crew. Gathering their belongings, the passengers formed a queue to exit the aircraft and the doors opening, the unperturbed young man who was in the front, led the way. He politely thanked the cabin crew with a charming but insincere smile as he made his way off the plane.

Having collected his suitcase from baggage reclaim, the young man went over to the Europcar car rental kiosk. The necessary paperwork completed, he donned his aviator sunglasses and made his way out of the airport. He quickly found the bay where his car had been parked, a nondescript grey coloured estate. Having keyed an address into the satnav, he drove off.

It would be well over an hour before he reached his destination. Sitting back in the seat, he turned the radio on and started to think about what lay ahead. He congratulated himself that he had allowed adequate time for arrangements to be made thus ensuring his plan would be faultless.

He wanted revenge and nothing was going to stop him achieving his goal. He would make them pay. They thought they could fuck up his life. Well, he was going to show them that no-one messed with him and got away with it. After he had enjoyed the satisfaction of making them suffer, he was free to achieve whatever he wanted in life. Upon this reflection, a cruel smile spread across his handsome face.

Chapter 1

It was the evening of Wednesday 3rd March. Lily Anderson turned the key in her front door and let herself in. It was pouring with rain and she was drenched. Her car had gone in for service and she had had to take the bus to and from work. On top of this she had forgotten to take her umbrella and her long hair was hanging in sodden strands down the sides of her face. She couldn't wait to get into a nice, warm shower, pop a ready meal lasagne in the microwave and wash it down with a glass of chilled Pinot Grigio.

Closing the door, she picked up the post from the mat. Nothing of any interest there. A couple of statements and advertising leaflets. She threw them on the hall table and took off her jacket, hanging it up to dry on one of the pegs on the wall.

Going upstairs she pulled off her clothes and stepped into the shower allowing the hot water to cascade down her face and over her body. She smiled, enjoying the relaxing feeling the sensation gave her. After a few minutes, turning the tap off, she opened the shower door and reached for her towelling robe.

Padding downstairs again, she put her lasagne in the microwave and opening the fridge door she took out the half empty bottle of wine and poured herself a generous measure in a large wine glass.

Wandering into the lounge while her lasagne cooked, she picked up a photograph from the mantelpiece and looking at it for a few seconds a tear fell down her cheek. She was looking at a picture of Jamie, her late husband, and thinking how happy they had been until he had succumbed to a particularly aggressive type of cancer. He was twenty-eight when he died. That had been two years ago. It had been the most awful time in her life, the worst. She remembered their shock, the disbelief and denial that such a thing could happen when he was so young, so full of life. These things happened to other people not to them. They had cried together, hugged each other and cried some more. Finally, they had accepted. Accepted that life was fragile and that very soon Lily would be on her own so they had set about enjoying every single precious second until the terrible moment they had to say goodbye. She recounted the gut-wrenching emptiness, the overwhelming sense of loss that she had experienced and, if she was honest, still experienced, although less frequently as time had gone by.

Colleagues at work had been wonderful. The Council had let her have two months off fully paid which they didn't have to do and for which she would be eternally grateful. Everyone had been so kind and she felt she should have let them in a bit more. She had kept herself to herself for the most part. It wasn't that she didn't want to see them outside work or be a bit more 'transparent', the favoured word of recent times, it was just that she was essentially a private person. She determined to try to change things, be a bit more friendly in the future.

Placing the photograph frame carefully back in its exact position she returned to the kitchen and taking out her meal from the microwave, she sat at the small kitchen table.

Having cleared up, she watched a programme about seals on a remote Scottish island for an hour and then switching off the lights she made her way to bed.

A little while later, a clicking sound could be heard near the back door of No.105 Avon Street. The clicking sound ceased suddenly and the back door handle turned down. A figure entered and quietly shut the door. Moving slowly but surely across the kitchen floor, the figure moved into the hall and up the stairs. A stair creaked. The figure stood completely still. After a few seconds it advanced up the stairs, hesitating at the top. Then seeing one of the bedroom doors ajar, the figure pushed it open a little more and came to stand at the bottom of the bed where Lily slept soundly, totally unaware of the stranger in her bedroom.

The figure moved to stand by the bedside and looking down at the woman, produced a white cloth from a trouser pocket. In a flash the cloth was covering her mouth and nose. Lily was awake now, trying to scream, her eyes staring wildly, her whole body thrashing about for a few seconds before she passed out.

The figure took the bedspread off the bed and lay it on the floor. Pulling Lily off the bed, the figure placed her unconscious form on the bedspread, rolled her up into it and carried her downstairs, out of the back door, through the side gate and zapping the car boot bundled her in, closing the lid quietly. Getting into the driving seat, the driver quickly shut the door, fastened the seat belt and drove off at a speed that would not attract attention.

Waking up, Lily blinked several times, trying to focus. Her head felt muzzy, her throat dry and scratchy. Her brain coming into gear, fear started to grip her. Where was she? What was this place? She gazed at her surroundings as she lay on her side, on the hard, concrete floor. Her mouth was gagged and her wrists, that were bound behind her back, were hurting badly. Her feet were bound together at the ankles and every now and again, when she moved, a searing pain shot up her leg from where the ropes were cutting into her flesh. Her breathing began to get more and more rapid. Panic was rising from her stomach and she tried to scream. She felt sick but tried to calm herself, taking deep breaths to avoid having a full-blown panic attack. She tried to remember something about how she had come to be in this place. Yes, it was coming back to her now. She had been asleep. Something had made her wake up and her heart skipped several beats as she recalled the figure bending over her. A figure dressed all in black. She had tried to scream but something was covering her nose and mouth. Then there was nothing. He must have drugged her. She struggled with the ropes that bound her, gritting her teeth against the pain.

A door opened and closed. She stopped moving and lay completely still, hardly daring to breathe.

"So, you are awake?" said an unfamiliar male voice.

He laughed but there was no humour in it.

"I don't expect you to answer with a gag in your mouth. You are probably wondering why you are here. Unfortunately, there is a strong possibility that you will never know the answer to that question but you will make matters worse for yourself if you don't do exactly what I ask. You can nod your head if you understand" he said.

She nodded slowly.

"Good! I am going to untie the ropes and take the gag out of your mouth. If you scream, cry out, or make the slightest sound or if you try to run away, I will slit your throat without a moment's thought. Is that crystal clear?" he asked in a voice that made Lily shiver.

Again, she nodded.

He untied her and took out her gag. She sat up, rubbed her wrists and then her ankles.

She sat staring fearfully at him, her eyes flicking from his head to the knife he held in his hand.

He got up from where he was crouching and walked over to a bundle of material lying on the floor. Picking it up he came back over to her.

"Take your pyjamas off and put these clothes on" he commanded pointing his knife at her.

She hesitated.

"Do it!" he menaced.

Shivering and shaking she took her pyjamas off. There was an orange short sleeved jumper which she put on. Then she picked up a long piece of material that looked like a sarong. She held it in her hands and looked at it for a moment.

"Put it on!" the man commanded.

"How? I don't know how you want me to put it on"

"Just wind it round your waist and over your shoulder. Come on! Stop wasting time!" he said harshly.

Trembling, she fumbled with it but eventually managed to secure it round her waist and over her shoulder.

"Now put the wig and headdress on!" he ordered.

She struggled to put on the blonde wig but eventually succeeded and then placed the headdress over the top.

"It's an African costume" she said more to herself than to him.

"Yeah, you look like royalty, like a queen in it!" and he laughed again but it was a laugh devoid of humour.

He picked up the ropes and walked towards her.

She shook her head.

"No, no" she said.

He waved the knife at her.

"I said no noise, or else" he said.

He tied her wrists together tightly causing her to whimper as the rope cut into her flesh again. He pushed her roughly to the ground and tied her ankles. Finally, he gagged her.

He left her lying on the ground for a few minutes which seemed like hours to Lily whose breathing was becoming increasingly more rapid every second that went by. Her mind was blank with fear and tears streaked her face. She could hear a scrunching sound but she couldn't make out what it was. The man came back holding the long, sharp-bladed knife in one hand and a bowl of something in the other. He knelt beside her.

Taking hold of one of her hands he started to make a cut on the palm with his knife. He did it slowly seemingly enjoying the muffled screams of his victim enduring unspeakable agony. He proceeded to make four long cuts on each of her hands and feet. Lily fell in and out of consciousness. The man took the bowl of glass and proceeded to rub fragments into her wounds with a scouring pad. Lily went rigid with pain, her eyes wide with shock, she was screaming but the gag only allowed for strangled sounds. Finally, she passed out.

Standing up, the man dragged Lily over to a chair and sat her on it. The movement caused her to gain consciousness. He took the gag out of her mouth. Taking a piece of plastic covered rope which was lying in the corner of the room he came up behind Lily and placed it around her throat. He pulled it tight and Lily struggled to breathe. She was choking, her tongue was coming out of her mouth and she was going blue. She was going to die. She knew it now. Choking, she was struggling for breath. Suddenly, the rope loosened. She was gasping, trying to breathe.

She blacked out for what must have been seconds. Coming to, she spluttered and choked. Her neck and throat felt as though they were on fire. Now it was easing a little. She was feeling better. Maybe she wasn't going to die after all. Maybe this monster was going to let her go. Even as she thought it, she knew, deep down, that wasn't going to happen. Then the rope tightened.

Her eyes wide with fear, she choked again, the rope was getting tighter, she couldn't breathe, the pain, struggling to stay alive, struggling to…………………………

The figure bent over Lily, whose lifeless head was lolling forward. He felt her neck and her pulse. She was dead. He walked over to a table pushed up against the side of the room and picked up an object. He got a sharp knife and etched something onto it. Putting the object in his pocket, he crossed the room, picked up the bedspread and rolled Lily's corpse into it. It was dark outside. He looked furtively from side to side assuring himself that no-one was about before putting the body in the car. He studiously avoided main roads with cameras, drove with care and within the speed limit. He couldn't risk some zealous traffic cop stopping him.

Arriving at his destination, again he looked around before extracting the body from the car. At this time, the early hours of the morning, there wouldn't normally be anyone around and sure enough tonight was not an exception.

He lay the body down, carefully arranged her dress and taking the object from his pocket, he placed it in her hand. Satisfied, he went back to his car and drove to his torture chamber. He sat for a moment when he got back and congratulated himself on his successful murder. He had so enjoyed seeing the bitch suffer. Leaving the clues would prove a challenge for the police to solve, if they ever did. Smiling, he changed his clothes, washed in the small sink in the corner, and after combing his hair, slipped out into the night.

Chapter 2

DI Jack Allan was breakfasting with his fiancée. It was six-thirty in the morning on Thursday 4th March and he had already been up an hour undertaking his keep fit regime which had considerably decreased both in time and enthusiasm since Vanessa had moved in. She had changed his life immeasurably and most definitely for the better. He had never been happier but one of the casualties had been his dedication to arguably being the fittest police officer in the Cambridge Constabulary. Vanessa had made some changes too. She used to like croissants and jam plus a large latte to start the day. Now she joined Jack in consuming a healthy nourishing nuts, seeds and fruit-filled breakfast, washed down with a smoothie.

"I've been thinking about our honeymoon and wondered if you fancied the Seychelles?" asked Vanessa taking a sip of her avocado, cherry and spinach smoothie.

"Okay. I'll leave the final decision to you but I was thinking about maybe Hawaii or Maui?"

"Ummm. Yes. Maui is less commercialised and ...."

Jack's mobile interrupted Vanessa's answer.

Jack held up his hand to her, signalling that he had to take the call, at the same time as answering, "Allan".

"Sorry to disturb you so early, Jack. There's been a murder at Wandlebury Country Park. All a bit bizarre but you'll see when you get here" said DS Julia Szymanski who Jack had had a great deal of trouble in persuading to call him by his first name when they were talking together and out of earshot of other members of the Force.

"Okay, thanks Julia. I'm on my way" replied Jack and hung up.

"Sorry, darling" said Jack walking round the table to where Vanessa was sitting. She stood up, putting her arms round his neck. They kissed as though they were being parted forever and then smiled at each other, their foreheads touching.

"No worries, it'll be me next time!" she said.

Jack got washed and dressed in a matter of minutes. Grabbing his keys and phone he rushed out of the apartment, down the stairs, into his car and switching on his blues and twos, he drove off at speed.

Szymanski was standing at the crime scene when he arrived. She walked up to the cordon while he was donning his protective gear.

"Morning again, sir" greeted Szymanski, already dressed in nitrile gloves and boot covers.

"Morning, Julia. What have we got?" asked Allan.

"Well, as I said it is quite bizarre as you will see" she answered, lifting the cordon so that Allan could pass through.

"Who found the body?" Allan asked.

"A dog walker. A Mr......" Szymanski referred to her notebook.

"A Mr Parsons, Jake Parsons".

"Have a check run on him, Julia".

"Already have, sir, he's not known to us. Lives locally".

"Okay, good work".

They walked towards the body; a woman on whose head was a brown and orange turban and whose body was clothed in an orange short-sleeved top with an orange and brown wrap. Her hands and feet were streaked with blood.

Stewart Strange looked up as they approached.

"Poor woman was strangled as you can see from the ligature marks round her neck" the coroner said pointing to two separate thin red marks "asphyxiation is the probable cause of death. I will have to examine the body further to confirm that, of course. The other marks on her are the four deep cuts on each of her hands and feet. In addition, there are marks on her wrists and ankles suggesting she was tied up".

"Any sign of sexual assault?" Allan asked.

"I will need to examine the body back at the lab before I can give a definitive answer on that. No ostensible defence wounds but again I would have to confirm later when I have examined the body further. What I would say, though, is the woman was probably taken by surprise from behind".

"Any identification?" asked Szymanski.

"Nope, but something of note is that she is wearing a wig. She's naturally a brunette but the wig is blonde".

"Doesn't really go with the African get up does it, sir?" commented Szymanski.

"No, you would think the murderer would leave her as she was with dark hair" said Allan thoughtfully.

Strange got up.

"Well, I'll be off now but I should have something to tell you later today".

"Yes, sure, Stew. Thanks. Be in touch later".

Allan and Szymanski bent down over the body to take a closer look and Allan rubbed the side of his nose which he always did when he was thinking hard.

"What have we here?" exclaimed Allan suddenly and he extricated a small black wooden object. "The Queen from a chess set! You were right to use the word 'bizarre', Julia! We have a Caucasian woman dressed in what appears to be an African outfit, who has abrasions on her hands and feet and clutching a chess piece!"

Later that day Strange rang Allan.

"If you've got a minute, can you come over to the lab?" Strange asked.

"On my way!" replied Allan who dropped what he was doing immediately and summoned

Szymanski. The two detectives arrived at the pathology lab twenty minutes later.

"I think you will be appreciative of the speed at which we have uncovered some hopefully useful information!" said a beaming Strange.

Allan smiled and nodded looking at the coroner enquiringly.

"Firstly, I have identified the body through dental records as that of Lily Anderson, twenty-five years of age".

Szymanski took out her notebook and scribbled the details down.

"Secondly, time of death was between midnight last night and two o'clock in the morning. Thirdly, there was no sign of sexual assault. Fourthly, we found some white threads from a cloth of some sort around her mouth. We tested the fibres and found them to have chloroform on them.

He tied her up as can be seen from the marks on her wrists and ankles where the ropes have cut into her flesh and we have found rope fibres in some of the abrasions. He then cut the underneath of her feet with crushed glass. We found fragments of glass in every abrasion. When he rubbed this into her hands and feet, it must have been excruciatingly painful. A form of torture. Why, is for you to find out.

So, it is fair to assume that she passed out from inhaling chloroform in a place as yet unknown and subjected to horrific torture. The cause of death was asphyxiation due to strangulation with something like a thin plastic rope such as a washing line.

However, she was not only strangled once; she was, in fact, strangled twice. The first time the murderer didn't kill her but caused her maximum distress. The poor woman must have struggled for breath, perhaps losing consciousness for a second or two, choking and spluttering. A truly terrifying experience. Then the murderer went in for the kill. Any questions?"

"Many but not any that you can answer, unfortunately, Stew. Thanks for the information. See you, but hopefully not too soon!"

The pathologist gave a wry smile and nodded.

When Allan and Szymanski got back to the station Patel came up hurriedly.

"Don't tell me! The DCI wants to see me urgently" said Allan.

"Yes, sir, how did you know that was what I was going to say?" Patel asked with a crestfallen expression.

"Can't think, Dev" replied Allan with a poker face and Szymanski tried to hide a smile.

Allan climbed the stairs two at a time. He never relished seeing his new boss, DCI Tom Clarkson. He knocked on the door.

"Come in, come in" was the answer.

Jack shut the door behind him as he entered and walked across to where Clarkson was standing with outstretched hand.

They shook hands, Clarkson with a broad grin which did not match the expression in his eyes. Indicating that Allan should sit on one of the chairs in front of his desk, they both sat down.

DCI Clarkson was medium in height, stout with a shaven head and had eyes that were very close together. When he smiled it was more of an insincere grin. He had a reputation of being a snake-in-the-grass and consequently was not well-liked. There had been several occasions on his way up the career ladder when he had side-stepped responsibility for an incident, managing to blame it on someone else. In each case there had never been enough evidence to prove what had happened and so far he had been able to climb the ladder unscathed and had made it to DCI level.

"There's been a murder in Wandlebury Country Park, I understand" said Clarkson.

"Yes, sir, a woman called Lily Anderson, twenty-five years old, strangled twice".

"Twice?!"

"Yes, sir, apparently according to Strange, the victim was strangled to near death, tortured and then killed by strangulation the second time".

"Horrible! Anything else of note?"

"Yes, she was found dressed in African clothing. She had cuts caused by a knife to her hands and feet that presented further lacerations made by fragments of glass which had been rubbed into the wounds. Two further things of note were that she was clutching a chess piece, the Queen, and she was wearing a blonde wig which was curious considering she was wearing an African costume".

"Very nasty and not a little bit strange! Were there any eyewitnesses do we know? Does she have any family, friends, colleagues? Have family been informed? Where did she work?" asked Clarkson.

"We don't know as yet, but we are working on it. As soon as we have informed the family, an appeal should go out for eyewitnesses, don't you think, sir?"

"Yes, of course, I will be doing that after you have spoken to the family. Keep me informed on progress".

"Yes, sir" said Allan getting up to go.

As he reached the door, Clarkson called him.

"Jack, we haven't managed time to speak properly. I know we haven't always seen eye to eye about things but I do hope we can let bygones be bygones and move on to work together as a team?" and he gave one of his most insincere grins.

"I'm sure we will do our very best to work together in the spirit of professionalism, sir" replied Jack turning and walking out of the door, closing it quietly behind him.

On getting back to his office, Allan had a quick look at his emails and then strode into the outer area where his small but effective and loyal team of seven, comprising DS Julia Szymanski, DC Dev Patel, DS Barry Wright, DC Sophie Callender, DS Max Garcia, DS Mike Townsend and DC Peter Purcell were sitting engaged in their work. They all turned to face their boss with expectant expressions as he walked in and proceeded to outline details of the murder of Lily Anderson.

"Okay, everyone, so we have a case with distinct peculiarities attached to it and obviously, we need to find our murderer as soon as.

Barry, as a matter of urgency, can you establish who her family are and then take Sophie with you to give them the sad news. Can you let me know immediately that's been done, please, because then the DCI can organise an appeal for any witnesses to come forward.

Max, can you find out where she worked and can you and Mike interview her colleagues. See what you can find out about her work and personal lives.

Dev and Peter can you go through her financial affairs and any phone calls she made the day before and the day she died.

Meanwhile, Julia and I will find out where she lived and if that was where she was tortured and murdered. Let's get to it!" and Allan moved quickly into his office with Szymanski closely on his heels.

Closing the door, Szymanski sat on a chair in front of Allan's desk.

"Jack, while you were in with the boss, I managed to find out where the victim lived. 105 Avon Street".

"Julia, you're a star! Pick me up tomorrow morning at eight o'clock sharp and we'll go straight there!".

When Julia got home that evening, she had the flat to herself. Sally had taken Leo round to her mother's house for a birthday celebration. Julia had been invited, of course, but she had cried off saying that she couldn't commit due to work demands and she didn't want to disrupt proceedings by arriving late. If Julia had said otherwise Sally would have felt obliged to hold things up so that her partner could join in. The real reason that she had wriggled out of going was that she didn't get on with Sally's mother. Doreen always looked at her with a lingering, sad look as though to say if it wasn't for you my Sally wouldn't be in a gay relationship. It was all Julia's fault as far as Doreen was concerned. She was traditional in outlook and she didn't understand gay people. The upshot was that Julia had feelings of guilt which were groundless, she knew that, but nevertheless that's how Doreen's attitude affected her.

Julia sighed as she got a large wine glass out of the cupboard, a bottle of Chardonnay out of the fridge and poured herself a generous glass. She held the glass up to eye level and looked at it with appreciation. It was a half-decent wine. In fact, so decent that she would need all her self-taught discipline to stop her from partaking of the whole bottle.

She moved into the lounge and sat down on one of the squashy sofas. She ruminated for a while, sipping on her wine and had to admit the truth. It wasn't really Doreen that was making her feel the need to imbibe, it was the events of almost two weeks ago when out of the blue an old friend had turned up.

She had known Sylas Bukosky on and off since university. They were both Polish but each of them loved Britain so much that they admitted that they both wanted to become British citizens and were filling in the necessary paperwork. The friendship had flourished until one day Sylas made a pass at her and she had to tell him that she was the other way inclined. Sylas hadn't spoken to her for a couple of months after that but as they were both attending the same lectures and were in the same hiking group, eventually Sylas came round. It was she who had made the first move at reconciliation, saying how much she valued their friendship. After that, things went back to normal. They both achieved British citizenship but she had lost touch with him a few months after leaving university for quite a while. Sometime later, they had bumped into each other quite by chance and had met once or twice for a drink and a catch-up. Subsequently, Sylas had decided to return to Poland whilst remaining a British citizen.

Then out of the blue Sylas had turned up. She put her head back on the cushion, stared at the ceiling, her wine glass clasped in both hands and recalled that evening.

"Can you answer that, Julia, I'm just changing Leo" Sally had called on the second ring of the doorbell.

"Yes, sure" Julia had replied.

When she opened the door, she had found herself looking up at Sylas.

"Oh, my goodness. Sylas!" she had exclaimed.

"That's an encouraging welcome! How about 'great to see you, how are you?' or something like that?" he had said sarcastically though smiling at the same time.

"Sorry, Sylas, you just took me by surprise! Come in, come in!" she had said and had ushered him into their flat.

Sally had come out to see who it was and Julia had introduced them.

"So, how are you? What's going on?" Julia had asked when they had sat down with a cup of coffee.

Julia had had a strange feeling that he was adopting a troubled expression rather than it was genuine. It had been just a feeling and she had quickly dismissed it putting it down to being a police officer in her leisure time too.

"I'm just in a bad place at the moment and I know I shouldn't ask this from you but I would really appreciate it if I could doss down here for a few days until I get myself together?" he had said with a charming, winsome smile.

Julia and Sally had both been taken aback.

"Well, we'd love to help but as you can see this is a one-bedroom flat and three of us are living here already. I don't think it's really feasible" Sally had said coming in straightaway to nip this request in the bud.

"I really would appreciate it, Julia" Sylas had said looking directly at Julia and seemingly totally ignoring Sally's reply.

There had been an awkward silence.

"If it is only for a couple of days Sylas but as Sally has said we are short of space as it is. You would have to sleep on one of these sofas and you would need to keep to the house rules. We'll outline those. Would that be okay, Sally? I've known Sylas for a long time and what are friends for if not to help out when needed?" replied Julia.

Sally had shot Julia a furious look but in the end had just nodded agreement.

The next evening when Sylas had gone out, Sally had hit the roof. "It is already almost unliveable in the flat as it is" she had raged, "too small for the three of us and now we are taking in some friend that you haven't seen for ages! It's just not on!". She had been so angry she had smashed a vase. Eventually, she had managed to calm down after the two of them had talked away a couple of hours and Sally had seemed to accept the situation.

Since then, things had got worse and worse. Sylas seemed to be up all hours. He said he had trouble sleeping because of the problems he currently had which were on his mind constantly. He said it wouldn't be long before he returned to Poland and he appreciated her understanding which made it difficult for her to chuck him out. Julia was worried about Sally who she knew was becoming more and more cross, although she was doing a good job, at least for the moment, keeping her anger to herself but someday soon Sally was going to explode. Julia was thankful this evening that Sylas had obviously gone out.

She sighed again and then heard Sally's key in the latch. She put the wine down on the coffee table and went to greet her partner.

Chapter 3

It was a breezy but bright and sunny morning on Friday 5 March. As Szymanski drove, Allan made a call to forensics to attend at 105 Avon Street. The previous evening, he had asked for a cordon to be put round the property and as they drove up the road he saw that his request had been actioned.

They arrived about the same time as the forensics team and donned their gloves and boots.

Starting up the stairs each of them took a bedroom. Szymanski quickly established that there was nothing of interest in the large spare bedroom or the smaller one but before she could start on the bathroom, Allan called her to the main bedroom.

"This is where the victim was chloroformed, Julia. I can smell it on the pillowcase and, looking at the decorative pillows over there on the armchair, there should be a bedspread to match. I think the bedspread was used to wrap the unconscious woman in. There's no sign of blood or glass and there's no sign of a struggle so this is not where she was tortured or killed".

"No, I agree, but we haven't checked the rest of the house yet".

"Ummmm. Let's do that but I have a hunch she was taken somewhere else".

In the lounge they looked through the sideboard drawers.

"I've found some photos, Jack. They seem to be of her husband or boyfriend". Szymanski showed them to her boss.

"Yes, and there's a picture of the same man on the mantelpiece so I guess it was her husband. I remember she had a wedding ring on".

"Okay, so where is he? Hopefully, Barry will have located him" continued Allan.

"Ummmm. When we were upstairs though, I went through the wardrobes and there was no evidence of anyone else's clothes but the victim's. Do you think they were separated?" asked Szymanski.

"Maybe. We should know soon" replied Allan.

"There is nothing really personal here apart from the photographs. Her mail seems to be either just junk or bills".

They checked the bathroom, dining room and kitchen but found nothing that suggested a struggle having taken place.

Allan's mobile rang.

"Barry! What have you got for me?"

"Well, sir, sad really. Sophie and I have come up with exactly zilch relatives. Her parents are both dead. Died in a car crash when she was nineteen. Her husband died of a particularly aggressive cancer a couple of years ago and there are no children. It seems she was completely alone in the world".

"Yeah, that is sad, Barry. Thanks for your efforts in finding out so quickly. I'll update the DCI straightaway so the press conference and media appeal can be arranged as soon as possible," Allan ended the call and punched in another number.

"Tom Clarkson" the DCI answered brusquely.

"Hello sir, DI Allan. Apparently, Lily Anderson had no living relatives. She was totally alone, so all clear for the conference and appeal".

"Thank you, Allan, I'll organise it, if possible, for this evening. It might make the nine o'clock news bulletin" and the DCI hung up.

****

While Allan and Szymanski were at the victim's house, García drove in silence to the victim's workplace. Townsend always found García, as did the other members of the team, extremely difficult to make small talk with. If he tried she, more often than not, answered in monosyllables and so he hadn't bothered to try. Instead, he flicked through his texts and the news on his mobile.

Earlier, he and García discovered that the victim had worked in a library as a senior library assistant in Wandlebury Road, opposite the park and it hadn't gone unnoticed by them that Wandlebury Park was where Lily Anderson had been found. Mike had spoken to the librarian, Pat Salford, conveyed the terrible news, and then arranged to speak to the five members of staff who worked there.

When they arrived, they took over the small staff room to conduct the interviews.

"Good afternoon, Ms Trott, isn't it?" Townsend addressed a small mouse-like woman of around sixty who blinked a lot and kept swallowing hard.

"Yes that's right, Detective Inspector, Pauline Trott. You can call me Pauline if you like" she whispered.

"There's no need to be nervous, Pauline and I'm actually Detective Sargeant Townsend and this is my colleague Detective Constable García. I expect Ms Salford has told you that your colleague, Lily Anderson, was found murdered early this morning?"

"Yes, it's terrible. She was such a nice, sweet person. I can't think that anyone would want to hurt her and only two years ago she lost her husband. They were devoted to one another, you know, then he got cancer and died three months later!" Pauline shed several tears wiping them away with a tissue.

"So, she was well liked here at the library then?" asked García.

"Oh yes indeed! Everyone liked her. There was nothing to dislike about her".

"Do you know what she did in her personal life. Did she belong to a sports club, for instance, or did she have a hobby?" García continued.

"No, no, I don't think I ever heard her say anything about what she did after work or on the weekends".

"She never mentioned a boyfriend, someone she was seeing?" asked Townsend.

"No, definitely not. She never mentioned anyone," said Pauline shaking her head vehemently.

"Okay, Pauline, thank you very much for talking to us. You have been very helpful" said Townsend.

"Oh! I do hope so Detective Sargeant," she replied and got up to go.

She reached the door and then turned.

"There was just one thing now I come to think about it" she said.

"Yes" said Max, failing to mask her impatience.

"Well, Lily had a stalker a few months back now. Anyway, you probably know this already because Lily reported it to the police but I'm not sure it was ever followed up".

"Thank you Pauline" said Townsend.

"Well, that's most interesting!" commented Townsend when Pauline had closed the door.

"Indeed! I've made a note to find out more about the stalker when we return to the station" replied García.

When Townsend and García interviewed the other four members of staff they found that they all agreed there had been a stalker and that they knew very little about Lily's personal life.

After popping into Pat Salford's office before taking their leave, Townsend and García made their way back to the station.

"Hello guv" said Townsend when Allan picked up his call.

"We've interviewed the staff and none of them knew a lot about the victim. She didn't talk much about her personal life. As far as they knew she led a quiet life and didn't have any friends. Colleagues were aware of the tragic loss of her husband to cancer and she was generally liked by all. However, we did uncover one potentially interesting piece of information about Lily. Apparently, she had been bothered by a stalker a few months ago. We've accessed the records and a man called Percy Parker was picked up and interviewed three months ago, it having been alleged that he had been stalking our victim. There wasn't enough evidence to hold him and the matter was dropped".

"Yes interesting. Possibility he could be our man. Have you got his address?" asked Allan.

"Yes and that's interesting too because he lives at 92a, Wandlebury Avenue, in the upstairs flat, which is just off Wandlebury Road" Townsend replied.

Allan was jotting down the address on his wrist with a ballpoint pen.

"Okay, thanks, Mike. Julia and I will make our way over there now. You and Max join us there as soon as you can" and Allan ended the call.

Minutes later, Allan and Szymanski arrived at the house which was divided into bedsits. The frontage was run down and in need of some TLC. The paintwork was peeling, the front garden was overgrown with weeds and two of the dustbins had their contents spilling out onto the path.

Kicking a couple of cartons out of the way, Allan and Szymanski reached the front door and pressed the relevant bell. Townsend and García had just drawn up outside.

A couple of minutes later, the door opened and a dishevelled figure stood before them. He stared at them with vacant eyes.

"Wot?" he said

"Mr Parker?" Allan asked politely.

"Yeah?"

"I'm sorry to disturb you but we need you to come down to the station with us" Allan said.

"Why, I ain't done nuffink wrong" said Parker sniffing loudly and wiping his forearm across his nose and mouth.

"We need you to come down to the station, sir" reiterated Szymanski.

"Okay, okay just a minute! I gotta turn the telly off" he said and closed the door.

They waited on the doorstep for a couple of minutes.

"Mike, Max round the back quick. He's done a runner!" Allan suddenly shouted.

They all went round to the side gate just in time to see Percy disappear over the back fence. García was the first over, followed closely by Allan and then the others. Clothes scattered from a washing line, being wrenched first by the pursued and then by the pursuers. Over garden fences and out to the side alley between the houses. They raced down the street after him, across the road, holding up traffic from both directions and attracting a lot of angry, blaring horns. Then into the park. García and Allan were steadily gaining on Percy and then García lunged forward and caught Percy by the waist bringing him to the ground.

Allan read him his rights while García handcuffed him. Townsend was bending forward, his head down, his hands on his knees, trying to catch his breath.

Once back at the station, Allan and Szymanski got their papers together for the interview with Parker.

On entering the room, Allan and Szymanski sat down opposite a hostile Percy Parker.

Turning the tape on, Allan and Szymanski introduced themselves and indicated that Parker should do the same.

"So, Mr Parker, I would like you to describe your movements from eight o'clock in the evening on Wednesday 3rd March until yesterday, Thursday 4th March at four o'clock in the morning?".

"I went round to a friend's house all evening on Wednesday from about seven o'clock, had a few beers, played a few games on the computer like. Then I went home and went to bed. So, at four o'clock on 4th March I was in bed asleep" Parker replied, sitting back in his chair, his arms folded in front of him.

"What is your friend's name?" asked Szymanski pen poised over her notepad.

"Melvyn. Melvyn Stott".

"And what time did you arrive at Mr Stott's place?".

"I dunno. Sometime that evening".

"And what time did you leave?"

"About one o'clock in the morning".

"That was quite late to be just playing games and having a few beers" commented Allan.

"Not really. It was just a few hours".

"From seven o'clock in the evening to one o'clock in the morning?" asked Allan.

"I didn't say I got there at seven o'clock, I said I got there about seven o'clock. Now, come to think about it, I was having my dinner and watching the telly until about eight-thirty", Parker said defiantly.

"So, you got to Mr. Stott's house then at about what... ten o'clock?".

"Yeah about that. I dunno. I can't really remember" Parker replied sulkily.

"Did you drive to your friend's?" asked Szymanski.

"Yeah".

"What car do you own, Mr Parker?" asked Allan.

"A Peugeot".

"What type of car is it?"

"What do you mean?"

"Is it a saloon, for instance?"

"No, it's an estate car".

"Do you know a Ms Lily Anderson, Mr Parker?" asked Szymanski.

"Who?" Parker seemed genuinely puzzled.

"Ms Lily Anderson. Do you know her?" and Allan produced a photograph of the victim.

Parker looked down at the photograph which had been placed on the table in front of him. He shook his head slowly.

"No, I don't think so" and he looked up and stared at the officers.

"What do you mean you 'don't think so'. Do you or don't you know or have you or have you not ever seen this woman?"

"No, I've never seen her. I don't know her", Percy said sullenly.

"And your friend – will be able to corroborate that you were at his house between ten o'clock in the evening to one o'clock in the morning?"

Percy nodded.

"I guess so" he said.

Having switched off the tape, he and Szymanski left the room.

"It would seem a perfect alibi but I would like forensics to take a look in the back of his car. An estate car would be perfect to put a body in quickly" said Allan as they walked back to the office.

"Just a point I picked up on, sir. Parker looked blank when we asked whether he knew Lily Anderson".

"Yes I picked up on that too. He is either a very good liar, a good actor or he isn't our guy" replied Allan thoughtfully stroking the side of his nose.

"I'll check Parker's alibi with this Melvyn Stott," said Szymanski and walked off to her desk while Allan gathered the rest of the team together.

"Okay everyone so what Julia and I have discovered is that the victim's house was not used for the murder. It would seem the murderer used chloroform to knock out Lily Anderson, wrapped the body in a bedspread and transported her to an unknown place where the torture was carried out. We are currently holding a suspect, Percy Parker and Julia is checking his alibi at this moment. It has been established that Mr. Parker does own an estate car and he was questioned a few months ago regarding suspicions that he had been stalking Ms Anderson. There was insufficient evidence and therefore it wasn't followed up. Ah, here's Julia" and he looked across the office at his approaching DS.

"Unfortunately, sir, the alibi does check out and according to Melvyn Stott, Percy left around 2.15 am".

"That's a bummer" exclaimed Allan.

"Unless they were both in on it" suggested Wright.

"Or Parker asked Stott to give him an alibi if he was arrested, perhaps suggesting some minor incident?" Callender chipped in.

"Yes the alibi could be dodgy. It's all conjecture though. However, I do think it's worth surveillance. So, Mike and Max when we release Parker can you follow him and park discreetly in view of his house?"

"Yes, sir" they said unanimously.

"In the meantime, what else have we uncovered?"

"Anderson was well liked at work but no-one knew much about her. She seemed a bit of a recluse. The only thing was the stalker. Other than that, nothing much" said García, and Townsend nodded in agreement.

"Thank you Max and Mike. Barry we've already spoken but for the benefit of the rest of the team?" said Allan.

"Sophie and I could find no evidence of family and friends. Her parents died in a car crash when she was nineteen and her husband died of cancer. No children" said Wright.

"Dev, Peter?"

"Nothing of interest on her mobile and there is no landline. Her finances seem to be in perfect order, no financial worries" said Patel.

"Thanks Dev. Okay, Parker is now under surveillance and needless to say look for anything that he does that could allow us to call in forensics to examine his car" Allan addressed García and Townsend.

"Barry put a trace on Parker's landline, if he has one, and mobile plus one on Stott's. Dev and Sophie, do a door-to-door in Avon Street. See if anyone spotted a car the evening of the murder, what make etcetera and who the driver was. Peter, check CCTV along the route that Parker took from his house to his friend's, if the alibi is true and he did go there, timing is obviously important. In the meantime, hopefully someone will come forward with information. That's all for this evening. Get some sleep. We've got a busy day tomorrow".

Townsend and García had already left for surveillance duty on Parker. Patel, Wright Callender and Purcell packed up quickly, jackets were taken off chairs, keys collected and very soon only Allan and Szymanski were left. Allan was looking at the incident board while Szymanski was getting ready to leave.

Suddenly, Allan turned round to face her.

"Julia, you got a minute before you go" Allan said turning to her, his sentence not begging anything but an affirmative answer.

Julia followed, closing the door behind her. They sat either side of Allan's desk.

"How are things going, Julia, at home I mean? You seem a bit on edge."

"Sorry, Jack, if I seem a bit lack lustre. I am perfectly okay".

"Really?" and Jack just looked at her.

"Okay, no not really".

"Are you and Sally having problems again?"

"No, it's not that. It's…..well…..it's…. An old friend of mine has come over from Poland to stay and it's not ideal. We thought it was going to be for a night or two but he's been with us now for two weeks. As you know, our place isn't big and he has been kipping down on our bed settee in the lounge".

"Can't you just tell him to go?" asked Allan with a concerned expression.

"It's difficult. He's had a rough time lately. He won't say what exactly happened. He doesn't want to talk about it".

"Okay. How did you get to know him?"

"We both studied at the same university. We both took up British citizenship and he lived here in the UK until very recently. Then he decided to go back to Poland just for a while. Something happened along the way, I don't know what or where, he won't open up, at least not to me, but it's obvious something is wrong. He seems in very low spirits. Anyway, he has come back to the UK and he is staying with us".

"What does he do for a living?"

"I'm not entirely sure. I'm hoping he will sort himself out soon and then everything will go back to normal. It's just that we are used to it being only the three of us. I'll remember to put a smiley face on tomorrow, boss!" she grinned. "By the way, how are you and Vanessa getting on with your wedding plans and have you decided where you are going on your honeymoon?"

"We're good, thank you. Don't ask about the wedding and we're sorting the honeymoon very shortly!"

Jack got up from his chair, Julia following suit.

"Anyway, it's nice to catch up Julia. Must go, we're having dinner with Vanessa's parents! Hope you manage to have a good evening and we'll see what tomorrow brings!"

"Hope you do, too, Jack!" replied Julia with raised eyebrows.

Allan just grinned.

Chapter 4

It was late afternoon on Friday 5 March and a woman struggled with the stiff breeze blowing her blonde bob over her face. She kept raising her hand to push the stray strands behind her ears. Heavily pregnant she steadied the wayward shopping trolley against a convenient pillar in order to secure her hair in a knot at the back of her head. Steering the trolley to her car, she opened the boot and started to unload her shopping.

Of course, she wanted this baby but right now, feeling like a billowing whale, short of breath and wanting desperately to pee again, she cursed their holiday seven and a half months ago. A tear unexpectedly escaped from her left eye as she thought how, whilst she had been abroad enjoying the Mediterranean sunshine, her mother had passed away. She thought how much she would have liked her mum to know that she would be a grandmother but obviously that was not to be.

Finishing her unpacking she closed the lid of the boot and wheeled the trolley to a park. Back at the car she opened the door muttering under her breath, thanking heaven the weekly shop was over. Climbing into the driver's seat, she carefully negotiated accommodating her huge belly, and switching on the ignition she drove to the exit, totally unaware of the unassuming dark grey estate, two cars behind her.

The car followed her at a discreet distance to her home, 15 Willow Drive. The car drove on a short way and stopped on the right-hand side of the road from where the driver had a clear view of the woman. The driver took a notebook out of his pocket and wrote something down, then picking up his camera lying on the passenger seat and pointing the lens towards the woman, he proceeded to take a number of photographs.

The woman was carrying the bags in relays to the house. When she had finished she closed the boot, zapped the car and disappeared into the house.

The driver sat for a few moments and then picking up his extortionately expensive professional camera, he started to examine the photos. Scrolling through the pictures he nodded and a satisfied smile crossed his face as he viewed the woman from different angles. Zooming in, the registration plate of the car became distinct. He looked up, still smiling, pleased with his work.

Putting the camera carefully in the glove compartment, he got out of the car and walked over to the driveway where the woman's car was parked. He bent down behind the boot. Then he walked back to his car, opened the door, climbed in and moving off from the curb, disappeared round the bend in the road.

Thirty minutes later the man parked his car in a residential street, retrieved his rucksack from the back seat and put his camera in it. Picking up his wallet and the remains of a 500ml bottle of water, he zapped the car. He walked up the street until he reached an unassuming block of flats and headed to the entrance. Once inside, he took the lift, turned left on arrival and fishing for the front door key in his jacket pocket he let himself in.

He walked through to the lounge area and placed his camera carefully on a coffee table in front of one of the sofas. Walking over to a cupboard he located a bottle of scotch and poured himself a large measure. He wandered over to the window.

He still had his jacket on, his right hand holding the glass of whiskey, his left in his pocket. He was deep in thought. His eyes were seemingly fixed on the view from the window but in fact he was blind to the view. His thoughts were focussed. He had placed a tracker on the woman's car so she wouldn't be able to go very far without him knowing. Finally, he took off his jacket, hung it up in the hall cupboard and strode into the bathroom. At the sink he looked in the mirror and decided it was probably time he had a haircut. His hair was looking unruly. Not a good image. He always liked to look as immaculate as possible.

Picking up his glass he poured himself another whiskey and took out the laptop from his rucksack. He sat down and started to type an email.

Meanwhile, back at Willow Drive, the woman had successfully unpacked her shopping and realised it was nearly time to put the dinner on.

Their dog, a liver spotted spaniel came padding over as, opening the fridge, she got out a pack of lamb mince and unwrapped it. His large brown eyes pleaded for the meat he could smell so tantalisingly close on the kitchen side. She bent down carefully with one hand on her bump and fondled the top of his head and ears.

"Sorry, Spot, dinner for you isn't 'til later!".

They had named their pet Spot, simply because of the large spots on his spaniel coat. They had joked about it at first, just as they had about the idea of naming him Deefor short for 'D for Dog'. Then somehow, the name Spot stuck. He was a true spaniel in nature, devoted to them both but more so Phil. She smiled at the thought of Spot always sitting faithfully by Phil's side when he was working from home.

She walked over to the fridge and poured herself an orange juice. Phil would be in from work soon but she just had time to catch her breath before preparing dinner. She sat down at the kitchen table and looked around.

It had been a sudden decision to move to Cambridgeshire. Everything happened so quickly really, she mused. A position for an associate director had arisen at Phil's firm and he had been approached. The position was based at the headquarters in Cambridge. At first both were torn, more on her side than his. Phil was keen to climb the career ladder. This would be a wonderful opportunity that he didn't want to pass up not least because along with the promotion would come a welcome increase in salary, especially with their baby on the way. Jane didn't want to leave her friends or her job but amazingly it transpired that she didn't have to leave her firm. When she had spoken to her manager, he had been totally sympathetic to the extent that he offered hybrid working with the occasional visit to the office, not more than once a year. That and the fact that she no longer had family in Wiltshire and her brother lived in Cambridgeshire, sealed their decision. So here they were in a beautiful house that just seemed to have been waiting for them.

She twiddled the mug around as she thought back to when they were house hunting in the area. They had viewed around ten houses before this one and were beginning to lose heart. Then they had viewed 15 Willow Drive, in Little Farnham, a village just outside Grantchester and set back from the quiet road which was a cul-de-sac. The mellow bricked house with leaded light windows faced a row of willow trees that framed the village green and was adorned with wisteria. The mature garden at the back had fruit trees and a beautiful magnolia shrub. The kitchen was state of the art and had been recently fitted which was the icing on the cake. They didn't even mind when the owners insisted on the asking price. They just knew this was the house for them.

She snapped out of her reverie when she heard a key in the door and then Phil's familiar voice called out.

"Hi darling!"

"In the kitchen!" she called.

"How was your day?" they greeted each other in unison.

They both laughed.

"Just glad it's Friday!" he said striding over to her and kissing her with one hand on the bump.

"How was yours?" he asked holding her by the shoulders at arms-length and looking into her eyes.

"Bump was restless, and shopping was a bit of a nightmare but apart from that fine!" she grinned.

"Tell you what, why don't you put your feet up and have a little nap while I cook you a culinary delight?" he said walking over to where an apron was hanging on a hook.

"Wouldn't hear of it! I'm not an invalid!" she waved her hand in the air dismissing his idea.

"Oh! Are you saying you don't like my cooking! I'm affronted! I insist that I have the opportunity Mrs Blake, to prove otherwise!" he said standing with his hands on his hips in mock offence.

"Okay. I give in! You're wonderful!" she beamed and kissing him lightly on the lips, she disappeared to the lounge.

Over dinner of moussaka, mediterranean vegetables followed by raspberries and chocolate ice cream, they talked about the arrival of their baby and the impending family wedding.

"So, has your brother revealed the date and venue for the wedding yet?" he asked.

"No! Plus I don't know for sure, it's more what they are not saying, but I wouldn't be surprised if they want a very simple wedding and that's definitely not going to go down well with Vanessa's parents! Apparently, according to Jack, they want a full-blown affair with all the trimmings!" and Jane grimaced.

"Well, there certainly won't be *any* wedding, if they don't get the date in diaries!" he retorted.

"It's not from want of nagging on my side. I said all this, but Jack just said, 'all in good time!', I mean what can else can I do?" she shrugged her shoulders. "By the way, this is a delicious meal. I think we'll do this more often!" she added, smiling.

"Thank you, I aim to please. Glad you're enjoying it but not sure about doing it more often. Now and again maybe?" he grinned.

"Okay, I'll settle for that!" she said, returning his grin.

There was a silence for some time while they savoured the delicious taste of chocolate and fresh raspberries.

"Do you want to know what *I* really want to know?" she asked at length.

"Go on!"

"What I really want to know, is whether Vanessa has chosen her dress yet and if so, what it's like!" she said putting down her spoon and dabbing her mouth with her serviette.

"Jane, that's hardly the most important thing, is it?" he was laughing as he spoke.

"Yes, it most definitely is!" she replied giggling.

"Well, it's no good having a beautiful dress with no date and venue to wear it!" he quipped.

"Shall we compromise and agree that all three things are equally important!?" Jane suggested.

"Deal. Let's shake on it!" he said with a mock serious expression and offering his hand over the table.

"However," he continued crossing the room and picking up his mobile "I think this would be the perfect time, while we are on the subject, to give Jack a call as his best man and ask him about the venue".

Accessing his contact list he tapped on his brother-in-law's number.

"Hi Phil, how you doing?" Jack's voice came over a bit crackly and indistinct.

"You're obviously out, mate, the connection's not good but I can hear you. Are you working or can you talk?"

"No not working. We're on our way to dinner with Vanessa's parents" replied Jack.

"Good luck with that then! We wish you fortitude!"

"Cheeky bugger!" chipped in Vanessa laughing.

"Well, you have to admit, Vanessa, Jack's going to need all the help he can get! After all he doesn't command a top accountant's salary to keep their daughter in the manner to which she is accustomed!" said Phil laughing.

Phil heard Vanessa snorting in the background.

"Yes, I tend to agree that I need Lady Luck on my side this evening. Anyway, what can I do for you, sir?" asked Jack.

"Your good sister and myself were talking about your upcoming wedding and it occurred to me that, as best man, I need to know something about the event. After all you were intimating last time we spoke that it's only a few weeks away and most people have booked their venue months, if not years, in advance. I'm guessing you must have made arrangements?"

"Ah, yes, well…. look………. we need to meet up for a drink and I'll fill you in!" replied Jack.

"Sounds mysterious!"

"Can you make sometime next week, say Thursday evening?" Jack replied without answering Phil's question.

Jane was mouthing something furiously at her husband. Phil held his hand up and nodded his head indicating that he understood.

"Yes, I'm good for that but Jane would like to come along too, so let's make it drinks for four?"

"Sure. Come round to our place for seven-thirty. Obviously, subject to work demands!".

"Understood but hopefully, see you both then!"

"Look forward to it!"

Phil clicked off.

"Looks like all will shortly be revealed. You're just going to have to contain yourself in the meantime!"

Jane folded her arms and made a moue.

Chapter 5

It was Friday 5th March and he was feeling on top of the world. He was still living off his success with Lily Anderson. His next victim was another woman living on her own. He'd done his research so well, he thought, applauding himself.

Then he sniggered. He'd been following the sad old cow to Alcoholics Anonymous and back to her prim little house.

He'd followed her from her boring work at Bodmin Pharmaceuticals back to her home. Sometimes he felt she knew she was being followed when she kept looking in her driving mirror but he had turned off and double-backed on those occasions to avoid detection.

He arrived at her address and clambered over the back fence.

It was early evening and quiet everywhere. There was no-one to be seen. He carefully cut the glass in the kitchen window, removed the pane and opened the window. Letting himself in, he silently moved through the kitchen into the lounge and back into the hall. No-one was about. He started up the carpeted stairs and stood for a moment or two outside Emily Henderson's bedroom. There was no sound, so he slowly opened the door which was ajar. The lump moved as it coughed. A chesty cough. Obviously, she had gone to bed early feeling unwell. How convenient, he thought.

Taking out a cloth from his pocket, he crept over to the bed. Bending over her, he was about to apply the cloth to her face when her eyes opened wide and she started to scream. He tried to put his hand over her mouth but she turned her head and started to pummel him with her hands and kick with her feet. Screaming, she managed to punch him in the chest which winded him. Getting off the bed she ran towards the door but quickly recovering, he grabbed her ankle and she came crashing to the floor. Her hands were opening and closing in an effort to grab hold of something but there was nothing for her to cling to and his strong grip steadily pulled her back towards him. She gave a last desperate kick as he released one of her ankles. He cried out in pain releasing the other ankle and she scrambled to the door on her knees at first and then used the door handle to stand up. Picking up the bedside lamp, he wrenched it from its socket and raising it high in the air he hit her hard on the back of her head. She lay motionless. He hadn't wanted this. He hadn't wanted her to die now. She hadn't suffered enough yet. He bent over her. She was breathing. He needed to move her fast but first he held the chloroform rag over her mouth to make sure she didn't wake up before he could get her in the car. He pulled off the bedspread and wrapped the unconscious Emily in it.

A couple of hours later Emily woke up and found herself lying on a concrete floor. She was dressed in her pyjamas and barefoot. She felt very hot like she had a temperature and coughed a bit. Not being tied up, she slowly stood up and looked around her.

There was a chair with two pairs of restraints attached and a table to the side with what looked like broken glass. She walked over to it and frowned as she looked at the mortar and pestle with bits of glass in the bowl. The room looked like someone's very large garage with a sliding door at the end but when she ran over to it ready to bang on the door and scream for help as loudly as she could, she found herself faced with a clear plastic wall. In the gloom she hadn't been able to make it out but as she came up close and started to run her fingers over it, she realised that it was solid but for a door at the end which she found to be locked.

Tears of fear started to gush down her face as she remembered what had happened. She shook as she thought of the masked face so close to hers and shuddered as she recalled how desperately she had fought to overcome the assailant and how hard the blow on her head had felt. After that, she had no recollection.

She felt the back of her head where the blow had been struck. The blood had dried but the area felt extremely tender and her head still ached. In fact, her whole body ached.

Suddenly, she knew she had to get out and fast. She started to scream and the more she did the louder her screams became.

The outer door opened from the bottom as the door slid up just enough for a man to slip under it and pull it back down behind him. In the gloom, Emily couldn't make out more than the figure was dressed in black.

Instinctively, she backed away, cowering in the far corner of the room. He moved towards her.

"You're awake then?" he said in a soft voice that caused Emily to involuntarily shiver.

Emily nodded.

"That's good. Now, we can do this the easy way or the hard way. It's up to you, Emily" he said advancing towards her.

She could see him clearly now. He had taken off his hood revealing his striking blonde hair. His eyes were as cold as ice and she felt as though he could see through to her soul. She shivered again, fear overcoming her. She started to scream. He was in front of her now and slapped her hard across the face. She screamed again and he punched her so hard in the stomach she fell to the ground, curled up in a ball and threw up.

He dragged her to her feet and slung her on the chair. She was struggling now, fighting for survival but he was too strong for her and he clipped on the restraints round her wrists and ankles.

A horrible smile crossed his face.

"There now that wasn't too difficult was it? It would have been so much easier for you if you had accepted your fate quietly" he said.

Emily started to scream uncontrollably again.

The man fetched a long piece of cloth.

She knew what it was for.

"Please, please, don't do this. Why are you doing this to me? Why? Why? No!" pleaded Emily.

The man gagged her without seeming to hear any of her questions or pleas and walked over to the table.

He walked back towards her slowly, brandishing a large knife. He ran his thumb and forefinger along the blade, looking at it lovingly and then looked at his victim, a cruel smile flitting across his face.

Reaching where she sat, Emily's head shaking wildly from side to side, trying to scream through her gagged mouth, he bent down and turned one of her restrained hands towards him palm up. She couldn't move her hand away and the tears started to stream down her cheeks. He slowly cut a line into her palm. Her whole body went rigid and then shook. The muscles in her face tensed. Her eyes shut now with her lids screwed up against the excruciating pain. He cut another and another until there were four long cuts. He went round to the other side and started to repeat his actions on her other hand. Emily's face flopped to one side after the second cut. She couldn't take the pain any longer.

The man walked over to the table, selected a small bottle and undoing the screw top he held the bottle under her nose. She came too with a start, blinking furiously. Her breathing was rapid and her face screwed up with the pain but she remained awake. Satisfied, the man put the bottle back, picked up the knife and finished his work on her hand. Then, he knelt down and picked up one of her feet. Emily realised what he was going to do and tried to kick her foot and then tried to push her toes downwards so that he couldn't reach the sole of her foot, but he was too strong and yanked her foot up slicing the sole with the knife. Again, he made four cuts. Emily's throat was straining with her screams and every so often, her torturer looked up at her and smiled.

"Won't be long now, Emily. We're nearly done here" he said, eventually, in a strange, sinister voice.

Blood was streaming out of her wounds onto the floor.

The man got up and once more walked over to the table. He wiped the knife clean with a cloth.

Then he picked up the mortar and pestle and, picking up a few of the fragments of glass, he started to crush them. He added a few more and then examined the mortar. Satisfied, he walked over to her with the mortar in one hand and a scouring pad in the other.

"Now the real fun begins, Emily" he said, as though they were about to embark on some sort of enjoyable game.

Emily's eyes were wide with terror and she shook her head violently from side to side, when the horrific realisation of what she was about to endure, dawned on her.

He began with the first hand and slowly but firmly rubbed the crushed glass into her wounds with the harsh pad. Before he reached her second hand, she had passed out. Again, he used the smelling salts and her muted screams filled the air. Her screaming suddenly stopped, her body went limp and Emily went into a state of shock when he reached the third cut on the second of her two feet. This time smelling salts failed to bring her round. The man finished his torture and put the pad and mortar back on the table.

He took the thin, plastic covered rope hanging on a hook on the wall above the table and walking over to his victim he put it round her neck. He pulled it little by little, tighter and tighter, letting it slack a bit now and again. When this happened,

Emily was able to gasp, choke and splutter, struggling to catch her breath. Then, he let the rope go completely slack. She gasped, gulping in air, trying desperately to survive. Calming down she began to breathe more easily and the thought occurred to her that she might be okay, that he was going to let her go. Suddenly, the rope tightened again but this time the rope only got tighter.

After a few minutes Emily's lifeless head lolled forward.

Chapter 6

The evening of Friday 5th March saw Jack and Vanessa driving to her parents' house. They had just been chatting to Jane and Phil on Jack's mobile.

"We should have told them that we aren't having a big wedding" Vanessa turned to Jack who was driving.

"No way! You know that my sister would be on Facebook and Twitter as soon as she knew. That would mean your parents would likely get to know and all hell would break loose".

Vanessa groaned.

"If only my parents weren't so traditional and more flexible. They want a church wedding and enormous reception so that they can show off to all their friends. It wouldn't be for us; it would be for them!"

"Nevertheless, we need to let them believe that that's what we are going to arrange for next year. If we don't and tell them the truth they will cause an inordinate amount of trouble, mainly for you. When we are married it is a *fait accompli* and I've no doubt they will come to accept it" said Jack pragmatically.

"I feel a bit guilty about not inviting my parents though, and I feel terrible about having to lie" said Vanessa more to herself than Jack.

"Yeah, well, if you're having second thoughts, we could arrange a traditional white wedding for next year" he said glancing across at her and grinning.

"Absolutely not!" she said vehemently, turning to look out of the window.

"Don't feel guilty about not inviting them. After all, there will only be five of us at the wedding, you, me, the registrar, Jane and Phil. It's not as though we were having a big gathering, and they were excluded!"

"No, you're right! I did say a 'bit' guilty!" she smiled as she turned to look at him.

Jack grimaced and turned in through the open gates, up the gravel drive and parked outside the substantial Edwardian house.

As they got out of the car, Edward, Vanessa's father came out to greet them, his hand outstretched towards Jack.

They shook hands.

"Good to finally meet you, Jack" he said with a lukewarm smile.

"Likewise, sir" he replied looking his future father-in-law directly in the eye.

After Vanessa had given her father a kiss and a hug, the three walked up the six stone steps into the house.

The lounge was large and square, one of two lounges, it was the room that guests were shown into, decorated in green and cream with long brocade green, gold and rose curtains. The large, comfortable cushions were attractively arranged on the green sofas and matched the curtains. The whole room had a restful, tasteful, expensive ambiance.

Edward indicated that they should sit on one of the sofas side-on to the fireplace while he took a seat on the sofa opposite them.

"My wife, Felicity, will join us shortly. In the meantime, what would you like to drink. We have a rather nice malt or if you prefer a sherry, brandy, vodka, martini?" said Edward addressing Jack.

"The malt sounds great" replied Jack, picking up on Edward's preference.

"Martini for me, please, dad".

"Splendid!" he exclaimed and strode over to an impressive drinks' cabinet.

As he did so, Felicity appeared at the doorway.

Tall, elegant with beautifully styled and discreetly coloured dark brown hair, she glided over to Jack and held out her hand.

"How wonderful to meet you, Jack" she smiled displaying a perfect set of very white teeth but while her mouth smiled, her eyes displayed disappointment.

"Likewise, Felicity" Jack said mimicking his exact same words of greeting to her husband a few minutes earlier.

She sat down on the sofa opposite her daughter.

"I'll have a sherry on the rocks, darling, please" she said.

Edward grunted, serving the ladies first. He handed Jack a glass of malt and sitting down he sipped his own glass of the same. Looking at it appreciatively, he put it down on the coffee table.

"So, Jack, I understand you are a detective. Am I correct?".

"Yes, sir."

"And what is your rank?"

"Detective Inspector, sir".

"Actually, Jack could have been a Detective Chief Inspector by now, but he likes to be where the action is and doesn't want a boring desk position. Jack's amazing at his job. I can personally vouch for that" cut in Vanessa giving her father a stern look.

"I'm sure he is, darling, but one must progress in one's job and climb the ladder, so to speak" commented Felicity.

"One day, surely, your sights will be on the position of Commissioner, Jack?" Edward asked, his eagle eyes piercing through Jack.

"Possibly but for the moment I enjoy what I do, sir" said Jack quietly, his manner totally composed.

There was an uneasy silence, both Edward and Felicity gave little coughs and discreetly looked at their watches.

"Vanessa was about to be engaged to a very nice young man. He was an accountant with a very prestigious firm, at a level where he commanded an excellent salary. Such a shame it didn't work out" Felicity sighed and then sipped her drink, looking despondently into the distance.

"Mum! That's not true! We weren't anywhere near getting engaged – at least I wasn't. We dated for a couple of months and that was it. If you remember, I had finished it with George a few months back! Now I have met Jack and I have never been so happy!" snapped Vanessa.

"Your mother just wants the best for you, darling. She just feels that a policeman's salary is not going to give you a good lifestyle" her father replied.

Turning to Jack he continued, "What about when Vanessa has to give up her career as a doctor to look after children? No offence intended Jack. I'm sure you are a decent chap. Just not what the doctor ordered!" Edward raised his glass to his lips chortling at his own joke.

No-one spoke for a moment or two. Then Vanessa got up, her blush spreading rapidly across her face.

"That's the most insulting thing you have ever said to me, dad. How could you, in this day and age, even suggest that I would contemplate giving up my career! Neither of us will be giving up our careers and I will be financially contributing to our 'lifestyle', as you put it, just as much as Jack. It's a partnership we will be going into not, as in your case, a man and his domesticated wife situation!" Vanessa stared down angrily at her father.

"There's no need for rudeness, Vanessa!" reprimanded her father in a stern voice.

Jack reached out for Vanessa's hand and pulled her gently down to sit beside him.

"May I suggest that we all calm down" he said looking at each of them in turn.

Edward looked as though he was about to say something but, in the end, refrained.

"I apologise if I don't meet your expectations of a future son-in-law" said Jack ditching the 'sir' "but I can assure you that no-one could love your daughter more than I do. I will do my utmost to make her happy for as long as we live. I do, in fact, earn well above the national average and, I can assure you that our combined salaries will be sufficient for us", he said turning to Vanessa who nodded in agreement. They were still holding hands.

Edward and Felicity exchanged glances.

"Well, you certainly seem very happy, and, in the end, I suppose that is all parents can wish for. Shall we head in for dinner, darling" said Edward addressing his wife.

Felicity sniffed and looking resigned at her husband's words, slightly inclined her head.

"If you all want to go into the dining room, I will fetch the hors d'oeuvres," she said getting up and walking out into the hall and across to the kitchen.

Felicity came back a few minutes later with a tray laden with tiny toasts topped with a sliver of sliced smoked salmon and cream cheese garnished with dill. There were murmurs of approval as she allowed each guest to help themselves from the proffered tray.

Conversation turned to wedding plans.

"So, have we just a year to plan the wedding, Vanessa?" enquired her mother.

Vanessa shot a sheepish look at Jack who gave her an encouraging smile.

"Well, yes, we will be looking at venues very shortly" she said turning to her mother.

"I would have thought you would have done that already, darling, after all most people book their wedding reception venue over a year in advance!"

"We're on it, Felicity. Vanessa and I are in the process of making a selection within a couple of weeks, aren't we?" and Jack turned to Vanessa placing a hand on hers.

Vanessa nodded enthusiastically.

"Then there's the guest list, your dress, of course, and what about the church. I'll have a word with the Reverend Taylor next week. Do you want me to book it for you?" asked Felicity.

"Let them sort it out, dear. I'm sure they are more than capable. Save us the work. It is not as though they are very young!"

"It's traditional for the wife's parents, Edward, to organise their daughter's wedding" she retorted.

"Really, don't worry, there will be enough time but we're not exactly sure of the date next year so hold fire on booking the church, Felicity," said Jack.

His future mother-in-law looked crestfallen, and Vanessa felt a bit of remorse.

"So where are you looking to live, Jack?" asked Edward, changing the subject.

"For the moment Vanessa has moved in with me but we are looking at buying a house in Ely. Another thing on the ever expanding To Do List! Realistically, we're not sure when we will finally get round to it," Jack laughed.

"Ely is a good choice.   Friends of ours live there. You never know you might move near to them. Small world!" exclaimed Edward.

Jack and Vanessa were simultaneously thinking – a good reason not to move there then! Ely was very definitely off the list!

There were a few minutes silence as Felicity served the second course, guinea fowl with parsnips, carrots with a hint of ginger, sprouts with bacon bits, dauphinoise potatoes, accompanied by a thick, spicy red wine gravy.

"This looks delicious, mum" commented Vanessa.

"Yes, it does, and you must give Vanessa the recipe!" added Jack, who rapidly regretted that he hadn't suggested that the recipe be given to both of them.

"Or maybe you might give the recipe to both of us because either one of us may wish to cook dinner", added Vanessa shooting Jack a malicious look.

"Yes, of course, that's exactly what I meant" leapt in Jack.

Felicity tried to subdue a smile, Edward guffawed, Jack went red in the face and Vanessa bore a self-satisfied smirk.

They all enjoyed the delicious meal. Felicity, being the first to finish, turned to Vanessa.

"So, the subject of children was mentioned a little earlier. I take it you are planning to have a family?" she asked.

Jack swallowed the wrong way and needed a couple of glasses of water to stop his coughing.

"Maybe that is a bit premature, dear?" suggested Edward.

"Not at all. These things should be discussed before marriage. After all, it's no good if Vanessa wants children and Jack doesn't, is it?" she retorted.

"Or maybe the other way around, mum" commented Vanessa.

Her mother looked shocked.

"Yes, we both want children but it's not high on our agenda at the moment" said Jack, having fully recovered from his coughing fit.

"Well, that's very good news" said Felicity shooting her husband a defiant look.

Dessert was a homemade lemon and sultana cheesecake with double cream.

"I don't think I will eat for a week after this, and I definitely don't think I can eat another thing this evening!" commented Vanessa when the Belgian chocolates were handed round together with the coffee.

"Oh, I can always manage a Belgian chocolate" said Jack grinning.

They moved back into the lounge and continued talking late into the evening.

At ten thirty-three Jack's mobile started warbling. He took the phone out of his jacket pocket, hanging on the back of his chair and glanced at it.

"Sorry, do excuse me, I have to take this. It's work" he said glancing round the table and putting his hand lightly on Vanessa's shoulder.

He moved towards the door of the dining room and walked into the hall shutting the door softly behind him.

"Hi Julia, as you know I am at Vanessa's parents' house for dinner" said Jack with a slight irritation detectable in his tone.

"I realise, sir. I do apologise, I wouldn't have disturbed you but there's been another murder and you are needed straightaway," said Szymanski.

"Do we know who? Where?" asked Allan immediately alert and forgetting about his irritation.

"Unidentified as yet, sir. The body was found where the old chalk pits were. Now called White Earth Nature Reserve. Near Lower Madden. Pretty gruesome by all accounts".

"Okay, I'll be there as soon as I can".

"Right, apologies again for disturbing you".

"Can't be helped. No worries, Julia".

He clicked off.

He re-entered the dining room, his face full of apology.

"I'm so sorry everyone but I have to go. There's been a murder and I'm needed straightaway."

"Quite understand Jack. Duty calls!" said Edward, a warm smile spreading across his face as he stretched out his hand.

They shook hands.

"Thank you so much for a most enjoyable evening. The dinner was superb, and it was a great pleasure to meet you both. I'm only sorry that I have to dash away" apologised Allan looking from one to the other of his future in-laws.

"Thank you, I'm so glad you enjoyed the meal. We were both delighted to meet you at last and hopefully it won't be too long before we meet again" said Felicity, as Jack kissed first one cheek and then the other.

Edward and Felicity's cold attitude towards Jack seemed to have evaporated, at least for the time being.

"Will you be okay to call a cab to take you home, Vanessa?" Jack asked.

"Sure. Of course. Take care. See you at home when you get there! Don't forget I am on early shift tomorrow!"

They walked into the hall and wrapping their arms round each other tightly, they kissed.

Once in the car, Jack switched on the engine and drove away at speed, blues and twos on as soon as he cleared the gates of the driveway.

During the thirty minutes or so drive from the village of Halton, where Vanessa's parents lived, to White Earth Nature Reserve on the east side of Cambridge, Jack thought of how much his life had changed for the better since he met her.

She had brought him a happiness he would never have believed he could experience. It was something that happened to other people but not to him. He remembered when he had gone down on one knee in the Le Jardin de Paris restaurant. Yes, he had wanted to impress her, that restaurant being by far the most expensive in Cambridge. He so desperately wanted her to say 'yes', he almost messed things up completely. His mouth had dropped or so he felt, when she had smiled at him and said the magic word.

After that, they had had an amazing holiday in Dubai, sun, sea and steamy sex. He grinned as he remembered how they couldn't get enough of each other. It was the same now – just that work got in the way!

He smiled again as he thought about the way his dedication to getting up in the early hours and hitting the gym for his workout every day had diminished to three times a week. He was having too much fun; he was too much in love to have time to work out every day. Somehow though, he didn't miss it one jot.

If someone had told him a few months ago that his enthusiasm for working out would be far less because of a very special woman, he would have scoffed at them. How wrong would he have been?

The crime scene at White Earth Nature Reserve was floodlit when Allan arrived. A police cordon had been erected around the area and a number of police vehicles were parked to one side.

Szymanski was striding towards him. Jack got out of his car.

"What have we got, Julia?" he asked.

"Again, bizarre, sir. Found by a dog walker, a Mr Josh Finlay" she said referring to her notebook.

Allan, having kitted himself with boots and gloves, followed Szymansky to the incident spot.

Pulling up the cordon for them both pass under, Allan saw before him a woman's body. She was dressed in a red top and brown mini skirt. Her feet were shoeless. Her feet and hands had been cut and there were streaks of blood on them.

Strange was bending over the body. He spoke without looking up.

"Definite similarities to the Anderson case. If you look at the soles of the victim's feet, they have been cut, hence the streaks of blood and there are fragments of glass in the lacerations. The same applies to her hands. She doesn't have a wig on though, but that could be because she is naturally a blonde. She is also holding a bunch of keys in her hand which is curious but similar to the last victim who was also holding a strange object, the chess piece", he said straightening up and addressing Allan.

"Cause of death?" asked Allan.

"These marks on her neck seem to indicate strangulation, but I would have to confirm that later after I have examined the body at the lab" Strange replied, picking up his bag.

"Speak tomorrow, Stew" said Allan. The coroner nodded briefly in acknowledgement and left.

Allan extracted the bunch of keys from the dead woman's hand and looked at them curiously.

"Obviously, this is a clue as was the chess piece. Thoughts, Julia?"

"Not sure about the keys or the Queen piece, sir, but I do think the hair colouring is significant. It could be that the murderer hated a blonde female in his life at some stage?" suggested Szymanski.

"Good point, Julia, you're probably right" and he counted the keys, then slowly turned them around in his hand.

"Seven keys. What do they open, I wonder. Bag them, Julia".

Taking out his mobile he proceeded to call all the members of his team one by one. Apologizing for the late hour, he informed them briefly that they had another murder case to solve requiring all hands on deck. Weekends and holidays were cancelled for now and as such, they should report for duty first thing in the morning.

Chapter 7

Arriving at the station on Saturday 6th March, Allan strode into the office and was greeted by a cacophony of phones ringing. There had been hundreds of calls since the Lily Anderson press conference had been held and the appeal had gone out. Regrettably, none of the calls had come to anything.

"Sir!" Patel hurried up with a smile on his face.

"Sophie and I did our door-to-door and I think you're going to like this. A nosey neighbour in Avon Street, she lives opposite number 105, saw a man coming out of that house on the night in question carrying a big bundle that looked like a rolled-up carpet!"

"Was this neighbour able to describe the man?" asked Allan.

"Yes" Patel referred to his notebook.

"Tall, full head of blonde hair, scruffy. That fits the description of our Percy Parker, doesn't it, sir?" he said excitedly.

"Yes it certainly does. We need to bring him in again for questioning but before we do, we need to find out who this latest victim is and whether there is a connection between them and Parker".

Allan's mobile rang.

"Morning, Stew. What have you got?" he asked brusquely.

"Got a minute to come over?"

"On my way!" replied Allan who did an about turn out of the office.

Strange looked up with a satisfied smile on his face as Allan entered the lab.

"First, you'll be pleased to know that we have been able to identify the victim. Dental records show that the woman before you, is one Emily Henderson. The two ligature marks around her neck" he said pointing to them "indicate that she was killed in the same fashion as Lily Anderson as do the marks on her feet and hands. She was twenty-four years of age. Bizarre case for you to solve, eh?" said Strange, as Allan stood gazing down at the corpse.

Allan examined the body, looking at the marks on the victim's hands and feet together with the strangulation marks on her neck.

"In your opinion was the woman strangled with the same type of plastic covered rope?" he asked at length.

"Yes, indeed, it has all the hallmarks of the same assailant as that of Lily Anderson" he replied.

"Time of death?" asked Allan.

"She has been dead for only a relatively short period of time. Time would be between five o'clock yesterday afternoon and nine o'clock last night".

"A different time to the other murder, then?" mused Allan thoughtfully.

"Yes. Looks like someone is either unemployed maybe or on variable shifts" replied Strange.

Back at the station, Allan called together his team and having reviewed information so far gathered, he proceeded to outline actions going forward.

"Barry, Sophie, find out where Emily Henderson currently worked and delve into her work history".

"On it, sir" they both replied in unison.

"Did anything come out of the trace on Parker and Stott's phones, Barry?"

"No, unfortunately not, sir".

"Okay. Dev and Peter, I want you to go through all her financial affairs, telephone calls both on mobile and if there was a landline – ditto".

"Yes, sir" Patel said and Purcell nodded agreement.

"Anything from CCTV?"

"No, sir. Parker's car doesn't show on any of the main routes to Stott's house".

"Mike and Max, I take it nothing unusual has surfaced from your surveillance of Parker?" asked Allan.

"No, sir, nothing of note so far" replied Townsend and García shook her head.

"Okay, keep on it. Dev has spoken to one of Anderson's neighbours who has described a man with a strong resemblance to our suspect, so hopefully we are on the right track. Any other information of interest gleaned from the calls following the appeal?" he asked.

Everyone shook their heads.

"Okay. Let's get to work. Julia, I'm going upstairs to update the boss. Apparently, he has come in to work on a Saturday, doubtless for some very good reason" he said sarcastically. "In the meantime, first off, get the keys dusted for fingerprints, though I doubt there will be any, and then get them over to a locksmith to establish what sort of locks they would fit. I think two of them are front door keys. Then find out where the victim lived and when I get back we'll get over there".

"On it, sir".

Allan made his way up the stairs to Tom Clarkson's office and knocked on the door.

"Come in!" barked Clarkson.

Allan went in, closed the door quietly behind him and walked over to the chair indicated by his boss.

"Sir, I'm sorry to disturb you, I'm sure you are extremely busy but I heard you were in the office today and I just wanted to update you on the situation regarding the Anderson case".

Clarkson sat back in his chair with a smile that did not reflect in his eyes. He twiddled his pencil one hand on each end of it. He nodded at Allan indicating that he should continue.

"There's been another murder, sir. Emily Henderson is the victim. Also, in her mid-twenties. There are similarities to the Anderson murder in that there were two ligature marks on both victims.

Both were holding a peculiar object in their hands. This time it was a set of seven keys. We are contacting a locksmith to establish what the keys might be for. However, whereas Anderson was wearing a wig, this victim was not, plus she was dressed in normal clothes. The victim was found by a dog walker late evening, yesterday. The appeal unfortunately didn't bring forward any witnesses regarding the first victim but the house-to-house enquiries did come up with a witness and the good news is that the description fits that of Percy Parker. We are still working on the validity of his alibi though CCTV hasn't come up with anything as yet, which means he either didn't use his car to get to Stott's but that begs the question, how would he then move the body or, more likely, he used a route that didn't involve CCTV cameras. Surveillance on Parker has been organised and we are investigating any connection between Parker and Henderson, sir" Allan finished.

"Another murder, Allan. You will have to work faster and longer hours to get ahead of this killer. Everyone has always sung your praises so I hope you are going to live up to expectations. You obviously wouldn't like to feel that you had failed in your duties, would you? Of course not. Well, thanks for the update and get back to me as soon as with some results" Clarkson looked at him smiling, his eyes glittering like a snake.

"I have cancelled all leave, sir, and the team are working hard to solve this case as fast as possible," Allan bit his lip refraining from saying anything he might regret.

Back in the general office, Julia waved to him to come over.

"Okay, sir, I've got a locksmith to come here this afternoon to have a look at the keys and Sophie will oversee. As you feared there are no fingerprints other than that of the victim".

"Good work, Julia! Where are we off to?"

"Emily Henderson lived at number 106 Beacon Street".

"Get a cordon round the building, Julia and we'll head off now" said Allan picking up his keys and identification.

"Already arranged, sir" replied Szymanski.

"Always ahead, Julia, well done!"

She smiled and they strode out of the office together.

Once at the house, which was a small, neat, two bedroomed affair, Allan took the stairs and went straight to the master bedroom. He sniffed the pillow of the unmade bed and turned to Julia who had followed him.

"What does that smell like to you, Julia?" he said handing it to her.

"Chloroform?" she suggested after taking a few sniffs.

"Exactly. This is the same killer".

Sometime later, having examined the whole house, Szymanski went to find Allan.

"Sir, it looks to me like Emily Henderson didn't have any family or friends. There's nothing to suggest any personal life other than some AA sessions that she attended. Same type of person as Lily Anderson?"

"Yes, it would seem this killer is targeting women that have virtually no personal life and will be alone when he attacks".

"There is an address for the AA sessions so we could make our way over and find out how she was doing?"

"Let's go!" agreed Allan. On the way Allan established that a Professor Tim Millett lived at the address where the AA sessions were held, along with his son, Seb.

The old Victorian house was situated in Newnham, a leafy suburb in west Cambridge where the streets were wide and tree lined.

Allan rang the bell and they waited a few paces back on the bottom step.

The man that answered resembled an absent-minded professor. He didn't really look at the police officers but rather above their heads as though not to let anyone disturb the train of thought in his mind.

"Can I help you?" he asked in a less than interested voice.

"Good afternoon, Professor Millett?" asked Allan.

"Yes and you are?"

"DI Allan and DS Szymanski, sir" announced Allan, both detectives showing their identity cards, "Do you organise AA sessions here at your house, sir?"

"AA?" asked the professor.

"Yes, Alcoholics Anonymous sessions" confirmed Allan.

"Ah, yes, of course. No, I don't" he replied coming down to earth from his thoughts now and looking at the two detectives.

"So, there are no AA meetings at this house, sir?" asked Szymanski.

"I didn't say that officer. You asked me do I organise AA sessions and I replied truthfully that I don't. However, my son does" the professor replied rather pompously.

"I see, sir" replied Szymanski politely, privately thinking that the professor was proving to be a proverbial pain in the arse.

"Would it be possible to speak to your son?" Allan asked managing to keep a pleasant smile on his face.

"I'm afraid not. He isn't here at present, but if you give me your contact details, I will ask him to call you upon his return".

"And when might that be, sir?" Szymanski asked.

"We are not in the habit of living in each other's pockets, so I really couldn't say" replied the professor in an off-hand manner.

"Understood, sir, but are we talking hours, days, weeks or months before he is likely to return?" said Allan who failed to mask the rising irritation in his voice.

"Hours or days, I would say. Can I ask what all this is about?" He looked directly at Allan.

"I'm sorry, sir, but we need to speak to your son" and Allan handed Professor Millett his contact card.

"Thank you for your time today and if you could ask your son to call us as soon as he returns, I would be much obliged" he then turned and, without looking back, left along with Szymanski.

The professor turned the card over in his hand several times and looking up, he stared at the retreating officers, a thoughtful expression on his face before turning and shutting the front door quietly behind him.

Once back in the car, neither had a chance to speak before Allan's mobile rang.

"Hello, sir, we've looked through the victim's financial affairs and there is nothing untoward. Regarding her mobile, there were a couple of calls the day of her death but nothing significant," said Patel.

"Good work, thanks, Dev" and Allan hung up.

While Szymanski was driving, Allan called Townsend.

"Mike, was Parker definitely in all evening yesterday?"

"Yes, definitely, sir. No question".

"Okay, so it would seem that Percy Parker fits the description but how did he commit the second murder if he was in all night. There's no way out from the back?" Allan asked.

"Not for him because he lives in the upstairs flat" replied Townsend.

"Unless he climbed out of one of the windows and jumped into the garden and over the fence at the back?"

"That is a possibility, sir!"

"Good, then Parker may still be our man. You and Max keep him under surveillance. I take it you have brought in uniform to help with that?"

"Yes, sir, we've organized that" replied Townsend.

"Good" replied Allan. Next he called Wright.

"Barry, how did you and Sophie get on in finding out about family, friends and colleagues?"

"I tried ringing you, sir, a moment ago but your line was busy. Bit of a sad story really. Seems that Emily Henderson was a recovering alcoholic. She had been abandoned by her parents when she was a baby and grew up in foster care. Never got to be adopted – the one that got left behind for no ostensibly good reason. When she was eighteen she took a job as a receptionist in Bodmin Pharmaceuticals in their offices just outside Cambridge in the Grantchester business park on the A603 and has been there ever since".

"Good work, Barry! Julia and I will head off to the business park first thing on Monday. Time to call it a day! See you at the station tomorrow early!"

"Okay, Julia, you caught most of that I'm sure. Between you and me, it is imperative we find the murderer quickly because I have a nasty suspicion that we may have a serial killer on our hands" Allan grimaced at the ugly thought.

"Yes, Jack, I was beginning to feel that way too!" Szymanski agreed.

As she drove back to the station to pick up Allan's car, he gave her a sideways glance.

"How's it going with your Polish friend? What's his name?" he asked.

"Sylas…….Bukosky. He's still with us. I'm going to have a word with him about finding somewhere else to stay. I don't think he has decided whether he wants to stay in Britain or go back to Poland. He still hasn't told us what happened to make him leave Poland but hopefully he will open up when I speak to him. It's not that I'm not sympathetic but it's difficult space-wise" she explained.

"Don't beat yourself up, Julia. It's your home and I think he owes you some sort of explanation or he needs to leave and get on with his life. Anyway, here we are. Good luck with it. I'm sure you'll sort things out. Sorry I have to rush off but I did promise Vanessa I wouldn't be late if at all possible. She's cooking up something special for dinner and a couple of friends are coming round. The way the case is progressing long hours would seem to be ahead of us! No Sunday lie-ins for a while! See you tomorrow!" Allan got out of the car, into his and shot off.

Szymanski sat in the car for a few minutes. She was frowning, her mouth was set in a thin, straight line, her birdlike face taught with concentration.

Chapter 8

Monday morning, 8th March at nine o'clock saw Allan and Szymanski at the offices of Bodmin Pharmaceuticals. They had hoped to be there at eight-thirty but the rush hour traffic never got any better.

After two hours of interviewing Emily Henderson's colleagues that had gleaned very little about her, apart from her being, on occasion, quite difficult. People never knew whether she would be fun and lively or down and introverted. Some suspected her of bi-polar, others that she suffered from a drink problem that took its toll on some days. No-one really knew much about her personal life.

"Last one now. Who have we got next" asked Allan.

"Sandra Olsen" Szymanski replied and at that moment there was a tap on the meeting room door which the office manager had designated for the interviews to be conducted.

"Come in" Allan called out.

Sandra Olsen was a tall, willowy blonde in her twenties with a pretty face though very pale in complexion. Entering the room, she sat down on the chair indicated by Szymansky.

"So, Ms Olsen, you worked for how long with Ms Henderson?" asked Szymanski.

"I worked with Emily for about three years" she said taking her handkerchief from a pocket in the side of her skirt and wiping away a tear running down her cheek. After blowing her nose, she fiddled with the handkerchief in her hands which were clasped together in her lap.

"Did Emily have a boyfriend, do you know?" asked Allan.

"No, not as far as I know, although………….." and she stopped suddenly.

"Go on, Ms Olsen, remember this is a murder enquiry" encouraged Allan.

"Well, there was someone she used to have dinner with from time to time but I got the impression he wasn't a boyfriend, just a friend, if you see what I mean" she replied.

"What do you know about him? His name for instance, where he lives and where they met?" pursued Szymanski.

"His name was Ian something. I'm not sure she ever told me his surname. I've no idea where he lives but I do know that they met at one of the AA sessions" she said, still twisting the handkerchief round and round in her hand and sniffing from time to time.

"That's very helpful, Ms Olsen, thank you and we understand this is a very upsetting time for you. Do you recall Emily talking about anyone else in her personal life?" said Allan.

"No, no, I don't think so" replied Olsen slowly shaking her head, her face screwing up in an effort to remember.

"Well, thank you for your time, Ms Olsen and if you do think of anything else, anything at all that you feel may be of interest to us, or even if you remember something that would seem to be insignificant, please call me immediately any time, day or night, on this number" and he handed her his card, indicating his mobile number.

Taking the card, she nodded, got up and quietly left the room.

Allan and Szymanski gathered their papers together and walked down to where they had parked.

As they got in the car, Allan's mobile rang.

"Allan" he said briskly.

"Yes, hello, is this Detective Inspector Allan? I believe you asked me to call you. My father told me. My name is Seb Millett".

Allan put the phone on speaker so Szymanski could hear and take part.

"Yes, indeed, I did and thank you for ringing, Mr. Millett. I need to ask you some questions about your AA group, if I may".

"Fire away".

"Okay. One of your members, Emily Henderson, what can you tell me about her?"

"I'm sorry, I can't really talk about Emily. It's all in the name really; Alcoholics Anonymous" he replied with an apologetic tone.

"Emily Henderson was murdered yesterday so this is a murder enquiry and you are obliged to tell us everything you know about Emily and the people who attended the group sessions. Now we can either do this over the phone or you will have to come to the station for a formal interview. Which would you prefer?" Allan asked politely but firmly.

"Murdered! That's terrible! Who on earth would want to murder her? That's really, truly dreadful!

And she was doing so well," Millett stopped talking, ostensibly overwhelmed.

"Yes it is, but you can help us with our enquiries to catch the criminal who did this. So, I ask again what was she like?" asked Allan.

"She was for the most part a cheerful person, although she didn't really gel with many of the other attendees. She could be moody and I suppose most of the others found that difficult to deal with. Personally, I think in time the strain of keeping to non-alcoholic drinks would cease and, as a consequence, her moodiness would have lessened, making it easier for her to make friends".

"When you say she didn't gel with many attendees, who did she gel with?"

"Well, really, only one person. Ian Matthews. They seemed to hit it off and I think they went out to dinner a few times".

"What was Ian Matthews like? Was he doing as well as Emily in his fight against alcoholism?"

"I would say so, yes, although………….."

"Although what?" asked Allan abruptly.

Millett hesitated.

"I was going to say, although I know this is going to sound weird, I wasn't truly convinced that he had an alcohol problem. I mean he said all the right words but somehow they didn't ring true but he must have had an alcohol problem, otherwise why on earth would he be attending?"

"What made you think that he didn't have a problem with alcohol?" asked Szymanski.

"Difficult to say but he didn't show any emotion when he spoke about his struggle. He was totally in control of his hands and body. Often a sufferer will wring their hands or their hands shake but.... it was like.... it was like he was delivering a speech which didn't relate to him. He was talking about someone else. Yes, that was it really, that and the fact that he seemed to latch on to Emily straightaway. He wasn't really interested in anyone else but I suppose that is natural if he liked her a lot. Without a doubt, he is going to be devastated when I tell him what has happened" Millet said soberly.

Millett was interrupted by Allan.

"No, you must not ring Ian and tell him. We will need his address, please".

"What now?"

"Yes, please".

"You don't think............?"

"I don't think anything, Mr. Millett. Now, if I could have Ian Matthews' address, please"

"Thank you" said Allan as the text came through with the information "and thank you for your time, Mr. Millett".

The address for Ian Matthews was No 18 Holling Avenue, Arbury, one of the most deprived areas of Cambridge, situated to the north of the city. The house turned out to be a mid-terrace council house on a large sprawling estate.

Parking a little way up the road Allan and Szymanski walked back to the unprepossessing house with nets at the windows that had probably been hanging there for the past ten years and never washed.

No sign of a bell, Szymanski rapped loudly on the glass panel in the front door.

A woman answered the door. She was in her mid-fifties, peroxide blonde, thin apart from her ample bosom. A cigarette was attached to her lip, the smoke emanating from it causing her eyes to screw up. She was both heavily lined and heavily made up. One hand on her hip and one hand on the door, she peered at them with a hostile expression.

"Yeah?"

"Mrs Matthews?"

"No, you've got the wrong address" she said and made to shut the door.

"Detective Inspector Allan and Detective Sergeant Szymanski" announced Allan who put his foot in the door and they both showed their identity badges before she had time to retreat inside.

"Oh? What do you want?" she asked curiosity displacing the previously hostility.

"We believe a Mr Ian Matthews lives here?" Allan asked.

"No, no-one called Matthews lives here. I'm not Mrs Matthews and I don't know any Ian Matthews!" she said.

"We have been reliably informed, madam, that Ian Matthews lives here. Are you sure you don't know him. Maybe he lodged with you at some time?" pursued Allan.

"No-one has ever lodged here and I'm sure I don't know Ian Matthews. Is that all Inspector?" she asked in an aggressive tone.

"Sorry to have troubled you Ms….?" asked Allan

"Mrs Greene" and she shut the door.

Back in the car, Szymanski spoke first.

"So, Ian Matthews gave a phoney address".

"If, indeed his name is Ian Matthews. Sounds like if the address is false so might his name be. We need to find this man" and Allan rang Patel.

"Dev, I want you to find out everything you can about an Ian Matthews fast as you can and get back to me".

"On it, sir" was the reply.

No sooner had the call finished than Allan's mobile rang again.

"Sir, Sophie here. The locksmith has just left and he said that two of the keys fit front door locks. Of the other five, one would appear to fit a case, two would fit back door locks and two would fit garage locks".

"Thanks, Sophie" said Allan and rung off.

Allan then punched in a number on his mobile.

"Hello, Mr Millett? Detective Inspector Allan here. When is your next AA meeting?"

"This Thursday. Why?"

"I need you to let me know if, and when, Ian Matthews turns up. It is urgent. It is vital that you don't let him know you are contacting us and it is also very important that you contact us immediately. However, in the meantime, I would appreciate it if you could come down to the station to give a description of this man. Maybe this afternoon at 4.30 pm?" asked Allan.

"Okay. Will do on both counts, Inspector" and Millett hung up.

Allan punched in another number.

"Barry, I need you to take the seven keys that were found on the latest victim to each of the victim's houses and try the locks on the front and back doors and on the garage door if there is one. Get back to me as soon as you've done that, will you? Oh, and if you find a case try the small key on the ring too" he added.

"Will do, sir!"

"Thanks, Barry" and Allan ended the call.

Allan was about to say something to Szymanski when his mobile rang.

"Hello, sir. I'm afraid there doesn't seem to be any record of an Ian Matthews except for one who is ninety-one years old and in a care home. I don't think that's the one you're looking for!" said Patel.

"No! Why doesn't that surprise me! The man has given a false name and false address. Interesting. It would seem we have another suspect. Hopefully, he will turn up at the AA meeting, although I think it unlikely, but in the meantime I have asked Seb Millett to come down to the station to give us a description of him" he glanced at his watch "he should be with you in about ten minutes. As soon as we have the description we'll put it on the media platforms. We're coming back to the station now" said Allan.

It was early evening, before Seb Millett had left. Having got permission from his boss, Allan went through the procedure of submitting the description to the media channels.

Allan was packing up his papers, when Wright knocked on Allan's door. Being summoned, he walked in and closed the door.

"None of the four keys fit front and back doors of either of the victims, sir and there are no garages in either case plus I couldn't locate a case for the seventh key" said Barry.

"It seems we have a mystery then, Barry" Allan replied stroking the side of his nose and looking thoughtful.

"Yes, sir, why were a random set of keys left in the victim's hands?"

"If we could solve that we might well be on our way to cracking this case" said Allan.

The next day, Tuesday 9th March, Allan called Szymanski into his office.

"We do have a possible suspect in Percy Parker and now we have a potential second suspect whose identity remains elusive at present, but, nevertheless, I think it would be helpful to hear the thoughts of Roger Quinn, in case we are missing something crucial. We're potentially facing a serial killer and the assessment of an excellent profiler would, almost certainly, be to our advantage".

"Agreed, sir".

Allan was already on his mobile.

"Morning, Roger. I need your thoughts on a potential serial killer. Can you spare us an hour of your valuable time?"

"Depends if you are going to keep your word this time on that pint you owe me!" he said jovially.

"If I had a pound for all the people I owe pints to, I would, without doubt, be a very rich man!" Allan quipped.

"Of course, Jack. I'd be delighted to help if I can. As it happens I have had a cancellation this morning so I am at your disposal. Shall I come over toute de suite?"

"See you soon and, Roger".

"Yes".

"Thanks" said Allan.

"Don't mention it!" replied Roger laughing.

Thirty minutes later, Allan, Szymanski and Quinn were sitting in one of the meeting rooms downstairs.

Allan described the two murders to Quinn in detail.

"Thoughts?" he asked the profiler.

"You are looking at a sadist. He enjoys inflicting pain maybe because he is trying to offload his own pain about something onto the victims. His pain would seem to be concerning women in his life. I would suggest that he hates women and wants to see them suffer the way, to his mind, women have made him suffer. Maybe he has been let down by important women in his life, like his mother, his wife or lover for example. Although, with no evidence of sexual interference, it would seem to point perhaps to the cause of his crimes being associated with childhood, in particular, to his mother. He is giving you obscure clues which he doesn't want to help you and part of his enjoyment is playing a game with you. So far, he is picking on young, lonely women but other than that there doesn't appear to be any similarity. He is probably choosing lonely women because it is easier for him to commit a murder. That may be the only reason. It is possible that you may find the answer to who and where the next killing might be by working on the clues he is giving you. If you could, if you like, break that code, you will be a step ahead of him".

"So, in your view, a. he will strike again and, b. he is leaving clues and not just mumbo jumbo?"

"Yes to both" replied Quinn simply.

"Would you say that we are looking for a man in his twenties to late thirties and a loner" asked Allan after rubbing the side of his nose and reflecting on what the profiler had told him for a few moments.

"Yes again. He will seem introverted and totally absorbed. Undoubtedly, he will be focussed on his crimes".

"Thanks for your time, Roger, invaluable insight as always" said Allan as they all stood up. The two men shook hands.

"Looks like you have your work cut out, Jack. Good luck! I'm sure you will crack this crime as always".

"I certainly hope so!" replied Allan.

Chapter 9

It was a bright and sunny morning on Tuesday 9th March.

"Come on, boy, let's go!" called Jane. The bump seemed to have grown to a size out of proportion to her time. She was just over seven and a half months, and she could swear most people her size would be full-term.

She called again but there was no response. She walked all around the house but couldn't find him. She frowned and felt a slight unease.

Jane picked up her mobile and called Phil.

"Hi there, you okay?" she asked as her husband picked up.

"Yeah, just got in, what's up?"

"I can't find Spot; you didn't take him to work, did you?"

"No, he was in the kitchen the last I saw of him. He was whining at the door and wanted to go out in the garden, but I let him back in before I left" he replied.

She crossed the kitchen and opened the back door, breathing a sigh of relief when she saw their pet standing forlornly waiting to come in.

"Obviously you must have forgotten him – he was still outside in the garden! No worries – the main thing is he is okay. Hope your day gets better!" she quipped cheekily.

"No, I'm sure I let him in, Jane" and she detected a puzzlement in his tone.

"Well, you couldn't have. I've done things like that before. You were probably thinking about work and forgot! That's the only explanation, isn't it?".

"Ummm! I guess but that's really weird! Anyway, as you say, you've found him! Enjoy your walk".

"Love you!"

"Love you too!"

Jane clicked off.

"Come on, Spot, let's go for a walk" she said getting his harness on and attaching his lead.

The local park wasn't far up their road, and they soon reached it, Jane puffing slightly as she waddled along.

Strangely she still felt an unease about Spot being in the garden. Phil wasn't usually forgetful, it was totally out of character, and at the back of her mind something else was nagging her, she just couldn't put her finger on it.

Entering the park, she slipped Spot's lead and he shot off ahead of her, stopping now and again, to sniff at an interesting smell. As he circled around before performing his usual offload, Jane fished for a poo bag in her jacket pocket. She sneezed violently. The tree pollen count was very high this year although, as far as she was concerned, it was high every year. Crouching down she picked up the offending substance with the bag and made a knot in the top of it.

She heard a cyclist approaching but didn't look round. As he passed, he brushed her with enough force to cause her to steady herself against the tree trunk. Shaken, it took a couple of moments before she was able to turn in the direction the cyclist had gone. He was disappearing into the distance so there was no chance to admonish him.

She took a deep breath and calmed herself before continuing her walk.

The cyclist stopped outside Phil and Jane's house. He looked around to make sure no-one was watching. He knew that the owners wouldn't be back soon. One of them was at work and the other was on an hour's walk with their mangy pet. Parking his bike at the side of the garage, out of sight of the road, he took some keys out and let himself in. He was wearing his cyclist's gloves but he removed those, putting them in his trouser pocket and donning a pair of latex gloves.

Padding upstairs he went into the master bedroom, rummaged through Jane's underwear drawer, and picked a pair of matching panties and bra. He placed them on the bed. Standing back as though to admire them, he smiled to himself. Running nimbly downstairs, he took one of the knives from the block and placed it on the drainer. Then turning on the oven, he set it to 200 degrees. Picking up the post he placed it in the hall drawer.

Then he walked out of the house, locked the door, got on his bike and rode away.

Jane was looking forward to a cup of coffee. She had always enjoyed walking Spot, but it was becoming a real struggle now with Bump.

"Come on boy" she said as she opened the front door and let the dog go in before her.

She took her coat off, hung it on one of the hooks behind the door and looked at the mat for any post, surprised to see none. The postman had usually been by now and she was expecting a letter about her upcoming maternity leave. Why the company had to send it in the post when they could have given it to her in person when she was at the office or send it by email, was beyond her comprehension. With all the bemoaning of rising costs, that could be one cost saving exercise. She shook her head. It'll probably come tomorrow she thought, walking into the kitchen and grabbing the kettle.

She went over to the sink and stopped dead. What was that knife doing on the drainer? She was certain that she hadn't left it there and equally certain that Phil hadn't either.   Why was it so hot in here, she thought. Then, glancing over at the oven, she saw the little red indicator light was on. Turning the oven off, she put the kettle down, picked up the knife and put it back in the block. Then she picked it up again and calling Spot to her side walked from room to room pushing each door back as she went. Finally, she got to their bedroom. She dropped the knife, raising he hand to her mouth and let out a scream as she saw her undies laid out on the bed. She went down the stairs as fast as her bump would allow and dialled Phil.

"You aren't making any sense, Jane, slow down, take a breath" said her husband calmly when he picked up his mobile and heard her breathless, panicky voice uttering unintelligible sounds. She was half crying, half shouting but after Phil had asked for her to calm down so that he could understand what she was saying, she swallowed hard, took a couple of deep breaths and relayed the events again.

"I'm sorry, Phil, but I'm totally spooked. I know I didn't leave the knife on the draining board, and I definitely didn't leave the underwear on the bed. Obviously, you didn't. So, who did?"

There was a moment's pause. Phil was thinking.

"Was there any sign of a break in when you got back. Anything unusual? Was the front door locked? Did you have to use your key? Anything at all that looked out of place apart from the knife, undies and the oven being on?" His mind was working fast. He was worried but he didn't want to alarm his wife, so despite his barrage of questions, he kept his voice level.

Jane thought hard.

"No, nothing" she said shaking her head.

"Well, you said it yourself, darling, who did it? No-one would break in and do those things. What would be the point? Plus, if there wasn't any sign of a break in then …….." he could feel himself relaxing at Jane's answer.

"Then what? You think I forgot that I did those things?" she said fractiously.

"No….no….well…..yes…..maybe. I don't know, darling, but well, you are heavily pregnant. Maybe it's a hormone thing. Look, I must go. I'm sorry. Make yourself a cup of coffee, relax and have a good afternoon at the office. Not long now and you will be on leave and lead a relatively stressless life for a few weeks! Love you! See you tonight!" and she heard him blow her a kiss before he rang off.

Jane stood for some moments unable to move. She knew she hadn't put the knife on the drainer and she certainly had turned the oven on. Equally she knew she hadn't put her undies on the bed, but Phil was right, if there was no sign of anyone else being in the house then what was the explanation?

The landline rang in their hallway and pulling herself together she walked over to it and picked up the handset.

"Hello" she said.

"Hi Jane, its Ruth from People Management. You okay? I expect you're looking forward to going on leave now? Today is your last day, isn't it?" Ruth's friendly, down-to-earth personality came over in the warm tone of her voice and made Jane feel happier.

"I'm good thanks. Yes, this afternoon is my last day in the office and I am really looking forward to my leave. How are you?" she replied.

"Very well, thank you. Jane, we sent your maternity leave letter to you in the post first class yesterday, so you should have received it this morning?"

"No, no I haven't as yet. The post has normally been by now but maybe it's late today".

"Yes, no worries, but when you do get it. There is a mistake in the letter so just to say we are aware, and a replacement letter is being sent to you with the amendment. Just destroy the first one you receive and wait for the correct version. Many apologies, Jane".

"Thanks for letting me know. I'll look out for the amended one".

"Thanks Jane. Bye".

"Bye, Ruth" she said and replaced the handset.

Putting the kettle on for a much-needed cup of coffee and while waiting for the water to boil she went to the cupboard under the sink where she kept the dog food and treats. Calling Spot to her she made him sit and then gave him a marrowbone treat.

She felt much better after the coffee and began to convince herself that she was probably losing it a little with the stress at work at the moment and contending with the bump. Maybe she had done those things and had simply forgotten.

As she sat stroking her tummy, she thought about her brother Jack and Vanessa. She hoped things had gone well at the dinner at Vanessa's parents' house last Friday evening. She wasn't altogether sure what they were up to. They hadn't told anyone what they were planning, and they were very short of time. She wondered whether Vanessa's parents were aware now of the wedding plans. Well, they would also know soon enough when they went round to Jack and Vanessa for drinks on Thursday.

Hoisting herself out of her armchair, she put her mug in the dishwasher and went upstairs. She had earmarked the rest of this morning to go through the baby's layette and make lists of items she still needed. Reaching the top of the stairs she stopped suddenly. Her head on one side she slowly retraced her steps to the hallway.

Yes, she was right, one of the drawers in the antique hall table had been slightly pulled out. Barely noticeable but as they never used those drawers, subconsciously her mind had remarked on it. She reached out and opened the drawer. Her hand flew to her mouth, she took two steps back as today's post looked up at her.

With trembling fingers, she pulled out the letters, one of which was the letter from Ruth Sands. Throwing the letters on the tabletop as though they were contaminated, she walked back through the kitchen into the lounge and sat down. She shuddered violently at the horrible realisation that she had been right in the first place. Someone had been in their house. That was the only possible explanation. But why? Why had they done these strange things. Her brother was always saying there has to be a motive for someone's actions. What possible motive could there be for such bizarre happenings? The one possibility was that the someone was completely mad but why choose them, their house?

While Jane sat shivering and pondering on her sofa, she was totally unaware that she was being watched.

****

The last thing that the intruder had done before he left was to install two tiny cameras in their home. He watched her distress, a wide grin spreading across his face.

****

With the thought of her maternity leave so close, she should have been relaxing and enjoying this time before the birth of their first child. Instead, she was fraught with anxious dread. After discovering the letter in the hall table drawer, she finally got up from the sofa and rang Phil again.

"Hi darling" Phil sounded slightly irritated.

"Phil, I've just found this morning's post in the drawer in the hall table, and I know I didn't put it there!" her voice rose as she spoke ending in a high-pitched squeak. Tears were threatening to roll out of her eyes.

"Jane, you have to get a grip. I think your hormones are playing up and you are forgetting things. We already agreed that there is no way anyone could have got in and done these things. There's no sign of a break-in, no-one has our key, except Martha the cleaner and I would be astounded if it was her unless she's suddenly had a complete breakdown! Listen, Jane, I love you and everything is going to be fine. I will endeavour to get home early today. Try to calm down and just do all the things you were going to do. Enjoy! Very soon you will be a lady of leisure! I will be home soon, okay?"

"Okay, love you too! See you later" she managed to stifle the sob which was rising in her throat.

Phil hung up.

Jane rang work and said she wouldn't be in that afternoon; she apologised profusely as it was her last day but she was feeling a bit poorly. She felt horrible about not going in because she knew that her colleagues would have bought baby things and other presents. Her manager had been very understanding and suggested she pop into the office when she was feeling better.

The rest of the day Jane kept Spot close to her. She couldn't eat her lunch. She felt nauseous most of the time and lay down on the sofa in the afternoon, her hand on the bump.

The key in the door woke her up. She called out immediately, fear evident in her voice.

"It's only me, darling" Phil said as he strode over to the sofa and sitting beside her, kissed and cuddled her in his arms.

Jane burst into tears.

"Now let's have a cup of tea as Bump won't appreciate a glass of wine!" he said kissing the top of her head.

Jane swallowed hard, managing a grin while wiping away her tears.

A few minutes later, they were sipping their steaming hot mugs of tea.

Finally, Phil put his tea carefully on the coffee table taking time to collect his thoughts.

"Darling, I'm really very sorry that you have been so upset when you should be enjoying this time. Let's think about it again though logically".

"Maybe we should call the police, Phil" interrupted Jane turning to look at him, her eyes bloodshot and smudged with black mascara. She was twisting her handkerchief round and round in her clasped hands on her lap.

Phil placed one of his large hands on her two much smaller ones and shifted his seat so that he could put his arm round her shoulders.

"And say what, Jane? There's no evidence that anyone has been in here, is there? No signs of a break-in. No-one has the key apart from Martha. All they will say is to let them know if there are any developments and that they have noted it".

"But they could see if there is any DNA proving that someone else was here" she sniffed rubbing the tip of her nose.

"The police won't have the time to do a DNA test, and funds won't allow them to do it if there is no real evidence of a crime having been committed, which there isn't, is there?"

"Yes, there is though! Someone else must have been here because neither of us did any of those things!" she pulled her hand away from his.

"Okay, Jane. I hear you. So, what I suggest is that we have cameras installed in the house and outside too. That way, if this happens again, we will know what is going on. I'll make some enquiries now online and see if we can get someone down tomorrow. How would that be?"

"Yes, that would be good but I'm still nervous about being in the house alone during the day".

"Well, would you prefer me to check you into a Premier Inn for a few days?" he asked.

She hesitated for a minute or two then shook her head.

"No, no, I'll be alright" she said smiling.

"You have Spot here to protect you. Not that I think his protection will be needed because I don't think anyone came in here".

"If you go and find a company that deals in security, I will make us dinner. You're right, I need to pull myself together. Maybe I have got a hormone problem and that is the answer" and she put her arms round him and hugged him tight.

Phil went up to his study, sat down and opened the lid of his laptop but before he keyed in the password, he sat for a minute staring at nothing in particular in front of him. Then he set about finding a firm.

"Ummm!! That smells delicious! What are we having?" asked Phil as he crossed the kitchen and put his arms round his wife's waist.

"Moussaka and salad. Lemon mousse to follow" she said upturning her face for a kiss.

Phil laid the table and Jane served the moussaka, placing a large bowl of salad in the centre.

"That was fabulous. My compliments to the beautiful chef!" commented Phil finishing his meal and placing his knife and fork together on his plate.

"Why thank you, kind sir" said Jane laughing. She felt better about things now after a good meal and talking it through with her soulmate. She was beginning to think Phil was right and it was just a pregnancy thing.

"So, the good news is that I've found a local security firm that I think can help and I have emailed them, but the bad news is that I think it maybe a few days before we can get someone out and then probably a few more days before we can get the cameras fitted" and he made a down face.

"It's okay, darling. I feel better now anyway but I do think the cameras are a good idea" she said smiling and reaching across the table for his hand.

"Just a thought. When we are round at Jack and Vanessa's on Thursday, I might just mention it to Jack. What do you think?" asked Phil.

"What about the cameras?"

"No, well, yes, about the cameras but about all of it. Just to get his take".

Jane considered.

"Yes, okay, maybe. Let's think about it?"

"Okay".

****

The man was listening to every word, sitting on a bench in Wandlebury Country Park, his earphones attached to his mobile and looking at the live feed of Jane and Phil as they spoke. A horrible smile crossed his face as he watched and listened to Jane gradually relaxing into thinking she was at fault, that it had all been down to jangling hormones. Those thoughts would disappear very rapidly when he implemented the plans he had for her.

****

On waking up the next day, Wednesday 10th March, Jane felt a whole lot better and even more so when she entered the kitchen to find, before Phil had gone to work, he had set out a delicious breakfast of fruit, yoghurt, cereal and fruit juice together with croissants and small, tempting Danish pastries which he must have picked up on his way home yesterday evening.

She located her mobile and sent him a text ending in an emoji heart. Humming to herself she poured a cup of coffee which was keeping hot in the percolator and settled down to her gourmet feast. Without a doubt, she would put on weight if this breakfast was the order of the day, every day. It was so like him to try to think of something to cheer her up if she was down. Life was a lottery game really and she had been so lucky to have met Phil quite by chance in a supermarket car park of all places. She remembered she had dropped her car keys and was scrabbling around on the ground trying to find them. Phil had parked next to her and walking over to her had asked what she had lost. He had joined in her search for the keys and finally located them under his car. She had laughed in an embarrassed way, thanking him profusely and saying that she owed him. He had suggested maybe she would like to buy him a drink and that was the beginning of their love journey.

Finishing her musing, she cleared up her breakfast dishes and ran a few errands. She was looking forward to meeting up with Sue that afternoon for her first antenatal exercise class. Sue was one of her closest friends and was due to give birth at around the same time.

Arriving at the local community centre where the class was being held at one-thirty, she looked around the car park for Sue. Quickly spotting her, she called out, waving as she did so. They hugged each other, then chatting away about this and that, they walked into the building and headed for the room indicated on the board in the small foyer.

"I was a bit sceptical about these classes, I must admit, but I really think it has been helpful, don't you?" asked Jane as they walked out into the car park after the session.

"Yes, I enjoyed it too. Helped allay the fears!" Sue said laughing.

"Ummm! I'm nervous too. I just want to be the best mum!" replied Jane grinning.

Sue was staring across to the far end of the car park. Jane followed her friend's line of vision.

"That car, the grey estate, right at the end by the grass verge" said Sue shading her eyes against the Spring sunshine.

"Yes, I see it and there's a man standing beside it looking this way. What of it?".

"I'm sure he was there when we went in, and he was looking this way then".

"Perhaps he's waiting for someone?" suggested Jane.

"Perhaps, but unlikely he would be standing by his car. Surely, he would be sitting in his car. Strange!"

"Maybe he has been sitting in it but has got out to stretch his legs" replied Jane unconvincingly.

They started to walk towards their cars and then Sue turned and looked across at the man.

"He's interested in us, Jane. His eyes are on us not the entrance to the Centre".

"Well, we are going now, aren't we?" but an icy feeling of dread was beginning to rise in Jane's stomach.

"I think we should see if he follows one of us. I just feel uneasy. You hear so many peculiar happenings nowadays. It's a one-way street to the roundabout and you go right, and I go left. So let me go first and if he follows me, you follow him and if he doesn't and follows you, let me know and I'll double back and get behind him. Use your blue tooth so you can phone me if that happens. I think he will give up if there are two of us. It's probably nothing but just to be on the safe side. We need to find out while we are together whether to be alarmed or not. It will be easier to convince the police about him if we are both witnesses. We must be sure to take his registration number", and she looked at her friend to see her reaction.

Jane's face had become tense and the expression in her eyes worried. She quickly told Sue about what had happened the day before.

Sue kept calm, at least outwardly. They both glanced over to the man who was still standing by his car watching them.

"Listen stick to our plan and if it is to do with yesterday, he will follow you, yes?"

"Yes, okay. Let's do it!".

They went to their cars and Sue drove off first, as arranged.

Jane had difficulty keeping her hand steady on the key to fire the engine but managed it the second time.

The grey car slowly moved out but stopped to allow Jane to reverse her car. Meanwhile, Sue was still waiting at the exit into the road. Jane drove up behind her friend and the grey estate car lined up behind her. Sue drove off and at the end of the road entered the roundabout and turned left. Jane was in the right-hand lane. The grey car lined up behind her. Jane's heart was in her mouth but as soon as a space presented itself, moved into the right-hand lane around the roundabout and turned right. The grey saloon took the second turning and disappeared. Jane breathed a sigh of relief and rang her friend.

"He went straight on!" Jane exclaimed.

"Very odd but obviously nothing to do with us! I'm sure there's a perfectly good explanation to yesterday too. It must be our hormones playing up! Phil is probably right!"

They both laughed and drove to their different homes feeling relieved.

****

The man was rattled. Instinctively, he knew that bitch, Jane, was on to him. She and her friend were setting a trap. He was rarely rattled but the stupid cows had caused him to abort his plan. That wouldn't happen again. Next time he would make sure he achieved.

Chapter 10

He sat at a small desk in apartment, drumming his fingers and looking at his laptop screen. He was certainly leading a double life. One where he was a nondescript nobody, necessary to enact the revenge he was implementing and the other where he was quietly and unobtrusively building his future life.

Satisfied with what he saw, he got up and moved over to the expresso coffee machine. Tall and elegant in stature, he moved with ease. Observers would be forgiven for thinking that he had undergone plastic surgery, so chiselled was his jaw line. His eyes were hard to read but always astute. His blonde, carefully highlighted, hair was swept back off his face and down the back of his neck. It had been cut in a style that could be ruffled to give an unkempt look or brushed back for a well-presented appearance.

Picking up the cup of coffee from the machine, he turned back towards his laptop when there was buzz on his intercom. On the camera he viewed the person standing outside the door to the apartments.

"Come in" he commanded and left the door to his apartment ajar.

A woman entered, dressed in a white clinical top.

"You requested a manicure, sir?" she asked.

"Yes, you have precisely fifteen minutes to execute the task" he replied in an abrupt and slightly menacing manner as though, if she were a second longer with her task, her fate was sealed.

While his nails were being attended to, he sat and seemingly stared into space. Far from it, he was planning his next move. It was all a chess game to him. It depended on who made the right move at the right time. He had already made sure on a couple of occasions that he had made his move at the right time and gone in for the kill.

Feeling relaxed after his manicure, he poured himself a whiskey and looked out of the window over Cambridge City.

A while later, he opened his laptop. He needed to compose a few letters.

Chapter 11

It was ten o'clock in the morning on Thursday 11th March when Allan's mobile rang. Before he had time to lift the phone to his ear, the caller was already speaking.

"Hello, Seb Millett here. I thought you might like to know that Ian Matthews has turned up for the session today".

"We'll be there in ten minutes. Act as normal in the meantime and under no circumstances tell him that we are on our way. Thanks for calling" Allan hung up.

"Right, Julia, let's go and meet our elusive Mr Ian Matthews" said Allan as he strode out of his office and past her desk.

Szymanski dropped what she was doing and followed her boss.

The session had begun when Allan and Szymanski arrived twenty minutes later at the Millett's house. Having announced themselves on the doorstep they were ushered in by the professor and shown into a large comfortable lounge. The professor had left them for a little under three or four minutes when Seb Millett came in with a man who he introduced as Ian

Matthews. Millett then excused himself saying that he had to get back to the session he was leading.

Matthews was a tall, overweight man with unkempt, greasy hair, whose corduroy trousers were none to clean. He had on a creased shirt, the tail of which was hanging out of the waistband of his trousers and a pullover that had seen better days.

"We need you to come down to the station with us, Mr Matthews, although that actually isn't your name is it?" said Allan sternly.

"What....yes...of course....it's my name" the man stuttered.

"It's a criminal offence, sir, to lie to the police when a murder is being investigated" said Szymanski also with a stern expression.

"Murder?.....Murder? what do you mean....Murder? Who?" he stuttered, his eye twitching nervously.

"Come along now, sir, we're going to take you to the station" said Allan firmly.

"Okay, okay but I don't know anything about any murder!"

Allan and Szymanski stepped either side of him and they walked out into the hall. Allan dropped back as they went through the doorway. Suddenly without warning Matthews seemed to gather all his strength, pulled away from Szymanski's restricting hand on his arm, and pushed her to the ground.

While Allan was helping his colleague to stand up, Matthews had run down the drive and hesitating momentarily he turned right and kept running with the detectives now in hot pursuit.

They all pelted down the tree lined avenue, across the junction which was empty of traffic at that moment and straight on down the next road.

Matthews had long legs and was fitter than he appeared. Allan was gaining on him slightly but not enough to bring him to the ground.

Matthews lurched across the road in front of an oncoming van who made an emergency stop.

Allan managed to cross after him while the van driver was still recovering.

Szymanski stopped briefly and shouted into her mobile for backup, then continued in pursuit.

Reaching a main road, Matthews weaved his way through the traffic oblivious to the danger and the sounding of horns.

Allan was close behind and gaining now.

Matthews legged it up a side alley and Allan knew that even his level of fitness would eventually drop. He had to get his man now. He gave a sudden spurt, gained on Matthews sufficient to grab his legs and pull him face down on the ground.

Allan pulled the man's arms behind his back and cuffed him. Szymanski had now caught up, with back up close behind.

"Take him down to the station" he said to one of the uniformed officers.

"You okay, sir?" asked Szymanski.

"Never better, thanks Julia" and he beamed at her.

Back at the station, the two went to Allan's office to collect papers before interviewing their suspect.

"Did anything strike you about Matthews, Julia?"

"Apart from he looks like an alcoholic who is not recovering and that he knocked me over?" she asked, her thin mouth curling in a sardonic smile.

"Yes! Apart from that!"

"Yes, his build doesn't fit the description given by Lily Anderson's neighbour".

"The neighbour could be wrong of course on the build. Anyway, let's see what the interview brings, take a swab, run it though the database. Might come up with something".

They walked down the stairs to the interview room.

They sat down opposite the suspect and Allan turned on the tape.

"Firstly Mr Matthews, I need to know what your real name is. Before you answer, I must inform you that if you do not cooperate, we will be able to take a swab from your mouth and dental impressions in order to establish your identity. It might take some time but we will get there in the end. So, it would be far simpler if you just tell me your real name".

The man pushed a hand through his unruly hair then folded both hands in his lap. His whole demeanour was now one of resignation as he looked down and twisted his fingers.

"Do I have to have a solicitor now?" he asked.

"You don't have to. Would you like one?" asked Allan.

Matthews was silent for a moment and then shook his head.

"Okay" he said at last, "My name is Ray Mason".

There was a silence while Szymanski input his name into her tablet.

"So, you are an escaped prisoner, is that right, Ray?" she asked with a piercing look.

He nodded dejectedly.

"It was an accident. I will never forget it. He just came out from nowhere. I tried to stop but he just ran in front of me" and he put a finger and thumb in each of his eyes.

"You were seriously over the limit when the accident occurred, Mr Mason" said Szymanski in a clipped tone, her thin lips set in a tight line.

"What were your movements on Wednesday 3rd March in the evening until 4.00 am on the morning of 4th March, Mr Mason?" asked Allan switching subject.

"Wednesday 3rd March?" repeated Mason, looking vague.

"Yes, describe your movements on that evening until the early hours of the next morning".

"I don't know. I think I was….. Yes, I remember now, I did a bit of shopping in Tesco Express near me. Then I went home, had my dinner, watched a bit of telly and went to bed".

"Can anyone verify that?" asked Allan sitting back and keeping his eyes fixed on Mason.

"I live alone, so, no, but I'm telling the truth. I may have a receipt for the shopping," he added.

"Okay. Do you know either or both of these women? This is a murder enquiry so I strongly advise you not to lie to us, Mr. Mason" said Szymanski, a severe expression on her face as she passed photographs of Lily Anderson and Emily Henderson across the desk.

Mason looked down at the photographs.

He looked carefully at each one and looked up at both of the detectives in turn, a nervous expression on his face. He looked back at the photo of Emily Henderson. His hand visibly shook as he pointed to the latter.

"Yes, this is Emily. I don't know the other lady" he whispered.

"And how do you know Emily, Mr Mason?"

"She....she's not dead is she? She hasn't been mur.....?" and his eyes were welling with tears.

"Just answer the question, Mr Mason" said Allan cutting in.

"Okay. She comes....came...to the AA sessions that are held at Seb Millett's house. We somehow hit it off. Not like that, just friends, you know. So, we had dinner a few times. That's it really. She was really nice, I liked her" he said tailing off.

"You liked her, you got on and then what....you had a row. She didn't want to see you anymore. You then decided to kill her, is that what happened?" asked Szymanski.

"No, no, no. I didn't kill her! She was my friend! I would never do that!" he said and the tears started to run down his cheeks.

"Have a look at the other photograph, Mr Mason, are you sure you have never met this woman?" asked Allan having left a few minutes for the interviewee to calm down and pointing to the photo of Anderson.

Ray Mason peered down at the picture again and shook his head.

"I've never seen this woman before" he said at last.

"Can you account for your movements on Friday 5 March from late afternoon to midnight?" asked Szymanski.

"Yes, yes, I can. I stayed at my sister's house. She and her husband were going out for the evening. There was a darts match at the pub and so she asked me to babysit and stay over. I got there about four o'clock in the afternoon of the 5th. You can ask her if you like!" he said defiantly now.

"Don't worry, we will" was Szymanski's quick response.

"Okay, Mr Mason" and Allan switched off the tape having made the necessary closing interview remarks.

Allan and Szymanski left the room.

Standing outside in the corridor, Szymanski leant against the wall while Allan stood characteristically rubbing the side of his nose with an extreme look of concentration on his face, his other hand in his trouser pocket.

After a few seconds he stopped rubbing his nose and then put his hand in his other trouser pocket. He looked at his colleague and broke the silence.

"He has no alibi for the first murder. However, he has for the second if that proves true, although family can lie for their own. Quite apart from that though, my gut feeling is he is not our man. He didn't try to hide the fact that he knew Henderson and he seemed genuinely surprised and upset that she had been murdered".

"Yes, agreed, this is not our man. Another point is that he doesn't fit the description that Anderson's neighbour gave," said Szymanski.

"So, we are back with Parker. Now we've found there is a way out the back of his property he could be in the frame for the second murder but we would need to find holes in the Stott alibi for him to have committed the first murder and there must be some connection between Parker and Emily Henderson. Dig deeper, Julia, see if you can find that connection. In the meantime, I'll get Dev to check Mason's alibi for 5th March. If it checks out, we'll have him moved back to prison".

****

While Allan and Szymanski were dealing with a double murder, Allan's sister, Jane, was getting into the swing of being a housewife and soon-to-be mother. She had allowed herself a little time to go through the layette again and ran her hand along the rail of the cot gazing into the empty space and imagining a magical little being with tiny fingers and toes and a smile on its tiny face. She knew it would be hard work and a matchstick job for the eyelids but nevertheless it would be wonderful. She was looking forward to being a mum.

She called Spot and took him for a walk in the nearby park. Spot was four years old now and loved to bits. She and Phil had agreed that when the new baby came along they would have to be careful to ensure Spot didn't feel left out and unloved. Sometimes, understandably, that happened, but they were adamant they wouldn't break their beloved pet's heart.

Jane was puffing at the end of her walk.

"Come on, boy" she called as Spot found an interesting smell in their front garden. She turned her key in the lock and called Spot again as she opened the door.

Spot came bounding up on the hearing a second command but stopped at the front step.

"Come on, Spot, I'm gasping for a cuppa" she said holding the edge of the door.

Spot stood resolutely unmoving, his head lowered to the ground, his tail down between his legs uttering a low growl.

"What's the matter, boy?" she asked looking at him with a puzzled expression.

When he still didn't move, she grabbed his collar and pulled him in. She closed the front door but Spot, still growling, didn't move.

She was starting to feel spooked when the phone rang.

"Hi Jane, it's Sue. Fancy doing a bit of baby shopping this afternoon?" she asked chirpily.

"Erm....yes....okay".

"Everything alright, Jane. You sound a bit....I don't know....a bit....strange?"

Jane hesitated before she answered.

"Yes, yes, fine. That'll be good. What time and where shall we meet?"

"Come round to mine and I'll drive. Saves parking two cars! Two o'clock okay?" Sue replied.

"Good for me. I must be back by five o'clock though, because my brother and his partner are coming round for drinks this evening and I've persuaded them to stay for a meal. Hopefully, we will hear about the date for the wedding! Though, having said that, I'm half expecting that Jack won't be able to make it. It seems he is on a major murder case at the moment, but we shall see! Anyway, see you later!"

Spot was still by the door when Jane came off the phone. She went over and fondled the dog's ears and stroked him making soothing sounds. Eventually, Spot rolled over for a tummy tickle and then followed his mistress into the kitchen.

At 1.40 pm, Jane came down the stairs having freshened up for her afternoon's shopping. Spot wouldn't leave her side and whined as she opened the front door.

"I'm sorry, boy, you can't come this time. I won't be long. Just look after the house for us. Okay" and Jane shut the front door, locked it and got in her car.

The two women enjoyed an afternoon's baby shopping and were walking along the Centre's Mall when the most delicious smell of freshly brewed coffee wafted from the café opposite.

"I think I have shopped 'til I dropped now. Let's stop here and have a coffee" suggested Sue.

"Agreed" laughed Jane who was about to say the same thing.

They found a table and put down their many bags of shopping. Placing their latte and cappuccino on the table plus two large pieces of chocolate gateau, they sat down.

"Funny thing this morning, Sue, Spot was freaked out when we got home for our walk. He growled at the front door and wouldn't come in the house. Eventually, after I had stroked and talked softly to him, he calmed down. He still wouldn't leave my side though. He was very clingy and wanted to come with me this afternoon. It spooked me a bit".

"I knew there was something wrong when we spoke. Dogs do get like that sometimes though. Sometimes they sense something like a car accident for example that has happened miles away but they can pick up on it. It obviously wasn't anything for you to worry about anyway! I'm sure he will be fine when you get back!"

****

At 2.00 p.m. while Jane and Sue were enjoying their shop together, a man drove up and parked a little way up from 15 Willow Drive. He put on a fedora hat to cover his blonde hair and checked the fit in his rear-view mirror before getting out of his car. He looked around furtively, checking that no-one was watching. He looked at the upstairs windows of the houses opposite but he couldn't detect any net twitching so he walked at a pace slow enough not to arouse suspicion. He looked as though he was meant to be there especially as he was carrying a large briefcase.

Reaching the house, he again looked round and then walked to the back of the house. Putting on a pair of gloves, he produced a key to the backdoor that he had taken from a shelf in the kitchen earlier that day.

That wretched dog had sensed his presence then and now he heard him again. The spaniel was snarling and growling. The man was in the utility room adjacent to the kitchen. He opened the door into the kitchen just enough to throw in the piece of meat he had extracted from a small bag in his pocket. Within a minute there was silence and the man opened the kitchen door and walked in.

When he had finished his mission, he shut and locked the lobby door, strolled slowly back to his car and drove off.

****

After about an hour chatting about this and that, Jane and Sue left. Getting back to Sue's house, the two friends hugged each other, saying they would do a repeat very soon then Jane got in her car and drove home.

As soon as Jane opened the front door she knew something was wrong. Spot always came to greet her. There was no sound. Dead silence met her calls.

She tiptoed into the lounge. Everything was as she had left it.

She went into the kitchen and there was Spot, lying on the floor.

"Spot" she called walking over to him.

"Spot". No movement.

She knelt down and put her hand on the dog's head. No movement.

She put her hand against his nose.

"Oh, thank god!" she said, tears starting to prick her eyes. Spot was breathing normally as far as she could make out. Still, he didn't move. It was like he had been drugged.

She stood up and went into the dining room. All okay. She was curious now rather than fearful. She wondered what on earth was going on. Nothing seemed to have been taken. She looked all around. No, everything was as it should be.

She walked into the conservatory. She screamed and kept screaming.

****

Szymanski knocked on Allan's door and summoned she went in and sat down on one of the chairs in front of his desk.

"You're not going to like this, Jack, but there is no ostensible connection between Parker and Henderson. I've checked thoroughly and there is absolutely no evidence that they knew each other".

"Okay, so it could be a random killing. He was alleged to have been stalking Anderson but that would also appear to be random. He's still not off the hook. Anything else?"

"Yes. Dev has established that Mason's alibi checks out".

"Right. Arrange for Mason to be transferred back to prison. He is not our man. So, we are left with one suspect, Parker".

Patel knocked and put his head round the door.

"Sorry to interrupt, sir, but there is a call for you from your sister. I can't make much sense from what she is saying. She seems very distraught. Shall I put her through? Also, this was left for you at Reception" and Patel waved a white envelope at him.

"Yes, please, Dev and thanks" he replied as Patel handed him the envelope and went out, closing the door behind him.

"Shall I go, sir?" asked Szymanski.

"No, no, no need".

"Hello, Jane?" he asked as he picked up the call.

He could make no sense of what his sister was saying.

"You're not making any sense, Jane, but I'll be with you in about twenty minutes. Sit tight 'til then" he said ending the call, getting up and stuffing his phone, keys and the envelope in his pocket.

"Have to go. See you in a bit!" he said.

"Okay, Jack. Hope everything is alright".

"Thanks, Julia. So do I!"

Allan made it in fifteen minutes. He rang the doorbell and rapped on the door when he arrived at his sister's house.

Jane fell into his arms, sobbing.

"Okay, sis, whatever is it? What has happened?" he asked wondering what could have caused Jane such distress.

She just led him into the house, through the dining room and into the conservatory.

There on the floor lay a bloody carcass of a dissected cat. Its head had been severed, its paws cut off and its entrails were hanging out of a huge, long gash down the centre of its small body.

Chapter 12

Allan stood and stared at the brutalised limp form of the cat and something stirred at the back of his mind. He had seen enough bloody remains during his career with the police to enable his stomach to remain reasonably calm.

"Jane, have you walked in the conservatory? Have you touched anything?" he asked, his arm round his sister's shoulders and walking her to a dining room chair.

She sat down, blew her nose and wiped away her tears.

"No, I couldn't go near it. The poor, poor cat. How could anyone do such a thing!?" she asked looking up at her brother with a tear-stained face.

"I didn't know you had a cat, Jane?" Allan questioned.

"We don't. I've never seen this cat before!" she exclaimed.

"Bizarre! I think you should go to hospital, Jane. Does Phil know. Have you called him?" he asked gently.

She shook her head fumbling with the tissue in her lap.

"No, I only called you. Phil is in meetings all day so I thought you would know what to do!"

"Okay, don't worry. I'll call forensics and get them down here; then you must tell me exactly what happened. After that, I will drive you to the hospital. You've had a terrible shock and in your condition we need to get you checked out".

Having rung forensics, called his team and left a message for Phil, Allan turned to his sister.

"So, explain to me what happened, Jane" he asked drawing up a chair opposite her and putting his hands over hers.

Jane was still struggling to breathe normally. She kept swallowing hard so she didn't dissolve into tears again.

"I'd been shopping with Sue and then came home. I turned the key in the latch and I thought it was strange that Spot didn't come to greet me. Oh my god, Spot! Is he okay? I must……..".

"I'm sure Spot is fine. Continue".

"No, I need to know if he is okay".

Allan got up and went into the kitchen where Spot was still lying on the floor. The dog turned his head and looking up at him sleepily, yawned, blinked and then staggered to his feet. He walked over to Allan and licked his proffered hand. Slowly the dog moved over to his water bowl and had a huge drink after which he walked slightly unsteadily to his basket and sinking down, he lay his head on his paws.

Satisfied that Spot was fine, Allan walked back into the dining room.

"I'd hazard a guess that Spot was drugged. He is just a bit sleepy now, otherwise okay. So, Jane, you felt something was wrong when Spot didn't materialise as he usually does?"

"Yes, so I went into the lounge and everything seemed okay. Nothing missing and nothing awry. Then I went into the kitchen and found Spot. I couldn't wake him. I thought he was…I thought he was…." and she started to sob again.

Allan got up and put his arm around her shoulders, giving them a squeeze. Jane managed to control her emotion and her brother sat down.

"Sorry" she said.

"Don't be! It's perfectly understandable! So, when you're ready".

"Then I went into the dining room and all seemed to be normal but then I saw the cat in the conservatory. I couldn't move at first. I just screamed and screamed. Then I rang you. That's it!"

"Is there anyone who you have argued with recently, anyone Phil might have upset? Anything you can think of that has happened that you thought strange recently?"

Jane then relayed everything that had happened over the past few days.

"Did you take a note of the registration number of the car?" asked Allan after she had explained about the grey car at the community centre.

"No, sorry I didn't but it was a nice car, a grey estate, not sure of the make" she said apologetically.

"Anything else odd or anyone who you feel could have done this?"

"Only other thing was that before I went shopping, I went for a walk with Spot and when I came back Spot wouldn't come in the house. He was growling and I had to coax him in. Then he was clingy and didn't want me to leave him in the house when I went to the class. You don't think someone was in the house? Maybe someone was hiding in the house and that's why Spot was unhappy" she gasped putting her hand to her mouth in horror.

"Possibly. I'll do a thorough check now to make sure no-one is still here, although I would very much doubt that. I'll organise a car to patrol this street for a few nights so if this person tries again we'll apprehend them".

Jane nodded.

"Thank you" she whispered.

"Okay. You did well, Sis. I know I said I would drive you to the hospital but I can't. I've got to get back to the station. I called for an ambulance which I see has just arrived, and Phil, I'm sure will be on his way as I left a message on his mobile," he said giving her another hug.

"We were supposed to be getting together this evening and talking about the wedding," Jane said dolefully, sniffing and blowing her nose.

"Don't worry Jane, we'll arrange another time. The main thing, at present, is to get you checked out," Allan replied with a smile.

The paramedics came in at that moment and escorted Jane to the ambulance.

Shortly after, forensics turned up and started their work while Wright, who had just arrived, put a cordon round the house.

As Allan left for his car, he stopped and spoke to him.

"Organise a door-to-door will you, Barry, in case anyone saw or heard anything".

"Right you are, sir. Nasty business. Makes you wonder what goes on in someone's mind to do a thing like that!"

"You can say that again!" remarked Allan.

Back in his car, he was about to drive off when he heard a scrunch of paper and extracted the envelope that he had shoved in his pocket.

Tearing it open he unfolded the letter and stared disbelievingly at the typescript before reading it.

"I suspect you didn't expect to hear from me again, Detective Inspector Allan. But here I am, turning up just like an itch you can't scratch. I said you would never catch me and you never will. I'm absolutely certain you will be delighted to know the good news; I am not making any demands this time. The bad news is that I will stop at nothing to make your life totally unliveable. No doubt your sister was badly shaken up by the mutilated cat but that is just the start because next it will be that adorable little dog, Spot, I think his name is. Then I'll progress to your sister and brother-in-law and so on. I think you're getting the picture. I should enjoy your family while you can, Detective Inspector Allan, because all too soon, I'm sure you will agree, good things come to an end. Bye for now!

Allan lowered the letter slowly to rest on his knee. So Manning was still alive! He picked up his mobile and punched in a number.

"Julia, Manning is alive!"

"What? But….."

"There was a letter left in Reception for me earlier today. It's from Manning. Same typeface and he confirms his identity by what he says in the letter. Basically, he is threatening every member of my family and he has started by putting a mutilated cat in Jane and Phil's conservatory!".

"Sick...that's really sick!"

"Yes but it is also very concerning. Manning, as you know, is as cold as ice and very dangerous!"

"So do you think Fran Cooper made it all up about Manning saying he would commit suicide rather than be caught?"

"No. I think it is more likely that Manning deliberately and very cleverly spoke just loud enough to be heard by Cooper who he knew was listening at the door. He was paving the way for his getaway if his plans went wrong" said Allan bitterly.

"Okay. So, Jack, do you want me to organise a police presence outside your sister's house?"

"Yes, I had asked for a patrol car but I think we need to escalate that and, as you say, organise a continuous surveillance for the time being and Julia………..".

"Yes?"

"I need you to be the lead on this case while I work on the two murder cases. I'll get Dev on side. I want you do a door-to-door and find out if anyone saw anything unusual in my sister's street over the past few days and particularly yesterday. I'm not on this case! I'll give you the letter from Manning tomorrow, at the station. Are you okay with that?"

"Of course, Jack. Leave it to me".

"Keep me informed of progress. Get uniform to help you".

"Will do!"

When Allan got back to his apartment he felt in need of a workout. Vanessa was on night shift so dinner would be for one tonight.

Before the workout he indulged in one of his healthy smoothies, adding spinach, avocado, mango and almond milk.

Changing into shorts and a vest he attacked the treadmill. His mind was troubled in both his personal and working lives. First off he thought of Vanessa. She hadn't seemed quite herself lately but nothing he could put his finger on. She was definitely happy about the wedding and there was nothing wrong on the sex front but there was something. He had caught her face looking pensive and thoughtful when she didn't think he was looking. He had asked her about life at the hospital and she had said she felt exhausted sometimes but she would never swap her work for anything else. So, he concluded that there wasn't anything wrong there. For now, it was a mystery.

Then on the work front he was very worried about Jane and Phil but Julia Szymanski was a first-class detective and apart from himself he couldn't think of anyone he would rather have in charge of the case. He knew that the police handbook in the Station stated that, if a crime against a sibling had been committed, then the relevant police officer could still be involved in solving the case, but with Clarkson as his boss he felt more comfortable delegating it to Julia.

He moved on to the rowing machine and pounded away for a few minutes, clearing his mind of any thoughts.

Moving on to weights, his brain once more engaged gear. Something about that letter from Manning was eating at him. He was missing something. Something important. He worried at it for the rest of his session and then gave up, towelled himself down and jumped in the shower.

Feeling rejuvenated he set about chopping up some vegetables to go with the fillet steak. By nine thirty he had steak and vegetables in the frying pan. He opened a bottle of Merlot and poured a glass. Turning the steak over with the spatula in one hand he was about to raise the glass of wine to his lips with the other when his mobile rang.

"Sorry to trouble you, sir, but there has been another murder. This time the body of a woman has been found by a cyclist in Grantchester Meadows on the east bank of the River Cam," said Patel.

"Bit late for a bike ride isn't it? When did he call it in?"

"Apparently he does shift work but likes to keep fit, sir. Apologies again for the late hour but DS Szymanski asked me to call you, sir, as she is engaged on another case?" he added.

"Yes, that's right, Dev". Allan quickly looked at his watch – 21.45 the luminated figures told him. Turning off the hob and looking regretfully at his dinner and glass of wine he spoke to his DC.

"Okay, Dev, text me the exact location and I'll be there in twenty minutes".

"Yes, sir. I'll meet you there".

Again, floodlights met his eyes as Allan walked across the fields to where the area had been roped off. Strange was already there, as was Patel.

Strange looked up.

"I'll be damned if we haven't ourselves a serial killer, Jack" he said solemnly.

"What the hell is she dressed in?" Allan asked, staring at the dead woman.

"Well, the murderer seems to have a fetish for clocks this time but the mode of death is the same. She was strangled twice like the other two. She is dressed in extraordinary clothes and her hands and feet have been rubbed by glass".

Allan and Patel bent down to examine the body more closely.

"Each of the victims have been holding something in their hands. Lily was holding the Queen chess piece, Emily seven keys and now this woman, an orange. These are clues the murderer is leaving. He is setting us a puzzle to solve" said Allan rhetorically.

"We'll pick this up in the morning, Dev. Stew, speak tomorrow."

"Yes, sir" replied Patel.

"Look forward to it!" was Strange's wry comment.

Chapter 13

Next morning, Friday 12th March at eight-thirty, Allan assembled the team. Behind him was the white board displaying various pictures and writing. He clapped his hands and everyone immediately ceased their conversations.

"Good morning all" he said.

"Good morning, sir" everyone chorused.

"Last night our murderer struck again and with a third murder alone we would be suspecting a serial killer but with the similarities shared by all three victims there is no shadow of doubt".

There were a number of mutterings and glances around the room which were hushed by Allan's raised hand.

He pointed to the board.

Murder 1 – victim a woman, Lily Anderson, twenty-five years of age, holding a Queen chess piece and wearing African clothing. There were four cuts to her hands and feet and small fragments of glass had been rubbed into her feet and hands. Strangled twice. First time to within a few seconds of asphyxiation, and the second killed her.

Murder 2 – victim a woman, Emily Henderson, mid-twenties, holding a key ring with seven keys attached. No particularly odd clothing this time but exactly the same wounds and same glass element. Again, strangled twice.

Murder 3 – victim a woman, identity not yet confirmed, holding an orange and dressed in bizarre clothes, the material being printed with clock faces and again the glass element. Strangled twice.

All victims lived in the same neighbourhood so it is probable but not certain that our killer is local".

The team were nodding.

"The first murder makes you think of the film doesn't it 'African Queen'! There was a film called that wasn't there? Okay, sorry folks, I know this is serious. Sorry!" said Wright raising both hands apologetically as the others looked at him scathingly.

Allan was staring at the board and went on staring. Seemingly, he hadn't heard what Wright had said. Then he keyed something into his phone.

After a few minutes he spun round and faced the team, his face animated.

"No, no, Barry. You're a genius – an absolute genius!" he exclaimed excitedly.

"You've cracked the meaning, or some of it anyway, behind the objects the victims were holding and clothing that they wore" and he turned back to face the board.

"Look! The first victim wore African clothing and held the Queen in chess equals the film called 'African Queen'. The second victim was holding seven keys. I have just Googled and there was a film called 'Seven Keys'. The third victim was dressed in an outfit printed with clock faces and holding an orange which equals the film called 'Clockwork Orange'!" he ended throwing his phone on the desk and raising his hands behind his head.

"However, although we have a glimmer of what is going on in the murderer's mind we don't know why he is using films as a theme for his killings. More importantly we have no idea who he is and who he will strike next. Also, we don't know where he carries out the torture and murders. Nevertheless, it is a beginning. Well done, Barry!"

Everyone smiled and looked at Wright who was blushing with embarrassment.

Allan's mobile rang. He turned away into his office and took the call.

"Hi Stew! What have you got for me".

"You definitely have a serial killer on your hands, Jack. Same on all counts as far as torture and reason for death are concerned. However, time of death is different. The victim was killed between 1.30 pm and 4.30 pm on Wednesday 10th March. Established who she is, by the way, a one Stella King, twenty-eight years of age".

"Okay, Stew. Thanks".

"You're welcome! Good luck, Jack".

Allan hung up and went back to his team.

"Okay" he said holding up his hands to quieten the chatter.

"That was Strange confirming that we are indeed dealing with a serial killer. We now have a name for our victim, Stella King. Sophie can you find out everything you can about family, inform the next of kin and ask them for the usual identification confirmation. Can you also find out about any friends, boyfriends she had".

"Will do, sir!"

"Max can you establish where she worked and interview her colleagues".

"Consider it done, sir" replied Max.

"Peter can find out about her financial affairs and any phone calls made on the day she died".

"Will do, sir!"

Dev can you find out where she lived and get a cordon placed round it. We'll get over there as soon as".

"On it, sir!" and Patel walked quickly over to his desk.

"Mike, as soon as Dev finds out where the victim lived, can you do a door-to-door and find out if any neighbours noticed anything unusual".

"Yes, sir!"

Allan's mobile rang again.

"Allan" he barked.

"My office, please, Allan" said the unmistakeable voice of DCI Tom Clarkson.

Allan took the stairs two at a time and arriving outside his boss' office he knocked on the door.

Seated opposite the DCI, Allan looked at him expectantly while he finished his phone call.

"I understand that your sister has had a nasty experience involving a cat" he said with a smile that instantly made Allan wary.

"That is correct, sir. It was sufficiently shocking to suspect a possible threat to her and her husband, so DS Szymansky took the precaution of stationing a car outside their house for the time being".

"You well know, Allan, that I must be informed of any personal involvement with victims or anyone being investigated in a case?" he was sitting upright now, ready for the kill.

"Of course, sir, and that is why DS Szymanski is dealing with the case and not myself" replied Allan calmly. He knew that Clarkson had not made that clear at all but was glad he had had the good sense to delegate to Julia.

Clarkson visibly deflated but still tried to get the upper hand.

"But you did organise for the car to be stationed outside your sister's house and I knew nothing about that!" he spat the words out.

"No, sir, Szymanski organised that" he omitted to enlighten his superior that he had asked Julia to do it.

"That will be all then, Allan" retorted Clarkson and he ostensibly started reading a document on his desk.

Allan left, closing the door quietly behind him. He knew that this was only the start. Clarkson was out for his blood. Let the battle commence, he thought.

Patel got up as Allan strode past his desk on route to his office.

"Sir" he said.

He stopped and turned back.

"Sir, Stella King lived at 107b Carson Drive, not far from the other two victims",

"Good work, Dev" said Allan as he walked quickly into his office, grabbed his car keys and identification.

Meanwhile Callender had found a great aunt who knew there was a new boyfriend.

DC Callender arrived outside Stella King's only living relative's house at lunchtime. Ducking her head she looked through the passenger car window and took in the idyllic cottage on the outskirts of the picturesque village of Little Mole which lay to the south of Cambridge.

Getting out of the car she walked up the path of the long front garden and knocked on the door. Getting no answer, she knocked again several times and louder. Eventually Sophie heard someone slide a security chain and the door opened a crack. An elderly voice spoke.

"Yes, who is it, please?"

"Good afternoon, Mrs Pingleton, Mrs Mavis Pingleton, Detective Constable Callender, Cambridgeshire Police. May I speak with you please, concerning your great niece Stella King?" and she passed her identification through the crack.

The door closed a bit and Callender heard the security chain slide off. The door opened and the tiny, birdlike lady leaning on a stick, handed back her identification wallet. She stood aside and let Callender enter.

Leading her through slowly to the small, comfortable lounge situated on the right of the front door, Mavis Pingleton indicated one of the armchairs either side of the log fire.

"Would you like a cup of tea, officer?" she asked.

"No, I won't but thank you for the offer. Please, Mrs Pingleton, can you sit down".

"You may call me Mavis if you wish" said the old lady sitting down and looking at Callender expectantly.

"I'm very sorry to have to tell you, Mavis, that your great niece, Stella King, died last night".

Mavis sat unmoving, still staring at Callender and the latter wondered if the old lady had taken in what she had told her.

"Mavis, are you okay? Would you like a cup of tea?"

Mavis shook her head slowly.

"How did she die?" she asked quietly.

"I'm so sorry to have to tell you this, Mavis, but she was murdered".

"Murdered?" and she raised a hand to her mouth.

"Yes".

"Do you know by whom?"

"Not yet but we will find the person responsible. I think you should have a cup of tea now, Mavis. Can I get you one? You have had a very big shock" and Callender looked at her kindly.

Mavis nodded and Callender went to find the kitchen.

After Mavis had sipped some sugary tea and Callender had joined her companionably also drinking a cuppa, Callender set down her cup on the coffee table and took out her notebook.

"Can you tell us about your great niece. Do you know what was going on in her personal life?"

The old lady thought for a bit.

"She was a quiet girl. She worked as a cashier in Harrington Building Society. I didn't see much of her but she came round from time to time. Always brought a couple of delicious cakes for us to go with a pot of tea".

"Did she mention her friends and what she did in her spare time?" asked Callender taking another sip of tea.

"Not really, no, but she had met someone recently. A young man. She said they both had a passion for old films. They had met at a shop that rented out films, old ones".

"Can you remember his name or which shop that was?" asked Callender eagerly.

"No, she did say, but I can't. It may come to me but I can't remember at present. She did mention what he looked like though".

"Yes?"

"He was tall with blonde hair. Do you think that this new boyfriend murdered her?"

"It's too early to say but we would certainly like to speak with him so if you do remember his name or the name of shop where they got the films, please call me on this number straightaway, Mavis".

"Yes, yes, of course" replied the old lady nodding and taking the proffered card.

Chapter 14

Earlier on Friday 12th March, Patel had pulled up outside the drab Victorian semi-detached house. A cordon had been placed around it. Someone peeked out of the side of a net, that had been pulled slightly to one side, at the ground floor bay window. When Allan glanced over, the net quickly settled back into place.

Allan and Patel put on their gloves and shoe covers. Once in the upstairs flat they glanced around the immaculate room that did for a lounge and started to search every inch of it including a large cupboard, a letter rack and bookcase. Finding nothing of relevance they were about to move on to the bedroom and kitchen when a voice stopped them in their tracks.

"I hope you don't mind me intruding?" said the voice.

"Sir, you need to step back outside the door" said Patel quickly advancing towards the cringing figure wringing his hands who reminded Allan of Uriah Heep, a character in the book David Copperfield.

Allan moved towards him.

"I'm Detective Inspector Allan and this is Detective Sergeant Patel and you are?" asked Allan crisply.

"Oh, I'm just the neighbour who lives downstairs. I just wondered what had happened, Detective Inspector" he said in a sickly, sycophantic manner, still wringing his hands.

"How well did you know the person who lived here?" asked Allan.

"Oh! Has something happened to her? Stella I mean? You said 'did' and 'lived' in the past tense, Detective Inspector!" his face took on a solemn look.

"If you could just answer the question Mr.... er?"

"Palmer...Jo Palmer. I knew Stella a little. She was a lovely young lady. Didn't have many friends, although there was someone who she had started dating recently. I don't know who he was and I never met him but she seemed happier than she had done. So, what has happened to her, Detective Inspector?"

"Can you describe this man, Mr Palmer?" Allan was doing his level best to keep his irritation and dislike of the man out of his voice. He hoped he was succeeding.

"No, not really. He was tallish, I suppose, fairish or you might describe his hair as blonde, I suppose. He was thin, very pale skin. Other than that, nothing really remarkable about him. Oh, there was one thing though, Stella mentioned that they liked watching films, particularly old films".

"At a cinema?" asked Patel.

"No, I got the impression that they went to his place and watched the films but that was just an impression rather than fact" he simpered apologetically.

"I'm not really much help am I? Can you tell me what happened to her, Detective Inspector?"

"Where were you two days ago on 10th March, Mr. Palmer, between midday and six o'clock in the evening?"

"Me?" he looked like a hare caught in the beam of car headlights.

Allan and Patel nodded.

"I was at home, in the flat downstairs. My mother lives with me. I look after her. We watched some afternoon TV and had tea at about five o'clock. We read a little while after tea then we went to bed".

"Is your mother downstairs now?" asked Allan.

"Yes, Detective Inspector" replied a subdued Palmer.

"Can I ask, Mr Palmer, is your mother suffering from dementia or mental incapacity?"

"Why do you ask?"

"Just answer the question, please, Mr Palmer," said Allan firmly.

"No, no, she's physically frail but mentally she is as sharp as a razor" Palmer replied with a puzzled frown.

Allan nodded to Patel who disappeared downstairs.

"What's going on?"

"DS Patel will ask your mother to corroborate your statement of where you were yesterday afternoon. If she does, we won't need to detain you any further".

Patel arrived five minutes later and nodded to Allan.

"Okay, Mr Palmer, I would like you to leave us now. Thank you for your help and if you do think of anything you feel might be of interest to us relating to Ms King, then please ring me immediately" and he handed his card to Palmer. Palmer clearly didn't want to go without knowing what had happened but the stern look, on Allan's face, convinced him that go he must.

"Interesting the boyfriend likes old films".

"Why has he chosen films to make a statement?"

"He may have had a bad experience with films and a woman or women generally. Another question. Where is he getting these old films from? He could be a collector of films, of course, but my guess is that he is hiring them. Dev find out who in Cambridge rents out old films and who has rented the three relevant ones recently. We need to dig deeper into whether the other two victims, Anderson and Henderson, had met someone recently who was interested in old films".

Patel nodded and jotted the instructions down in his notebook.

They had just about finished the rest of their search when Allan's mobile rang. It was Sophie who relayed what she had learnt from Mavis Pingleton. Allan thanked her for the information, told her to go back to the station and turned to Patel who was looking at him with interest.

"So, from several sources now, including this Mavis Pingleton that Sophie has just interviewed, we have a description of the suspect being tall and blonde. Not much to go on but nevertheless progress. Sophie also found out that our victim worked at the Harrington Building Society," said Allan.

Allan punched in a number.

"Anything gained from the neighbours, Mike?" he asked.

"Yes, a Maureen Greenaway was looking out of her window and spotted a grey truck or large car, she was unable to confirm which, outside 107 Carson Drive at about nine o'clock in the evening. A tall, blonde man went into the house. She couldn't make out whether he entered Flat A or B. She stayed by her window to see if he came out but nothing happened in the next few minutes so her curiosity subsided".

"A long shot but she didn't by any chance take a note of the registration number of the vehicle?"

"No, sir. Unfortunately, not".

"Thanks Mike" and Allan hung up and punched in another number.

"Max, did you uncover anything from work colleagues at the Harrington Building Society?"

"Yes, although she was a very private person, apparently she did confide in one of her colleagues that she had met a man who she really liked and they had a love of old films in common. Apparently, she had described the man as interesting, charming, tall and blonde".

"Did she give any further description to this colleague? Facial features, did he speak with an accent?"

"No, nothing else".

Allan thanked Max.

Having established from Peter that there was nothing of note in King's financial affairs or any significant calls on her mobile, he rang Julia.

"Are you still interviewing Jane's neighbours, Julia? Any success?"

"No, I'm back at the station now and yes I have had some success. A Mrs Baker was driving back from her weekly supermarket shop and noticed a car she had never seen before parked on the opposite side of the road to where your sister lives.

Any unknown car or person, apart from delivery drivers, is unusual around there, as you know, being a cul-de-sac but what particularly drew her attention was that the engine was running and the headlights on.

She carried on a little further to her house and parked in her driveway.

Being nosy she wondered if someone had lost their way and started to walk towards the car. As she approached the car revved up hard and shot past her and she was left staring after it.

Before you ask she was so stunned that she didn't take a note of the registration number".

"When was this? The day that Jane found the cat?"

"No, it was about a week ago but I thought it might be pertinent to the case?"

"Definitely worth considering. Could she see who was driving or notice the make and colour of the vehicle?"

"It was only a fleeting glimpse but she thinks the driver had blonde hair, in his thirties maybe and the car was a grey colour, she wasn't sure of the model".

"Okay, something to go on. Just a minute, blonde hair?"

"Yes, that's right".

"Maureen Greenaway gave a similar description to Mike for the man that was seen entering Stella King's apartment on the night she was murdered and she said the vehicle he got out of was a grey truck or large car but it was definitely grey. This would potentially mean that the incident regarding the cat is linked to these murders. Several witnesses have come up with the description of a blonde-haired man in connection with the murders. Could this blonde-haired man, stalking my sister, be our serial killer" Allan said thoughtfully stroking the side of his nose.

Allan was lost in thought and was silent for a couple of minutes.

"Jack are you there?"

"Yes, just thinking. Something is lurking at the back of my mind. I just can't put my finger on it. Thanks for the information Julia. I'll see you back at the station," he said and rang off.

Patel had been standing listening to the conversation.

"Shall I drive, sir" he asked as they walked to the car.

Allan nodded still immersed in his thoughts.

"Just a minute, sir" called the Duty Sargeant as they entered the station building.

Allan turned back to the desk and took the proffered envelope. Once in his office, he tore open the envelope and slid out the A4 typewritten letter.

Hello again, Detective Inspector Allan. Any moment now you will get a harrowing phone call from your beloved sister but you will only be able to try and comfort her on her sad loss. This is the way it is going to be from now on Jack. The nightmare won't stop. It will go on and on. You really shouldn't have crossed me. It was the worst mistake of your life. Oh! Is that your mobile I hear ringing? Bye for now, Jack.

Allan screwed the paper up into a ball and smashed his clenched fist on the desk in front on him. His mobile wasn't ringing, of course. Manning couldn't know exactly when his mobile would ring. But then it did.

****

Earlier in the afternoon, Jane got Spot's lead and summoning him, she left the house and walked to the end of her drive then turned left towards the park. She felt much safer now that there was a police presence outside their house and returned the nod and smile of the policewoman sitting in the driver's seat. It was a short walk to the park and the sun was shining although there was a still an early Spring chill in the air. Spot was straining at the lead so Jane decided to let him run free.

"Go on then, boy!" she said as she unclipped the lead.

Spot dashed off, sniffing here and there at an interesting smell. She threw the ball several times and the dog raced after it, bringing it back to her for more of the same.

She threw it one last time and Spot true to form went after it. She bent down to tie the lace on her trainer which had come loose. Standing up she shaded her eyes against the sun. Spot hadn't come back.

"Spot, Spot, come on boy!" she called again and again but still no dog appeared.

She walked over the grass and found the ball she had thrown. Still calling and still no response an unease crept up from her stomach. She quickened her pace, puffing with the effort, towards the trees which formed a small wood around the park. She didn't need to go far before she caught sight of Spot and breathed a sigh of relief. She ran over to him. He was on his side.

She raised her hand to her mouth as she bent over him. She stroked his beautiful liver spot fur whispering to him. The dog didn't move, eyes staring sightlessly.

Tears were streaming down her face and she cried out in anguish as she looked down at her precious pet.

Shaking, she extracted her mobile from her pocket and rang Phil. He had a hard job making out what she was saying but when he finally understood he told her to go directly to the police stationed outside their house and tell them what had happened. As if on automatic pilot she managed to walk to the police car.

****

Allan answered his mobile. It was Phil and not Jane. After the call, Allan immediately phoned Szymanski. While on the phone to her, Allan described the contents of the latest letter he had received from Manning. They arrived at Jane and Phil's house within minutes of each other.

Jane was sitting sobbing uncontrollably on the sofa in the lounge with Phil next to her, his arm around her.

Allan walked quickly over to her and crouched down beside her, placing a hand over her clasped ones in her lap.

"Jane, I'm so, so sorry" and he just squeezed her hands tightly.

Jane continued to sob for some minutes. Then she gulped and the tears subsided. She gently pulled her hands from under her brother's and using the tissues she had been clutching she wiped her eyes, red from crying, and blew her nose loudly.

"When you're ready, Jane, you need to tell Julia exactly what happened as she is in charge of the case" Allan said quietly, getting up from his crouching position and squeezing her shoulder gently.

"Phil you need to follow Julia's instructions to the letter, okay?" Allan said turning to his brother-in-law and laying a hand on his shoulder.

Phil nodded, struggling to keep the tears away.

Allan indicated that Szymanski should accompany him out of earshot of the others.

"Julia, you need to get my sister and husband out of here to a safe house. Clearly they are next on Manning's hitlist!"

"Will do, Jack. I'll get them out today".

Chapter 15

When Allan had gone Szymanski got on the phone immediately to establish which safe house was available.

"Detective, I know what Jack said and I know he has our interests at heart but we need to stay here for the time being. We need closure on the death of Spot" and Phil began to swallow hard to stop the tears.

"I understand Mr. Blake but you must also understand that you are in grave danger. After the incident with the cat and now the deliberate murder of your dog, I don't mean to scare you, sir, but............." Szymanski was interrupted.

"No, we are not moving out of here until our dog's ashes are buried in the garden. We need to do this. I know my wife will agree" and he turned to look at Jane for her agreement.

Jane was nodding furiously still struggling with the lump in her throat.

Before Szymanski could comment, Phil continued.

"I know that we have to wait for forensics to confirm why Spot died suddenly and I know that the assumption is that he was deliberately killed on the basis of the cat incident, but we don't absolutely know that do we? It could be the result of natural causes. Maybe he had a heart condition that we didn't know about for example" he ended lamely.

Szymanski looked at him doubtfully.

"With respect, sir, I think you are wrong and I would strongly suggest a safe house".

"Well, unless you know something we don't, thank you for your advice, but we will be staying here hopefully with a police presence" said Phil firmly.

Szymanski debated whether to tell Phil about Manning's letter but decided not to. Walking outside, she rang Allan. A constable was standing outside the front door.

"I've hit a problem, sir" she said.

"Okay?"

"Your sister and brother-in-law are adamant that they stay in the house because they say they want closure on Spot's death. They want to bury his ashes in the back garden after forensics have finished their work".

"Understand, but they can come back and do that. They don't have to stay there in the meantime".

"I know, sir, but I don't think they will move out until they have buried their dog's ashes. They are happy with a police presence at their house".

"Well, I take it you have explained the seriousness of the situation?"

"Yes, I have, but I was wondering whether you wanted me to mention the letters from Manning?"

There was a pregnant pause while Allan considered.

"No, don't mention the letters, Julia, but reiterate how important we think it is for them to go to a safe house and if they still insist on staying, so be it. A police presence will have to suffice. Let's hope that's all it needs!"

"Okay, sir. Understood" and Allan ended the call.

Szymanski went back into the house where the couple were sitting, arms round one another, comforting each other in their grief.

"Excuse me, Mr and Mrs Blake I have spoken to DCI Allan and he says that he feels it of the utmost importance that you leave here immediately but at the end of the day it is your decision".

"We appreciate your care for our safety but we will be staying. Thank you and please do call us Phil and Jane. There is no need for formality".

Szymanski smiled and nodded.

Back at the station, Patel knocked on the door of Allan's office.

"The DCI wants a word, apparently. Could you go up straightaway?"

"Thank you Dev" replied Allan and then muttered under his breath.

"Why doesn't he just contact me direct!"

"What was that, sir?" asked Patel as he was just shutting the door.

"Nothing, Dev, nothing!" replied Allan getting up from his chair and moving swiftly towards him.

Patel stood aside, keeping the door open for his boss who strode out, up the stairs and was soon sitting on the opposite side of the DCI's desk facing Tom Clarkson.

"So, where are we with the serial killer, Jack? You must have got somewhere with it or is something else demanding your impressive detective skills?" he asked with a sneer.

"I would like to suggest a combined press conference and media appeal, sir" completely ignoring any implication that he was dealing with his sister's case through Szymanski.

"Another one? What are we going to say this time, Jack?"

"We believe a grey estate car is involved and that the description is a tall, blonde man who watches old movies from way back when".

"That's not a lot to go on".

"DC Patel is looking into shops that rent out old films and in particular the three films linked to the victims but it could be that the murderer gets these films from someone not listed. If we go to the media, a member of the public may recognise someone fitting the description who borrowed or rented those films from them recently. Maybe they also recognise the car that the suspect drove as fitting the description".

"Okay Jack. I'll have both a press conference and media appeal arranged for tomorrow at 1.00 pm. Make sure you're available".

"Sir" said Jack getting up and escaping quickly from the room.

Getting back to the main office, Allan beckoned Patel to come in.

"Dev, how are you getting on with findings on the film shops?" Allan asked indicating that he should take a seat.

"Nothing much has come up really, sir. No-one remembers a tall, blonde guy asking for those films".

"Right. I thought that might be the case so I suggested to the DCI that we hold a press conference to appeal to the public. Someone may know a man of that description who borrowed or bought the films from them privately".

Patel nodded.

"Hopefully, someone will, sir".

"It's very late, I think we should wrap it up for today" Allan said striding to the door and walking out of the office.

"Okay, team. Let's all head off home now and start again, fresh in the morning" there were nods around the room and the sound of chairs scraping into place under desks.

Driving home, through the green and pleasant Cambridge countryside Allan thought about the case. Something was bothering him at the back of his mind.

As he entered their apartment, he stepped on the post and stooped to pick it up. He quickly glanced through it, as he walked through to the kitchen area but stood stock still as he came to the last letter. With no postmark, it had to have been hand delivered. He tore the envelope open and read the familiar typeface.

Yes, I know where you live, Detective Inspector, so after I have finished with your sister and her worthy husband, I will start on your loved one, the delightful Vanessa. You remember the wonderful time I gave her not so long ago. This time it will be even more rewarding for me. So, take care of her for now and enjoy your precious moments with her. Bye for now. PS have you worked out who the serial killer is yet? Do you really think you have two dangerous criminals to catch? Perhaps being in a relationship with the ravishing Vanessa, and getting a tad older, you are losing your excellent detective skills.

His hand was shaking as he placed the letter on the kitchen side. At that moment, he heard the front door opening and he swung round half expecting to see Manning but instead it was Vanessa. She smiled at him and then frowned.

"What is it, Jack? What's the matter?"

Quickly recovering, he swiftly put the letter in his pocket. Smiling he walked towards her, his arms outstretched. They embraced and kissed.

"Nothing, darling, just the case I'm working on at the moment is taking its toll".

"Well, I stopped off at the supermarket on the way home and the result is I have a super meal that I am going to cook for you. Why don't you de-stress in the gym, while I work on it?"

He nodded and beamed at her.

Allan tried to blank his mind from the letter and from the cases altogether but something was still worrying him.

Later, Vanessa and he sat down to a sumptuous meal including a prawn and avocado starter with an unusual dressing, the ingredients of which Vanessa refused to elaborate on. Completely surfeited, having enjoyed conversing about their up-and-coming quiet wedding, Vanessa's face took on a more serious expression. I will be going away for a few days from tomorrow on a course. A cancellation has come up and I would be a fool not to capitalise on that. It's something not to be missed. The places are like gold dust!"

"Why so serious, Vanessa, that's great! Of course I will miss you but if it is important to you, I'm pleased you will have the opportunity".

Vanessa fiddled with her spoon. There was something she wasn't telling him. Allan waited patiently but when nothing was forthcoming he broke the silence.

"Where is the course?" he asked lightly.

"Just north of Edinburgh".

"What time do you leave tomorrow?" he asked, thinking it was a bit strange for a course to begin on the weekend.

"Six o'clock in the morning".

"How long will you be away for?"

"Five days".

There was still something troubling her.

"It's my turn now, Vanessa. Is something wrong? Has something happened? Has someone frightened you?" he asked, thinking perhaps Manning had already made his presence felt.

She looked up, a look of curiosity on her face.

"No. Nothing has frightened me! Why do you ask that?"

Allan shrugged. He was pleased she was not going to be there for a few days, away from the threat of Manning.

"No reason. Just my line of work that's all. There is something on your mind though, Vanessa. What is it? We are okay aren't we?"

"Yes, yes, of course" but there were tears in her eyes.

He reached across the table and put his hands on hers.

"Something has upset you. Is it your parents about the wedding?" he asked gently.

"No. It's nothing. I love you" and she leant across and kissed him.

"I love you too, Vanessa, so much".

Her tears gone and her smile returned, he smiled back and led her to their bedroom.

Chapter 16

The next day, Saturday 13th March, Allan was at the station early, Szymanski arriving a few minutes later, cancellation of all leave and weekends still in force. Allan waved her into his office.

"Look at this!" he said excitedly and handed Manning's latest letter to her.

Szymanski looked up, having read the letter.

"We need to step up protection for your sister and Vanessa needs protection too" she said, her thin mouth in a determined, straight line.

"No, you don't see the most important part of the letter do you?"

She re-read the letter and shaking her head, she looked at her boss with a puzzled expression.

"It's all in the postscript! He is the murderer, he is the serial killer, don't you see? He is telling me that he killed those three women!"

"But, Jack, what about the films and the numbers. How do they figure if he is the culprit?"

"I don't know. Maybe all that stuff is actually meaningless, just planted to mislead us. I think we are looking for Manning in connection with threats to my family and the murders".

"So, you are saying that the films, numbers and costumes are all red herrings?"

"Yes, unless there is a meaning from somewhere in his past that we know nothing about. The description of the suspect fits the description of Manning. Tall and blonde. That together with this letter suggests we go with this line of enquiry".

Szymanski was nodding her head.

"Yes that is true, Jack, the description fits and maybe you're right, Manning is telling us he is the killer".

Meanwhile, Allan was looking thoughtful. Suddenly, he jumped out of his chair and went into the main office where the board displayed the information on the case.

"Yes, yes, of course" he exclaimed, "Why didn't I see that before?"

"What, sir?" asked Szymanski with a puzzled expression and the rest of the team, who had also got in early, looked up from what they were doing.

"Look here, we've established the dates on which the films were first shown are 1951, 1961, 1971, so the next famous film, I would suggest, will have been showing in 1981. So, we need to find out who has rented a famous film in the last month which showed in 1981! We have the press conference and media appeal today so maybe someone will recognise the description of Manning as the person who rented, bought or borrowed one of the old films in question and more specifically one shown in 1981! The icing on the cake would be that they saw the suspect with his car and took the registration number".

At one o'clock precisely DCI Tom Clarkson and DI Jack Allan took their seat behind a long desk, in front of a myriad of microphones and journalists.

"Good afternoon ladies and gentlemen and thank you for your attendance today. I am DCI Tom Clarkson and here on my right is DI Jack Allan who is in charge of the investigation into the recent three murders of women in Cambridgeshire. We are here to update you on progress in apprehending the person or persons responsible for these murders and to appeal to the public for any information they may have that could help us with our enquiries. I am handing you over now to my colleague who will explain".

"Good afternoon everyone. I would like to start with an appeal to the public. So far we have two important leads.

The first is there is strong evidence to suggest that the person, and we're almost certain we are dealing with one suspect, has a fetish for old films.

Further evidence suggests that he is actively seeking old films which in turn suggests that the suspect is examining the films for precise details to be used in conjunction with the murders.

We are checking outlets for these films but it may be that this person has borrowed or bought certain old films from a private seller.

The films in question are 'African Queen', 'Seven Keys' and 'Clockwork Orange'. Also, any 1981 film.

I repeat, any 1981 film. If anyone has lent or sold any of these films to anyone in the last month, please can they contact us urgently.

The second lead is the description of the suspect. The suspect has been described as a tall, slim, blonde Caucasian man who we guestimate is between the age of twenty and forty.

He will probably be a loner, either unemployed, on shift work or engaged in work that entails odd hours.

Again, if anyone knows of, or has seen, a man fitting this description in the area of Wandlebury Country Park, Avon Street, White Earth Nature Reserve, Wandlebury South Street, Grantchester Meadows or Carson Drive, please contact the police urgently.

That is the end of the public appeal. We are proceeding now to the press conference and I would like to invite the press to pose any questions that they may have. I'm sure there will be quite a few" he added with grim humour.

He pointed to a woman with bright red hair in the front of the crowd of journalists.

"You are asking if anyone has borrowed or bought a 1981 film recently. What significance is there in this lead? There could be a great many film lovers who borrowed or bought such a film".

"I think that is unlikely. Every lead will be investigated and could result in us finding the suspect before he kills again".

He indicated a tall man standing at the back.

"Have you any clue as to the motive or connections between the women killed or is it your assumption that they were just a random pick by the killer?" he asked.

"I never assume! However, the fact that each victim has been dressed and/or is holding an item associated with a specific film indicates that the motive has something to do with the years or the films, the films themselves or films in general. The connection between the women, if there is one, is yet to be established".

Allan pointed to a further three journalists and answered the questions from each, before he and the DCI got up, Clarkson thanking everyone and ending the conference.

****

While the press conference and media appeal were taking place, Jane was coming to terms with the loss of their beloved pet, Spot. She was nervous in the house now but took consolation in the prominent police presence outside the house. Phil had instructed her to always have her mobile with her and putting her coffee cup on the kitchen table she gave the object a sideways glance to reassure herself it was right beside her.

She sighed as she slowly got up, absent-mindedly stroking the now humungous bump. Not long now and they would be a family of three. She smiled to herself and the thought made her happy despite the sorrow in her heart. Placing her mug in the dishwasher she put her jacket on and picked up her keys and handbag. She needed a few groceries and getting out of the house for a bit would do her good.

Shutting and locking the front door she made her way to her car, raising a hand at the policewoman sitting in the car outside their house. She fastened her seat belt, fired the ignition and drove off the driveway.

The quickest way to the supermarket was down the dual carriageway. The cars in front were quite slow so she signalled and overtook then returned to the left-hand lane.

There were cars ahead of her and she signalled to overtake but someone was in the outside lane so she braked to wait for a space. She pressed the brake pedal again. Her car was still going at the same pace and gaining rapidly on the car in front. She depressed the pedal again and again, each time more frantically. Nothing happened. Her foot wasn't on the accelerator and yet the car showed no signs of slowing. By the time she thought of switching off the engine it was too late. There was a terrible bang, the sound of breaking glass as her car went into the back of the car ahead which skidded over to the outside lane and the car coming up that lane went into it. The car behind Jane went into her.

There were altogether ten cars in the pile up. Jane was unconscious but the airbag and seat belt had kept her body from going through the windscreen.

****

Allan looked at his mobile as he walked out of the conference room. He had several missed calls and a message. He listened to his messages.

"Jack, it's Phil. I've been trying to get hold of you. You need to come to the hospital straightaway. It's Jane. There's been an accident. She was driving and oh ……! They are trying to save the baby!" his voice was shaky with sobs as the message ended.

Allan rushed out of the building and got in his car, calling Szymanski as he drove off.

"Oh no! I'm so sorry, Jack! Take care and it goes without saying, hope everything is okay!"

Allan got to the hospital eight minutes later and slung his car in a parking space. He found Phil pacing up and down in the corridor outside the emergency operating rooms. The two men hugged each other. Tears were streaming down Phil's face and Allan's eyes were welling up.

"It's all my fault. I should have listened to you. We should have gone to a safe house like you said. If we lose our baby I won't be able to live with myself. If I lose Jane………." and he broke off wiping one hand across his nose and mouth.

"It's no good thinking about what should or shouldn't have been done. What's done is done. We all have to make decisions. Some turn out to be the right ones and some not. It is not your fault, Phil. Until the necessary investigations are carried out we don't know that the accident wasn't just that, an accident. In the meantime, the doctors are doing all they can" and Allan but a hand on his brother-in-law's arm.

Phil nodded miserably.

It seemed like an eternity had passed and they had consumed several coffees when a tired looking surgeon emerged, still in his scrubs.

They both stood up and looked at him expectantly.

"Your wife is a lucky lady. She is shocked and has had a nasty bump on the head. She did suffer internal haemorrhaging but we managed to stop that. She is going to be fine" the doctor said smiling at Phil.

"The baby, our baby?" interrupted Phil in a whisper.

"The second bit of very good news is that you have a son, Mr Blake. Congratulations. He is healthy as far as we can see. We will do a few tests but I would doubt there is anything to worry about. He is a premature baby but his weight is 9lbs 3ozs and therefore doesn't need to be in an incubator. Mother and baby will be going home very soon, I'm pleased to say".

Phil, sobbing uncontrollably, sat down, his shoulders slumped and shaking.

"I'll leave you now but one of the nurses will be with you shortly to take you to your wife and to see your son" said the surgeon, again smiling kindly at Phil.

"Thank you very much for everything" he managed to reply.

"Congratulations on the birth of your baby son!" said Allan after they had sat in silence for a while.

"Thanks, mate" replied Phil placing the palms of his hands over his eyes and rubbing them hard.

"I have to go now but I will be back in a couple of hours to see Jane and meet my tiny nephew" Allan said standing up and clapping him gently on the shoulder, he took his leave.

Once outside the hospital, Allan rang Szymanski.

"I'm relieved to say, Jane is okay. She is in shock but she's going to be fine and the baby boy is good too."

"Oh, I'm so glad, Jack. Congratulations on becoming an uncle!".

"Thank you, Julia, I want you to get forensics over to look at Jane's car if they aren't already there. Tell them it is extremely urgent that I know whether it looks as though the car has been tampered with" he said.

"On it, sir!".

Chapter 17

When Allan got home that evening he felt in serious need of a workout. Changing into gym gear he set the treadmill for thirty minutes. While he was running, his mind went back to when, on his way home from the station, he had visited Jane.

Jane was still in shock, when he arrived, and recovering from the caesarean operation she had undergone. She looked pale, wide-eyed and fragile. He had walked over to her and kissed her gently on the forehead avoiding the nasty wound from the car accident. Tears were in her eyes as she spoke disjointedly, a sob escaping every now and again.

"I can't understand what happened, Jack. One moment I was driving along normally and the next the brake pedal wouldn't work. My foot was obviously off the accelerator but the car just wouldn't stop. It was as though it had a mind of its own. I couldn't control it. It wouldn't stop", she repeated and the tears were streaming now as she faced away from her brother.

"You are safe now Jane and you have a beautiful little son. Think of him and the many years you and Phil will have to enjoy him. Leave the accident to us. We will find out what happened but for now try to relax and get well. You will need to be extra fit to look after a tiny baby!"

She turned back to look at him.

"It wasn't an accident though, was it, Jack? Someone tampered with the brakes. It was the person who left that poor cat and killed Spot, wasn't it? Why would anyone do this to us? Who is this person? What do they want from us?" she demanded tearfully.

"I don't know!" lied Allan, "but I do know that you must let us move you into a safe house now. You can't go home. For the sake of your new arrival, you will need to trust me and follow my advice. Let me look after you, Phil and …….. By the way, what are you going to call my little nephew?"

"We are thinking Oliver Jack but nothing's definite" she managed a wan smile.

"Good names, especially the second one, of course" he laughed.

Jane gave a more relaxed smile.

"You get some sleep now, Jane. Is Phil still around?"

"Yes, he went off to the canteen I think".

"Okay I'll go look for him and take a peek at the little one" he said and gave her a reassuring wink.

Out of earshot he got on his mobile.

"Julia, you need to ask for a police presence outside Jane's room at the hospital. From how Jane described the accident, I think we are definitely looking at attempted murder. You will need to organise a formal statement from her. Perhaps you could do that? This has all come from you, of course, you understand".

"Of course, sir" Szymanski was standing in the middle of the general office, "I will come down now, and consider the constable organised".

"Thanks, Julia" and putting his mobile back in his pocket and, directed by a nurse, he walked down to where the room where new born babies slept to give their mother's the rest they needed.

The door was locked so he pressed the bell and very soon a nurse appeared. He spoke into the intercom and the nurse opened the door. He then produced his identification and explained his relationship to the baby. The nurse showed him the way to the relevant ward. Standing in front of the cot he looked down at the tiny form. The little fingers flexing, the tiny lips making bubbles. Allan resolved that without a shadow of a doubt he would ensure his nephew and the baby's parents would be protected from Manning's evil.

Leaving the room, he took the lift down to the hospital cafeteria in search of Phil and found him nursing a cup of coffee. A dirty but empty plate, together with a knife and fork on the table in front of him, bore witness to his much-needed meal. Allan sat down opposite him. Phil looked shocked and just stared at Allan for a couple of minutes.

"I'm so sorry, mate, that this has happened but on the bright side congratulations again on the safe birth of your first child!"

"Thanks, Jack" Phil replied smiling and looking down at his half-empty cup.

"DS Szymanski is arranging for a police constable to be stationed outside Jane's room but you will all be taken to a safe house very shortly. Needless to say, it is imperative that you all stay there until this matter is resolved".

"How long do you think that will take?"

"How long is a piece of string, Phil. Hopefully, not too long. We have eyes on a suspect".

"What I want to know, is why anyone would do this to us. I've been wracking my brains trying to think of someone who would want to hurt us, no, want to kill us. Jane and the baby could have been killed in that accident".

"Try not to worry about it, Phil. You need to be strong for Jane and the little one. I understand you are thinking of the name Oliver?" he added.

"We weren't going to tell anyone!" Phil exclaimed, surprise evident on his face.

"Oh! I'm sorry, I shouldn't have said!" apologised Allan.

"No, that's fine! Yes, it could well be Oliver and second name Jack".

Allan smiled.

"Listen I've got to get back to the station now but DS Szymanski will be here soon to take a statement from Jane, and the police constable should be there now. Take care, Phil and I'll be in touch soon".

Phil nodded as Allan put a hand on his shoulder and patted it.

That had been before he made his way home. It was now seven-thirty and Allan had moved on to the rowing machine. He was still thinking about the events of the day when his mobile rang.

"Hello, Jack, Julia. Had a call from Craig Miller, one of the forensic vehicle examiners, who confirms that the brake leads in your sister's car were cut but only to a certain extent so that they would not fail immediately but while she was part way through her journey.

He said that someone had calculated how long it would take for your sister to reach a main road where she would undoubtedly gather speed.

The accelerator had also been tampered with to ensure that it stuck and did not decelerate" she said.

"It's Manning without a doubt. Hang on Julia, I have to take a call from Dev" and he switched to the call holding.

"Hello Boss. Took a call earlier. An anonymous caller but they said they saw a car parked a little way up your sister's road on the day the dead cat was left in their house. They saw a man go into your sister's house. He was carrying something large, like an oversized briefcase or carrier. The caller didn't think too much about it at the time but then he saw a report in the local newspapers about the cat and Spot, so he thought he had better call us".

"Okay, well, that doesn't really help much does it?"

"No, not in itself, sir, but the caller remembers the registration number of the *grey estate car* and we ran the number plate. Guess what!?"

"Go on!"

"It's a rental car and the name of the hirer is a Mr N Naming at an address in Cambridge. An apartment block".

There was a silence on the phone for a few seconds.

"Well don't you see, sir!?" asked Patel excitedly.

"Erm"

"N Naming is an anagram for................"

Allan stroked the side of his nose for a moment and thought.

"Manning! Of course! Thanks Dev. Good work! Text me Manning's address. I'll be back at the station later" and he took Julia's call back.

"Sorry Julia" he said and explained what Patel had told him.

"You need to get an APB out for the registration. I will organise a search warrant for tomorrow. I'll call you," and he hung up.

Allan immediately phoned Stephen Simpson the magistrate for whom he had great respect and who would be the most likely to grant him a warrant quickly, if he presented sufficient compelling evidence.

"Good evening, Stephen, I'm sorry to disturb you at this hour but I urgently need a search warrant".

"Just before eight is not that late, Jack. Tell me why this is so urgent?"

Allan outlined the situation and reasons for the request. Simpson, after some consideration, agreed and confirmed that he would email the warrant to Allan within the hour. Allan thanked him and punched in Szymanski's number.

"I've put out an APB, Jack" said Szymanski before Allan could speak.

"Good! Now organise an ARU to meet us at Manning's address within the next half an hour. I'll text you the address now. We have the search warrant! I'll see you there!" and he hung up.

As Allan was rushing out to his car, his mobile rang. It was Vanessa calling. Reluctantly he pressed the red button.

Twenty minutes later the armed response unit, Allan and Szymanski, were at Manning's apartment.

"Police, armed police, open the door" an ARU officer called out.

There was no response.

"Armed police. We are coming in" and with that the door crashed open and the police quickly filed in. They went through each room of the immaculate flat.

"All clear! All clear!" they shouted as they found no-one. The unit filed out and left Allan and Szymanski to make their examination of the empty apartment.

"Clearly he is a fan of Far Eastern culture!" remarked Szymanski looking at several Japanese prints and paintings.

"We'll take this laptop that Manning has kindly left us!" Allan said sarcastically.

When they returned to the station they went straight to the techie guys to break the password which they did in a matter of minutes.

Returning to his office, Allan together with Szymanski explored the files on the laptop.

"Omg!" exclaimed Szymanski as she stared at the screen.

"Yes, Jane and Phil's house and how sick is this?" he said grimly as recordings of Phil and Jane in their home and pictures of the mutilated cat came up on the screen.

"This is concrete evidence, Jack, but what about the murders? And what about anything connecting him to the tampering of Jane's car?" Szymanski asked.

Allan sat back in his chair, stretched his arms and put his hands behind his head.

"I think it's time to head for home and catch a few hours' sleep. We are heading for a long day tomorrow that could start in the early hours if Manning is apprehended".

"Okay, I'll see you tomorrow then" said Szymanski getting up and walking to the door.

"Oh, by the way, Julia, how are things at home. Sally and Leo okay?" he asked.

Julia turned.

"Yes they are both fine except…… Oh! It doesn't matter. Yes we're all okay" she said.

"No, it does matter. Something up?"

"Yes, well, no. Well yes and no. We're fine but it's just, you know, I mentioned an old friend had come to stay, well he's still with us and I know he is upset about something but he doesn't keep to a routine and he is disturbing Leo sometimes. Not intentionally, of course, but he can't sleep and then he gets up and walks around and Leo hears him" she said taking a seat again.

"I suppose you need to ask him to leave but it is difficult?"

"Yes it is but you're right, of course. I will have to do that and soon! Anyway, nothing lasts forever and in this case I will make sure it ends in the not-too-distant future!"

Allan nodded and Szymanski smiled holding up her hand to thank him, then she departed.

As he was gathering his keys and picking up his jacket, Allan's mobile rang. Looking at the screen he saw that it was Vanessa and this time he pressed the green button.

"Hi, I'm sorry I couldn't take your call earlier, darling, I was in the middle of an urgent case" he said apologetically.

"Now why didn't I guess that?" she replied tongue in cheek.

"Okay, okay!" he laughed.

"So, how's it going? The case I mean?" she enquired.

"Oh, some definite progress but we're not there yet! But how is my wonderful woman?"

"Yes, really interesting stuff. I'm sorry I didn't ring you when I arrived but there was a get together at the hotel that went on until late and then I was so tired, when I finally managed to get to my room, I fell asleep!"

"No worries! Sounds like you're enjoying it," he said.

There was an awkward silence and Allan felt, once again, that Vanessa was hiding something from him and then she spoke.

"There's something I have to tell you but I can't over the phone" she said stumbling over her words.

Allan felt a chill creeping up from the pit of his stomach.

"Vanessa, tell me now. I can't wait days. There's something wrong isn't there?"

"I can't speak now, Jack. We'll talk when I get back. I have to go now".

"Love you" he said but she had already hung up.

It was midnight now as he drove home. His mind was in a whirl and he felt like his head was going to explode. He had two cases on his mind and Vanessa was hiding something. It sounded like the unthinkable. It sounded like she wanted to end their relationship. And yet, at the beginning of their conversation she had sounded like her normal self. They were laughing and enjoying each other. But had she met someone else? Had he missed something? Perhaps she had met another doctor at work. He let himself into their apartment and stood for a moment in the hallway completely motionless. He couldn't contemplate a life without Vanessa. He put his thumb and forefinger in the corners of his eyes to stem the tears. Then he did something that he wouldn't normally do. Instead of hitting his exercise machines to help him through a difficult case or time, he poured himself a whisky and then another and another. Finally, he slung himself on the bed fully clothed and crashed out.

Allan woke up to his mobile ringing. It was five o'clock in the morning on Sunday 14th March. His head was pounding.

"Allan" he barked into his mobile.

"Jack, Manning's car has been found in Wisteria Close. It's north of Wandlebury Park. No sign of Manning. Do you want me to get the vehicle transported for forensic examination?"

"Yes, do that as quick as you can, Julia. Let's see if there is something incriminating in the car to nail this bastard".

Jack was rubbing his face with his hands, walking over to the bathroom when his mobile let out a ping alerting him to a new message. Going back into the bedroom, he picked it up and accessed the email. He opened the attachment, blinking several times to convince himself he was seeing correctly.

"Good Morning, Detective Inspector or perhaps not such a good one for you. So, you have found my car at last. Well done! Not that you will find anything of interest in it. You don't really think I would leave you any clues as to how to find me do you? I have to admit it's rather inconvenienced me as I'm now forced to find another vehicle. No matter. I expect you are wondering how I got your mobile number and email address. I won't enlighten you but suffice to say it was a simple matter. Well, your sister survived her ordeal this time but next time I can assure you she won't and nor will her tiny baby. So good luck with trying to stop the inevitable! Oh, and good luck too with solving the murders. A serial killer on your hands. I am causing you problems, aren't I, Jack. By the way, how is the lovely Vanessa? Bye for now!

Allan lifted his arm high and threw the mobile on the bed angrily.

"If it's the last thing I do on this earth I am going to ensure you go down and never see the light of day again!" he shouted and when he stopped the sound of silence engulfed him.

Thirty minutes later, Allan was just leaving the apartment and his mobile rang.

"You're not going to like this, sir" Patel said.

"Hit me with it" replied Allan.

"There's been another murder".

"Where?"

"Midsummer Common. Another, as yet, unidentified woman".

"Okay, I'm on my way" Allan answered wearily.

When he arrived twenty minutes later Strange was already there. Having donned the statutory footwear and gloves, Allan walked over to where the murder victim lay.

Strange looked up as he approached.

"Looks like the same murderer" and Strange pointed to the object in the woman's hands.

Allan bent down to examine it more closely.

"Two glass eyes" he muttered as he extracted them from the dead woman's hand.

"Even more bizarre are the two arrows drawn on her cheeks pointing upwards to her eyes".

"What can you tell me about the time of death?"

"I can't confirm until I get her back to the lab but I would guestimate between midnight and four o'clock this morning. The glass scratches on her feet and hands together with the cuts on her feet and hands and the strangulation marks, make it almost certain that this is the same killer, Jack".

"Okay, thanks, Stew. I'll be in touch later" said Allan getting up from his crouching position.

Patel had come up to stand beside him.

"What do you make of it, sir?" he asked.

"I have had a message from Manning this morning and he obviously intends to carry on killing. We have to get this guy and we have to do it fast, Dev".

He rang Szymanski and filled her in.

"So, we need to combine forces now on this one. We will deal with this bastard as a team. With Jane, Phil and the baby now in a safe house, hopefully Manning can't get to them. In the meantime, round the whole team up for a meeting in one hour back at the station".

"Will do, sir" replied Szymanski and rang off.

An hour later the team had assembled, quietly awaiting their boss to update them which he did.

Allan finished by saying, "We now know the identity of the serial killer whose name is Roland Manning alias Mr N Naming. It is imperative we catch this bastard like yesterday. I have organised a temporary uniform presence outside Manning's flat and his car is in the pound, although I hold no real optimism for anything to materialise from its examination, particularly in light of the contents of the killer's last letter".

DC Callender, who had walked away for a few moments to take a call, came back into the room.

"Sir, sorry to interrupt, but we've just heard from a witness who said that she saw the driver of Manning's car. She thought he looked quite striking, tall with blonde hair. He turned and looked right at her so she can remember his features. She didn't really think anything more of it but when she returned from her shopping she remembered she had seen the media appeal and decided to phone us".

"Get her in, Sophie. We're making progress in gaining an up-to-date facial description of

Manning. When the photofit is finished have it distributed, Sophie. This rat soon won't have anywhere to hide" he said with venom.

"Sir, Strange on line 2 for you" called out Wright.

"Hi, Stew, what have you got for me?" asked Allan picking up the call.

"Time of death is confirmed as between midnight and four o'clock this morning. Dental records show that her name was Kim Watson, twenty-six years of age. She died of asphyxiation and was strangled twice. I'd lay money on it being the same killer".

"Thanks, Stew" said Jack grimly and hung up.

Allan wrote another name on the board, together with details of the crime scene.

Max, having read the details, took out her phone. Her thumbs were pressing buttons with the speed of light.

"Sir, this follows the pattern completely. The glass eyes is a clue for the film "For Your Eyes Only" released in 1981.

"Sick bastard" muttered Mike.

"Well, when we catch Manning we may find out what the significance was of the film element" ventured Barry.

Allan nodded but something was troubling him. Something was off. He folded his arms, frowning.

"Everything okay, sir?" enquired Szymanski.

Allan came out of his reverie.

"Yes, fine, Julia, just thinking that's all" he said with a ghost of a smile.

"Okay everyone, so as usual, even though we are almost certain that we know who the killer is, for the record we need to find out all we can about the victim of this latest murder plus, Mike, as a matter of urgency, can you establish who Kim Watson's family are and then take Sophie with you to give them the sad news.

Max, can you find out where she worked and can you and Barry find out the home addresses of her colleagues and interview them. See what you can find out about her work and personal lives.

Dev and Peter can you go through her financial affairs and any phone calls she made the day before and the day she died.

Meanwhile, Julia and I will find out where she lived and if that was where she was tortured and murdered".

Allan broke off to answer his mobile.

"What! When? I'm on my way".

"Julia you're with me" and he rushed out of the room, Szymanski following right behind him.

"You drive" he said as he got in the passenger seat when they arrived at his car.

Szymanski caught the keys, Allan threw to her.

"Where to, Jack?" she asked.

"To the safe house where Jane and Phil are" he said and then spoke on the phone.

Szymanski didn't ask her boss but put the blues and twos on. She expertly weaved her way through the thick Cambridge traffic.

"Do you mind me asking what has happened, Jack?" she asked, her eyes never leaving the road in front of her.

"A man was seen around the safe house dressed as a policeman. The police presence shouted and attempted to stop him but the man was let in and now he is in the house with Jane, Phil and the baby. If anything happens to them I'll......."

"Sir, I don't want to hear! Do you think you should be dealing with this? Perhaps leave it to me? Were you calling for a negotiator and armed response?" replied Szymanski calmly but firmly.

"Yes" he said quietly now.

When they arrived, a police cordon was already in place around the safe house which stood alone in a large garden, the nearest neighbour being about half a mile away.

Allan went up to one of the uniformed police.

"Have we heard anything going on in the house?"

"No, sir. It has all been very quiet. There has been no sign of any movement but the guy in there has a gun. He turned around as we were approaching and fired a shot at us".

"Anyone hurt?"

"No, fortunately, sir".

"Okay. We wait for the negotiator but if he doesn't appear within ten minutes, I will start the negotiations. Have the loud hailer ready" he commanded in a stern voice.

Szymanski had been within earshot of Allan's conversation with the officer.

"Sorry, sir, but I really don't think you should be involved in this. I know what the handbook says but it's too personal even so. Let me negotiate. I do have the experience. Please, sir" she said looking at him with a concerned rather than her usual no-nonsense expression.

"I'm perfectly capable of conducting the negotiations" he snapped turning to look at his subordinate.

Then his face went slack and he put both hands up in a placatory manner.

"I'm sorry, Julia. You're right, of course. You can lead if the negotiator doesn't arrive in two minutes" he said looking at his watch.

"But, Julia, I am staying and may have input into what you say to this bastard" he added.

Szymanski nodded agreement and couldn't prevent a sigh of relief escaping her.

With no negotiator turning up, Szymanski began. At Allan's request she addressed the guy as Manning.

"Good afternoon. This is Detective Sergeant Szymanski. I want to speak to Mr Manning, Mr Roland Manning. We are going to ring you on the landline and then we can discuss what it is that you want us to do. We are ringing you now, please answer".

After half a dozen rings, the receiver was picked up.

"Good afternoon. I will only negotiate with one person, Detective Inspector Jack Allan. Is he there?"

"I'm sorry but you will have to put up with me, Mr Manning. DI Allan is not able to be engaged in this negotiation but before we proceed, I want confirmation that Mr and Mrs Blake and their baby are okay. Can I speak with them, please?"

"With the greatest respect, I don't think you are in any position to ask me for anything, Detective Sergeant Szymanski. I think you will find that I am the person calling the shots".

Allan gently pushed Szymanski aside. She remonstrated that he should not speak but he ignored her.

"With the greatest respect, Mr Manning, unless I can hear for myself that the Blake family are unharmed you don't have anything to negotiate with, so if I were you I would consider the potential consequence of that very carefully" said Jack in an icy tone.

There was a silence for a few seconds and then Phil came on the phone.

"We are okay at the moment, Jack, but I think this guy means business...." Jack could hear his sister and the baby in the background as Phil was speaking.

"Sorry to cut you off, Detective Inspector, but you now know that they are alive and well. Let's get down to business, shall we?"

"So, what is that you want?"

"Oh, nothing much. I want £2 million to be delivered to an account of my choice. A light plane to take me to a destination of my choosing, safe transport to the plane, and finally, last but not least, I want you, Jack, to come into the house in exchange for the Blake family".

"I agree to all those terms but it will take a while to get together the money and the plane. I will walk over now, if you release the Blakes".

"Don't get ahead of yourself, Jack. I will only release them in exchange for yourself when I have the money in the bank account that I send to you. You will be my safe passage onto the plane".

There was a ping on Allan's phone. It was the account number from Manning.

A flurry of phone calls was made for authorisation of the money and organisation of a plane. Three hours later, Allan was in a position to confirm to Manning that his demands had been met.

"I can see that. I must commend you and the police force for a very efficient service, Jack. Now if you could start walking towards the house".

Szymanski lightly touched Allan's forearm.

"I don't like this, sir. It's all too neat and easy. Something's off".

"Yes, maybe, but if we can get my sister and her family out of there, we have achieved".

"But, sir, would you do this, would this be the right decision if this wasn't your sister and her family?"

"Honestly, as a policeman, yes, I would".

She released her hand and shrugged her shoulders lightly.

"Okay" she said softly.

Allan put on his bullet proof vest and started to walk towards the house. The armed police were positioned. The front door was opened as he arrived and Allan was unceremoniously hauled inside.

As the minutes ticked by, no-one emerged.

"Let the Blakes go, as agreed, Mr Manning or we will come in by force" rang out the commanding voice of Szymanski using the loud hailer. The negotiators had just arrived, too late to be of assistance.

Thirty seconds later the house lit up the sky. Orange flames and black smoke fanned out from all four corners of the house.

"Oh shit! Bloody hell!" were the cries from the police.

Szymanski was running towards the house along with several of her colleagues. Someone rang the fire brigade and ambulance services.

A few of the officers told Szymanski to stand back as they battered in the door with their shoulders. Furniture and bits of flaming plaster were flying everywhere. The baby could be heard crying.

The officers fought their way through the burning wreckage avoiding being burnt as much as possible. Phil and Jane had been tied to kitchen chairs. The police were coughing, choking on the smoke. They couldn't untie the knots. Someone grabbed the baby from the cot and picked their way out of the house. An ambulance had arrived outside and the paramedics raced over to the baby. They exercised tiny resuscitation movements of the baby's chest to no avail.

"One more try" said the visibly moved paramedic who was trying to save the baby's life, a strangled choking in her voice.

She applied the pumping motion again.

The baby coughed. His tiny fingers moved and he coughed again. Everyone clapped and a little oxygen mask was put on his little face. Everyone was wiping tears from their eyes.

The officers had managed to carry out the chairs with Phil and Jane attached. More ambulances had arrived and the officers were treated for smoke inhalation and burns. Phil and Jane were untied. Jane was unresponsive at first but with the care and attention of the paramedics both the Blakes' lives were saved and they were taken by ambulance to hospital for full assessment.

The fire brigade arrived and hoses were soon put to good use.

Szymanski had come out for air. She had used a scarf around her mouth and nose but nevertheless she was gasping, coughing, choking and feeling lightheaded. A couple of paramedics came over but she waved them away. She had to go back in. She had to find her boss. Where was he? Where was Manning?

The flames continued to surge into the sky as Szymanski bent forward, her hands on her knees, trying to breathe normally. She gradually stood up and then ran determinedly back to the house.

"No, you can't go in there!" said a fireman, catching her arm.

She pulled out her identification and flashed it at him long enough for him to read her name and rank.

"DI Allan is still in the house. I have to find him. NOW!" she cried shaking her arm free only to be caught again.

"It's too dangerous. We will find him. Don't worry! It's our job!" said the fireman.

"Yes and it's my job to support my boss and I need to get him out of there!" she said defiantly, her mouth in a hard straight line, her chin up, daring the fire officer to argue.

"I'm sorry, DS Szymanski, but it's out of the question. The fire department have the authority here until the fire is under control and we deem it safe for others to enter".

As she thought about her next retort, shouting could be heard from the burning building.

The fireman ran towards the house with Szymanski close behind him.

The sound of force being used against a door could be heard now.

"The bloody door is locked" said one fireman, presumably to a question from the one that had tried to prevent Szymanski from entering the building.

More sounds of battering and then the sound of yielding wood as the door collapsed.

"He's been tied up. Nasty wound on the head. Not responding".

Szymanski waved frantically at a paramedic standing beside an ambulance. He moved swiftly towards her at the same time shouting to his colleague to follow him.

Two firemen, faces obscured by oxygen masks, came out carrying Allan still tied to the chair.

They untied him and the paramedics lay him on a stretcher on the ground.

Szymanski stood with her hand over her mouth.

A paramedic was giving Allan CPR. Suddenly Allan was coughing. Again, there was clapping from those standing around. Allan groaned and then tried to get up.

"No, sir, you can't get up. We are taking you to hospital. That head wound is nasty and needs checking out plus you need to be observed for a few hours after that smoke inhalation".

"I haven't got time for all this. I have a murderer to catch!" and he struggled to get up but collapsed back onto the stretcher.

"That's as maybe, sir, but you aren't progressing with that today!" and the two paramedics picked up the stretcher either end, transporting him to the waiting ambulance.

Szymanski walked beside him.

"It could be, sir, that the murderer himself was killed in the fire" she suggested as Allan was put into the back of the ambulance and the doors closed.

Szymanski drove to the hospital. When Allan had been checked out and allocated a bed for the night, despite his best protestations to the nurses, the two detectives discussed happenings and the way forward.

Chapter 18

The next day, Monday 15th March, the team were at their desks reeling from the news from Szymanski about the events of the day before, when Allan walked through the swing doors sporting a large amount of padding on his forehead.

The whole team stood up and applauded their boss.

"What's this for? I haven't done anything to deserve a clap. In fact, rather the reverse. I can't believe I walked straight into a waiting trap and got myself knocked out, tied up and left to die!" he bemoaned.

A couple of the team squeezed his shoulder and smiled.

"Glad to have you back, sir" said Patel.

"That looks like a sizeable wound on your head, sir! Should you be back so soon?" asked Callender looking concerned.

"We've found a lot out about the latest victim, sir! When you're ready, of course, sir!" said Max and the rest of the team glared at her for being so unfeeling.

"What?" exclaimed Max looking round at her colleagues, totally oblivious to any insensitivity on her part.

Allan strode over to the white board.

"Listen, guys. We have a chance now to catch not only our serial killer and solve a cold case but also keep my family safe.

Julia will update us on the case concerning my family shortly.

Now we know that Manning has all but confessed to being the serial killer.

I had a call last night from the Chief Fire Officer who confirmed that his body has not been recovered from the wreckage and therefore we can only assume that he escaped. The CFO also confirmed arson. We can take from that the request for the money and the light airplane was not his goal. His goal was to kill my sister, her husband and baby. That would cause me maximum distress in my last few moments of my life, thinking that I could do nothing to save them. Then, ultimately, he would have the satisfaction of knowing that he had killed me. I'm guessing the motive was to get at me because I destroyed his 'empire'. This is all about me. He is taking revenge.

What I can't explain is what films have to do with anything but that is something we can find out when we catch and question him.

I have ordered an extensive search of the area around the safe house which is being organised as we speak. There is also an APB out for him on major roads, airports and ports. With luck he will be apprehended before close of play today.

We also know that he has left us clues that could lead us to who the next victim is. We need to work on that in case we cannot find Manning and, to that end, we will, this morning, go through what you have all found out about our fourth victim and try to make sense of it in relation to the information gathered on the other three victims" Allan paused for breath.

"You mentioned that we have a chance to solve a cold case, sir?" asked Mike.

"Yes. It came to me when I was sitting in that cupboard, drawing what I thought were my last few breaths".

There was complete silence as the team waited to hear.

"Manning is Qíang!"

"How do you work that one out?" asked Max.

"On three counts.

Firstly, there were fires at Misslethwaite Hall, Rosedene Grange and now the safe house. All fires were arson. All fires were concerned with killing those people who, in one way or another, were a threat or an inconvenience to Qíang.

Secondly, there was no sighting of Qíang after the fire at Misslethwaite and the reason was that he used his money made from the fraudulent scheme at his university to finance his cosmetic surgery. This new appearance is the one he was using as Manning after the Rosedene Grange fire and the one that has been described by witnesses concerning the current serial killings.

Thirdly, it explains the motive. Revenge against me. He felt I was the one responsible for wrecking his plans because I was the detective assigned to the case of the murder of his parents and questioned the shopkeeper who sold him the paraffin. Thus he knew he had to disappear which wasn't what he had intended at all".

"Wow! So, the son was responsible all the time! But how did he manage to go under the radar before he had cosmetic surgery?" asked Patel

"He is extremely clever. I suppose genius bordering on madness springs to mind although in this case I feel the border has been crossed. Also, as I explained, he had made a great deal of money from his scams" replied Allan.

"Why then didn't he have further work on his appearance. Surely, that would ensure no-one would connect him to Misslethwaite and Rosedene?" asked Max her voice crisp and matter-of-fact.

"Very simple. He has run out of funds for the moment".

"Which is why he was demanding the transfer of monies when he held your sister and her family as hostages" commented Barry.

"Possible but not likely because his aim was to cause me as much misery as possible and then let me die a horrible death. He never meant to use the light plane to escape or collect the money because, if he did, he wouldn't have been able to start the deathtrap fire. So those were bogus calls. Now, Julia, could you fill us in with what has happened regarding my sister and her family?"

"Yes, sir. Jane and Phil Blake have been taken to hospital suffering from minor burns and smoke inhalation. Baby Blake is doing well. No burns thankfully."

Szymanski paused for a couple of seconds.

"I'd like to add too, we are very fortunate to still have our boss with us" and she nodded and smiled, indicating Allan who also nodded in acceptance of her sentiment. The whole team smiled and there were grunts of agreement all round.

"DI Allan was found in a store cupboard tied to a chair and gagged. He was unconscious from smoke inhalation when they found him with a very nasty gash on his forehead. I think we are all agreed that the paramedics did a superb job in saving the victims' lives. There is an armed guard on each of the Blake's rooms at the hospital and they will be taken to a safe house in another part of the country as soon as the doctors have given them the all-clear".

At that moment, Patel, who had briefly exited the room to take a call, came rushing back in.

"Sir, they have found him. He checked into The Regency Hotel in Market Street and the desk clerk recognised him from the descriptions issued but he is using the name James not Manning".

"Julia you're with me. Dev, Barry follow on!" commanded Allan.

The four rushed out and within seven minutes they arrived at the hotel.

Everyone ran through the large, imposing lobby with its shiny marble floor matching the shiny marble walls.

Brandishing his warrant card at the receptionist Allan was given Manning's room number and the hotel manager immediately followed them to the stairs.

Having reached the third floor, they followed the manager to the suspect's room and Allan rapped loudly on the door.

"This is the police. Open the door, please, Mr Manning" he said authoritatively.

No answer.

"Open the door, Mr Manning or we will be coming in" commanded Allan.

No response.

The manager opened the door and all four detectives brushed past the manager and walked quickly into the room. Both the room and the ensuite were empty. There was a rucksack on the chair by the window.

"Did anyone see Mr Manning leave the hotel before we arrived?" asked Allan.

"Not as far as I'm aware but I will check, sir" replied the manager and rang his receptionists.

Meanwhile, Szymanski was examining the rucksack.

"He won't be going anywhere without this, sir" she said brandishing a passport.

Allan took it and looked inside.

"This is for his new identity, Mr Lee James with Manning's photo. As you say, he will need his passport. So, we wait!"

"No, sir, no-one saw Mr James, I mean Mr Manning, leave. His face seemed familiar to the receptionist although his name did not. When she realised who he might be, she immediately called you but after that she didn't see him again" said the manager.

"I'm very glad she called!" exclaimed Allan.

Two hours later, Allan and Szymanski were still sitting in the car awaiting the reappearance of the suspect. Allan in the driving seat.

"So how are things going at home" asked Allan consuming the last mouthful of banana, wrapping the skin neatly in a brown paper bag, and biting into an apple.

"Good, thanks. Well actually not entirely good" she said looking at her chocolate bar and feeling guilty about eating it but not that guilty. She took a huge bite out of it savouring the thick, creamy taste.

"Oh! How so?" asked Allan turning is his seat and looking at her enquiringly.

"Well, it's all good with Sally, and Leo is just fabulous" she said wiping some chocolate from around her mouth.

"Ummm! That was good! Much better than that boring old apple!" she said her wide, thin mouth curling upwards into a cheeky grin.

"Well at least I won't have to have my arteries scraped out in ten years' time" he retorted with an askance look.

Szymanski laughed.

"No, all's well with my two but it's a real strain with my friend. He is obviously in a state about splitting up with someone. I don't know for sure it is that, but he is showing all the signs. I just wish he would come out with it. Maybe we can all talk it through and he can get his life back together again!"

"He'll have to, I suppose. He can't stay with you forever! What did you say his name was?"

"Sylas. Sylas Bukosky. Okay, that's *my* life at the moment. What about yours. How is Vanessa? Are her parents clamouring for the date of the wedding?"

"Vanessa's on a course for a week. I so miss her. All quiet on the soon-to-be in law front at the moment. You know, Julia, something's off!" he said suddenly throwing his apple core into the brown paper bag.

"What with Vanessa or her parents?"

Allan was stroking the side of his nose thoughtfully.

"No with Roland Manning" he said absent mindedly, deep in thought.

"Something isn't right. He's fooled us. He's not coming back here! He's already at an airport with another passport" he exclaimed.

Szymanski didn't have time to reply.

Allan answered his mobile.

"Hold him. We're on our way" he barked and clicked off.

"As I just twigged, Julia, Manning or Qiang, or whatever his name is now, has been picked up at City airport" he said activating the blues and twos as he sped off.

"Manning played us. The rucksack and passport were left on purpose for us to find and assume, wrongly, that he was returning, while he made his escape".

"But, sir, if he hadn't finished his mission, which was to kill you and your family why would he disappear now".

"He doesn't know we aren't dead but even if he did, he is well aware that he would have to lie low until everything dies down before he resurfaces to finish the job" Allan said grimly, increasing his speed and swerving expertly around the traffic in front of him.

When they arrived at departures at the airport, they were greeted by an unexpected scene. Allan dumped the car. He and Szymanski rushed into the building. A steady stream of people was spilling out of one of the doors, channelled by barriers either side of them, onto the pavement and road. Allan and Szymanski squeezed past the file of people and showed their warrant cards to a security officer, who was examining passports and waving people through.

The officer momentarily stopped the passage of people to speak to Allan.

"The DI over there will fill you in, sir".

Allan and Szymanski walked in the direction indicated, leaving the security officer to carry on his check.

Showing their warrant cards once more, and introductions made, Allan asked where Manning was.

"We had him, Jack. We had him," said DI Nigel Fareham. The suspect went into the toilets with an officer outside the cubicle. He used some sort of drug because the next thing we knew we went in to find out what was taking so long and found DS Thomas on the ground out cold. No sign of physical violence and he was alive but unresponsive. An ambulance is on its way".

"Good but where is Manning?"

"We are searching. Every person who was in this building is remaining here until they have been checked out so he won't get far. He won't be able to leave this building".

"Don't be too sure about that, Nigel. I need to have the outside of this building searched thoroughly too. The planes, for example and any buildings".

"Jack, I am in charge here. This is my patch. I want to catch the suspect as much as you do. So, leave it to me and when we find him we'll hand him over to you but the operation to find him is my responsibility. Are we clear?" said Fareham.

"With respect Nigel, I know this suspect. He is as slippery as they come. If there is a way to escape he will find it and even if you don't believe he could get away, think again because you'd probably be wrong. So, I say again, I want the planes and any outbuildings searched. I take it you have cancelled all departures?"

"Do you really want me to answer that? What do you take me for, Jack?"

"Okay, okay!" said Allan allowing himself to grin.

"We'll get him! Don't worry!" said Fareham, slapping Allan on the shoulder.

Allan started to pace up and down, looking over now and again through the floor to ceiling windows onto the concourse and the planes lined up.

"I'll go and get a couple of coffees, sir" said Szymanski.

Allan didn't answer. He was thinking.

A few minutes later, Szymanski returned and handed Allan one of the drinks.

"Penny for them, sir" she asked as she sipped her cappuccino.

He didn't answer but was staring at something intently.

Szymanski looked in the same direction.

"That man – what is he doing?" he muttered more to himself than to Szymanski.

"The one walking over to the plane?" she asked, turning her head towards her boss.

"Yes. That plane has air stairs against it".

"I don't know, Jack. He looks like one of the staff. I assume he is doing a check or something like that?"

"But all planes have been grounded and, Julia, never assume!" he swung round, hurled his cup full of coffee into the bin beside him and raced over to where he could see his counterpart talking to another officer.

"Nigel, Nigel" he shouted across the concourse.

DI Nigel Fareham swung round and faced Allan who was racing towards him.

"He's down there, outside, in the Apron. I think he is going to try to escape in one of the planes".

"He can't do that without a pilot!" said Fareham who was already on his two-way radio.

Within minutes police were swarming outside onto the Apron. Allan and Szymanski joined them.

Soon the door opened in the aircraft with airstairs and Manning could be seen.

"I'll make this brief, everyone. I need a pilot provided to take me to whatever location I ask and in return I won't blow up a major public building in the UK" he shouted.

"Why should we believe you? We could just come up those stairs and arrest you?" shouted Fareham into a loudhailer.

"The answer is that you don't have to believe me. Not at all. You do just that! The problem with that is that I might, just might, be telling the truth. Think of all those people you would have sentenced to death because you didn't believe me! Can you honestly live with that, Detective Inspector Fareham. I think probably not! However, you have two hours, I think that is very generous of me, to make up your mind before you will find out whether I was telling the truth of not!" he sneered and closed the door.

Fareham turned to Allan.

"Is he telling the truth or not?" he asked bluntly.

"On balance I would say he probably isn't but I can't be sure. He might have put in place a plan, that if the worst happened, would get him out of that tight spot. I don't know but I think, unfortunately, we have to work on the premise that he is telling the truth".

"Okay, we can't provide a pilot. It's too dangerous. We have to take him by storm and we need to do that within two hours. If he comes out for a progress report we'll keep talking. In the meantime, we need to escalate this to bring in the SAS. I'll make a few calls" said Fareham.

"Good. We must take him alive. I want him to confess on tape to all the crimes he has committed" said Allan grimly.

Chapter 19

Approximately an hour and a half later, the light was failing as evening drew in. An SAS team had been assembled and were waiting out of sight of the plane's visual.

"Mr Manning can we speak. It's Detective Inspector Fareham" he said using his loud hailer.

There was no response.

"Mr Manning I need to speak to you before we proceed with your demands for a pilot" he said in a louder, more determined voice.

The door of the aircraft slowly opened revealing Manning who had a supercilious expression on his face.

"You are running out of time, Detective Inspector Fareham. You have less than thirty minutes before I press the button and all those people will die. Their deaths will be on your conscience forever. So, I do hope that you are not wasting precious time with pointless questions" he said curling his lip disdainfully.

"No, I can assure you I'm not but it's really important that we are certain you are not going to activate the explosion if we meet your demands.

How are we to know that you won't do that anyway? Also, we are concerned about the pilot's safety. Can you guarantee that he won't be harmed and will be returned to us safe and sound?"

While Fareham was stringing out the questions as long as possible, the SAS team of six quickly, quietly and efficiently made their way to the back end of the plane out of sight of Manning's vision.

The first team member started to unscrew a hatch and carefully lowered it to allow the team to enter the plane. They came up through the galley each signalling to the next officer when they were certain the coast was clear for entry. Stealthily advancing down the aisle of the plane they were completely silent. When they reached the curtain that divided the main cabin from the front galley, they could hear the conversation between Fareham and Manning.

"You have no choice but to trust that your pilot will return safely and that I won't detonate the bomb anyway. Those are risks you will have to take. Now you have less than twenty minutes to meet my demands. I suggest you get on with that!"

The leader of the SAS team drew the curtain back revealing the team in a ready position, their guns raised and pointing towards the suspect.

Manning, who was standing in the doorway had caught sight of their legs below the mid-length pleated curtain and had drawn his gun, pointing it not at the officers, but at Fareham and Allan standing below.

"Drop your weapon now! Drop your weapon" shouted the lead officer.

"If you shoot me, at the same time I will press the trigger to detonate the bomb and I will shoot dead one of the officers......."

Manning didn't have time to finish as the shot rang out and he fell from the open doorway thirty feet to the ground below. The blood from his head mingled with smashed skull fragments and the red liquid formed a quickly increasing pool.

Allan, Szymanski and Fareham stood in stunned silence for a few seconds.

Then Allan knelt down by the corpse and, putting on his blue protective gloves, he examined Manning's hands and pockets.

"There's nothing resembling a detonator here. It was a bluff! We should have....I should have known" he said bitterly.

"We couldn't have possibly known, sir" said Szymanski.

"She's right, Jack, you know she's right!" agreed Fareham.

"I wanted the bastard alive, damn it!" muttered Allan at last.

"Well, you've got your man. That's all that really counts, isn't it, Jack? Another bastard off the streets. Congratulations!" and Fareham slapped Allan on the shoulder.

"Yes, sir, well done!" Szymanski's thin lips curving upwards into a broad smile.

"Thank you for all your cooperation on this one, Nigel. I owe you!"

"That you do, Jack, but all in good time" he winked.

The six SAS officers walked over and shook hands with Allan and Fareham.

"Well done chaps! Thanks" said Fareham.

"I understand you would rather have taken him alive but we had no choice. Apologies but we couldn't let him have time to detonate the bomb or, for that matter, have a chance to shoot one of you" said the leader.

"Yes I did want him taken alive but I understand completely why you shot him and thank you. Good job!" said Allan smiling broadly and then turning to Fareham.

"Thanks again, Nigel, for all your help. The Press are here already, I see. We need to get back to the station to prepare a press release immediately," he remarked, looking up at the window overlooking the Apron.

"Of course," said Fareham ushering Allan and Szymanski towards the staff exit and out to their car before the Press realised what was going on.

Arriving back at the station, Allan made his way directly to the DCI's office. He knocked on the door and when summoned he walked in and sat down on the chair indicated.

"I hear that the serial killer is the same person that terrorised your sister and her family?" Tom Clarkson said with one of his over nice, dangerous smiles.

"Yes, sir, I'm pleased to say that the killer is now deceased".

"And you have proof that he was guilty of the murders and guilty too of the potential murder of your sister?"

"Yes, sir, I received a letter from Manning concerning threats against my sister and her family that also indicated that he was guilty of the murders. So, the cases are solved, sir.

In addition to those two crimes, I believe we have solved the cold case concerning the deaths of Professor Bingwen Zhang and his wife. Arson was used to kill them at their house and their son Qíang just disappeared into thin air until he emerged as Manning where another house fire conveniently killed Piers and Francesca Cunningham. Manning kidnapped my sister and family as revenge against me, and they were destined to be killed in a house fire too along with myself! The common factors in all three incidents are Manning and arson used against anyone that posed a threat to his plans!".

Tom Clarkson was tapping his pen on the edge of his desk, smiling but there was no warmth in the smile.

"So, you have deliberately disobeyed my order in line with police policy that you were not to be involved in your sister's case! I will have to ask you for your warrant card, Allan. As from today you are suspended, pending further investigation into your conduct" was all Clarkson said while unable to disguise the glee in his voice.

Allan made no move. He remained totally relaxed, sitting back in his chair and looking straight at his boss.

"Actually, sir, I don't wish to contradict you, but I think you will find that the policy here in Cambridge is that an officer may not be involved in any case concerning a spouse, child or parent but it does not extend to siblings. So, with the greatest of respect, sir, I won't be handing over my warrant card," Allan allowed a few seconds for this to sink in and then continued as there was no comment from a gobsmacked Clarkson.

"I think we need to move on now, sir, to the press release which is urgent and should be done this evening, even at this hour. I am happy to do the talking if you are okay with that, sir?"

Clarkson had now recovered his composure.

"Yes, quite happy, Allan. Make the necessary arrangements as quickly as you can!"

"Yes, sir" and Allan got up from his chair.

As he approached the door he turned round.

"Oh, by the way, sir, did you want me to find the clause in the our handbook that concerns involvement in cases concerning family? Just so as you know where it is, sir?" he asked with his most innocent and helpful of expressions.

"No, that won't be necessary! No mention of your theory and circumstantial evidence concerning the cold case and that's an order. Shut the door behind you!"

Allan closed the door quietly and once shut, grinned broadly. He had, of course, delegated his family's case to DS Szymanski in the first instance because he hadn't wanted to give his boss any ammunition he could use against him but subsequently he had established by consulting the police handbook that he was, in fact, able to investigate at sibling level.

An hour later DCI Tom Clarkson and DI Jack Allan strode into the conference hall filled with journalists and the press holding a mass of microphones of all shapes and sizes. The two detectives took their seats and when the signal came that the cameras were ready Clarkson began.

"Good evening ladies and gentlemen. We've called this conference to notify the press and the general public of the successful conclusion to our search for the person responsible for the heinous crimes committed against three defenceless women. The perpetrator was shot dead resisting arrest this afternoon at City Airport by a squad of SAS officers. I can release the man's name – Roland Manning. DI Allan?" and Clarkson turned to his colleague indicating he should continue.

"I have nothing further to add to what DCI Clarkson has told you other than to express my thanks to my team and all those involved in preventing any further horrific attacks by an evil individual. I'll take questions now" and he pointed to a red-haired woman at the back.

"Is it true that you shouldn't have been involved in this case at all because the same man tried to murder your sister and that means you had a personal interest?" she asked thrusting her microphone in his direction.

"I'm not sure where you got that information from but it is incorrect. If you were to look at the

Procedures Manual it quite clearly states that if an officer's parent, spouse or child is involved then they must stand back from the case. There is absolutely no mention of a sibling demanding the same action. So, yes, I should have been involved in the case," replied Allan calmly but firmly. He was thinking what a bastard his boss was, because undoubtedly he was the one responsible for leaking this to the Press and this was confirmed when he noticed a puzzled look from the reporter in the DCI's direction.

Allan pointed to a tall man with a shock of black, wavy hair.

"DCI Clarkson mentioned that three defenceless women had been murdered but I understand that a fourth woman has been found dead and the same murderer is suspected. Is that correct".

"I cannot comment at this time" was all Allan replied, which raised a murmur of curiosity from the Press.

Allan indicated a small blonde woman at the front of the crowd.

"What was the motive for the killings?" she asked.

"That is not clear at present and we may never know the answer to that" replied Allan avoiding mentioning the revenge theory and the debatable motive for the serial killings.

"What was the relevance of the items the victims were found holding in their hands?"

"I can't comment on that".

"That's it. Thank you for your time," said Tom Clarkson authoritatively getting up and walking out purposefully, closely followed by Allan.

Clarkson didn't look at or speak to his subordinate but took the stairs to his office.

When Allan walked into the general office, all the team were still there talking excitedly but stopped when their boss walked in.

"Great work everyone! I didn't expect you all to still be here! It's well gone eight o'clock! As you are, let's all repair to the Dog and Mouse. The drinks are on me!"

Everyone cheered and prepared to go.

In the pub, everyone's shoulders dropped, their faces relaxed, laughing at each other's ridiculous jokes.

Szymanski came and stood beside Allan who was texting on his mobile.

"Busy?" she said.

"Just catching up with Vanessa or trying to. Last time I spoke to her she said she had something to say to me that she couldn't say over the phone. I asked her to spill but she wouldn't, that it had to be face-to-face. I'm trying to prepare for the worst. That she's met someone else. That she can't cope with my hours. I don't know. I've put it to the back of my mind because of the case but it's flooding my mind now. She seemed so happy a few days ago. We were talking about the wedding and about how good it was that it would be a quiet one. We talked about the honeymoon. I just can't believe that she wants to break up but………………"

"Jack, stop! Your imagination is running riot. I understand how you must feel. It doesn't sound good admittedly but, as you say, it would be extremely odd if, only a few days ago, she seemed happy and looking forward to your future together, to suddenly cool off and want to end the relationship. Plus, it would be totally out of character. Obviously it is something important that she wants to say but try to keep an open mind and wait as she has told you to. Umm?" said Szymanski sympathetically but firmly.

"Thanks, Julia" he said with a lost and troubled expression, something that was alien to the norm for him. Then with a big effort and a shrug of the shoulders he seemed to pull himself out of the depths of misery he had fallen into.

"I was thinking about your friend who is out staying his welcome................." Allan began but the noise was getting so loud now that they would have trouble continuing the conversation so they took their drinks and joined in with their merrymaking colleagues.

Two hours later, no-one noticed the door of the pub open and a woman walk in. The atmosphere was thick with elation, merriment and loud voices. Beer and wine were both being eagerly consumed by Allan's team, together with a few others from the station, some friends and loved ones who had also joined.

She stood for some moments at the door, wondering if she should just go home and wait there. She was on the point of doing so, when Allan happened to glance across the pub and blinked twice to make sure he wasn't imagining it. Two seconds later he was rushing over to her.

"Vanessa! You weren't due home until Thursday! This is so good!" and he kissed her hard and long, then pulled away and held her at arm's length smiling. He grabbed her hand and pulled her towards his team.

"What are you having to drink? We can pick up the cars tomorrow. Tonight, we're all celebrating the closed cases. Not sure whether you will have heard on the news what has happened?" he stopped as he took in Vanessa's serious expression.

"What is it, darling?" he asked his voice just slightly slurring.

"Jack, I want to go home. I'm very pleased you have solved your case. Well done!"

"Won't you stay just to have one drink? Then we can go home!" he cajoled.

"Vanessa, I won't hear of you going home without partaking with us!" said Wright who had come over.

"No, really, thanks for the invitation, I wouldn't be very good company. Congratulations to everyone on your success. I wish I could stay but I need to get home" she added lamely, looking around at Allan's team and then turning to Allan.

"Jack are you coming?" she asked with only the slightest nod to a request rather than a command.

Allan looked puzzled and embarrassed.

"Sorry everyone, I think we need to get back but I'll put some money behind the bar. You all carry on and have a good night but I will be wanting everyone fresh in the morning. There are still some loose ends to tie up which need to be put on record" and he put his hand up to indicate he was going.

"Cheers boss. Thank you. Break a leg, boss" were the shouts as he made his way first to the bar and then to the door where Vanessa was standing waiting.

"I've phoned for a cab to pick us up and pre-paid on my card" she said when they had closed the door behind them.

"Okay, so do you want to tell me why we had to leave so suddenly?".

"Not really, Jack. When we get home" and she looked away down the street.

Jack had a horrible sinking feeling in his stomach but the cold night air was doing a lot to dispel the effects of the alcohol he had drunk that evening.

Fortunately, he had not consumed enough by the time Vanessa arrived, to be out of it. However, he couldn't shake the dread feeling in his gut, the awful foreboding that Vanessa was going to end it with him when they got back. Why had she come home early? Perhaps she just couldn't concentrate because she needed to tell him.

The cab came and they travelled in complete silence.

When they got in Jack went straight to the bathroom and was violently sick. He splashed his face with cold water and ran his wet fingers through his thick black hair. Staring at himself in the mirror he gripped the edge of the sink, giving himself the strength to hear what the dearest person in the world was going to say.

Coming out of the bathroom and into the lounge he found Vanessa sitting on the sofa. Two steaming cups of coffee were on the table.

"Thanks" he said sitting down on the sofa next to her and picking up his coffee cup. He took a small sip and replaced the cup.

"For the coffee" he added and sitting back in his chair managed what he hoped was an encouraging smile.

Vanessa sat for a moment not looking at him, then chin up and with a determined expression started to speak.

"First of all, Jack, I want to apologise for all the mystery. It wasn't my intention to worry you but I had to sort things out in my own mind before I spoke to you".

Jack was struggling to contain his emotion but digging the fingers of one hand into the soft seat of the sofa he managed to maintain his composure.

"You see, it's something I never thought would happen. It didn't occur to me. It should have done but it didn't. I should have told you but I didn't and I'm so, so sorry......" her words tumbling out in quick succession.

"Please, Vanessa, don't cry. Who is he? Is he that doctor that you always describe as a good friend?"

Vanessa gave him a bewildered look.

"I guessed that was what you had to tell me. You've been acting strangely over the past couple of weeks, so it was obvious that you had met someone else. I tried to persuade myself……………………." he broke off as Vanessa waved her hands rejecting his words.

"Stop! Stop! Jack! You couldn't be further from the truth. Of course there isn't anyone else. There could never be anyone else for me. Oh Jack! My love!" and the tears were streaming down her face as all the emotion she had been holding in check escaped like rivers streaming down her face. She flung her arms round him and they kissed and caressed. At last, they pulled away from each other.

"So, what could possibly be so terrible to tell me, darling?" he asked as he gently pushed the hair out of her eyes, his heart thumping hard with love and joy that she still loved him.

She took a deep breath.

"I'm pregnant!" she blurted out and started to cry again.

"But that's wonderful. That's great! Why are you crying?" exclaimed Allan as he put an arm round her shoulders and hugged her to him.

"Normally it would be wonderful, yes, but it's not because my aunt on my mother's side inherited the Lynch Syndrome gene and died at twenty-eight of stomach cancer. My mother has never been tested and neither have I, so I don't know whether I have the gene and therefore could pass the gene on. I should have told you but we said we didn't want children for a while and I just put it off. I know I was wrong. Especially as I am a doctor!" she managed to speak through her tears.

Jack was silent for a few minutes.

"What is the Lynch Syndrome gene?" he finally managed to ask.

"It……….it causes the person with it to have a significant risk of developing certain types of cancer. Some of those who have it, but not all, have a specific mutation that causes them to be more at risk of having a shortened lifespan".

He was hugging Vanessa to him but he froze at her words and an icy current ran through his veins. He felt stunned, numb. Thoughts were tumbling through his mind like a tsunami. Slowly he extricated himself from her and without thinking, as though on automatic pilot, he took his coat off one of the hooks and quietly went out.

He walked and walked, on and on. He had no idea where he was going, trying to think things through and understand what he was feeling. After around thirty minutes he sat on a park bench and as was his custom, he rubbed the side of his nose hard for several seconds. It was cold and he didn't have his gloves so he put his hands in his coat pockets. Finally, after staring into space and allowing his mind and body to calm down from the shock of what Vanessa had told him, he came to a conclusion and walked quickly back to the apartment.

When he got in he expected to find Vanessa asleep, worn out by the journey back from Scotland and the emotion of the evening. He was wrong. She was sitting nursing a cup of coffee, her eyes red from crying, her hair all over the place. She looked so vulnerable sitting there all alone. He mentally berated himself for being so selfish.

He walked over to her and put his arms round her.

"I love you. Whatever. I love you, Vanessa" and he kissed the top of her head.

She looked up.

"I thought you had left me!" she said her lips trembling.

"That's never going to happen!" he said smiling at her.

"I thought maybe the best thing would be for me to have an abortion but we don't know that our baby has inherited the gene or whether I have. I don't think I could live with always wondering if we had aborted a perfectly healthy baby. Then I thought maybe I could be tested but the results take three months to come through and I would have passed the legal time for abortion. I'm so sorry, Jack".

"Don't be sorry, Vanessa. I understand. Truly I do. It's my turn to apologise anyway. I should never have walked out this evening to indulge my own thoughts. I should have got a grip and stayed with you. I'm sorry. Now we've both been sorry, so I think it's time to move on and think about our baby positively. From what I understand you don't know if you have the gene and therefore you don't know that our baby has the gene. There is no purpose in knowing, at present, whether you have the gene or not, so let's enjoy the knowledge that we are going to be parents!"

They were sitting on the sofa now and smiling at him, she raised her hand to stroke his hair.

"I think I would like to know so that I can be prepared, if that's okay with you, Jack?" she said softly.

"Okay, if that's good for you then it's good for me!" he said catching her hand and kissing the back of it.

"I'll make arrangements tomorrow" she said.

Chapter 20

Allan left Vanessa sleeping when he went to the station early next day, Tuesday 16th March. He wanted to get the report written up as far as he could and then establish what the team had found out about the fourth victim, Kim Watson.

At nine o'clock he gathered his team together.

"Hope you all had a great evening yesterday after Vanessa and I left".

There were thumbs up and smiles all round.

"Now we're back doing what we do best. First off, I need to establish what we found out about Kim Watson really just for the record. Obviously, submit written reports but for the benefit of the whole team what was gleaned? Mike, Sophie, I take it the next of kin have been informed?"

"Yes, sir. Kim had a sister who lives in Cottenham. They weren't close but Zoe was clearly upset. There are no other relatives and Kim said her sister was very quiet and unassuming. Didn't have many, if any, friends. Sad", commented Callender.

"So same background as the other victims. Max? Barry?"

"Yeah. She worked in a chemist. We interviewed her colleagues. There were four assistants and two chemists. All said the same thing. She was very pleasant, kept herself pretty much to herself. Not much to say about her. Ordinary" said Max and shrugged his shoulders.

Allan nodded.

"Peter?"

"Nothing of note on the financial side, boss, and no calls of note on her mobile".

"Julia, you found out where she lived and put a cordon round it. Where did she live?" asked Allan

"Near Midsummer Common, 108 Denby Road to be exact" replied Szymanski in her usual precise manner.

"Sir, what was Manning's reason behind reference to films on his victims?"

"I'm not sure we will ever know that Dev".

"There doesn't seem to be any connection between the women either so I suppose they were randomly chosen were they?" asked Wright.

"It would seem so. Again, another unanswered question".

"Well, I'm just pleased the bastard is dead and no more women are at risk!" exclaimed García.

"Okay, everyone. Report writing unless something more urgent arises," Allan said.

Sitting at his desk and going over case notes, he suddenly scrabbled through a pile lying at the edge of his desk. Something was worrying him just as it had done previously when he couldn't quite connect that Manning and Qiang were one and the same and when he did, he solved the cold case and the current one.

A couple of minutes later he retrieved the case note he was seeking. His eyes got wider and wider until he threw the piece of paper on the desk and howled, raising his arms behind his head in utter disbelief.

His howl was so loud that both Szymanski and Patel appeared at the door of Allan's office.

"You okay, sir?" asked Szymanski.

"No, I'm bloody not. He's not our man. Manning! Manning is not the serial killer. He can't bloody be. It's not possible. The third victim, Stella King. He couldn't have murdered her. Manning and his grey estate were spotted by Jane and her friend Sue at the Community Centre car park then.

Their statements here confirm that. There wouldn't have been enough time for him to torture and kill King, place her in Grantchester Meadows and be at the car park at the time that Jane and Sue said he was," he shouted with a horrified expression, waving the statements in the air.

"But he admitted it, sir. He confessed in his last letter to you" said Patel.

"No, he lied and I fell for the lie because I knew he was capable of heinous crimes and I knew he was a narcissist. He liked to boast how clever he was. He played me. How could I have been so stupid".

"No, sir, he took us all in" said Szymanski.

"I have to go and face the DCI. We are still seeking a serial killer" Allan grimaced.

Szymanski and Patel moved out of the way quickly as Allan, with a face like thunder, charged out of his office and, taking the stairs two at a time, he arrived outside his boss's office seconds later.

A minute later he was seated opposite Clarkson who didn't speak but raised an eyebrow.

"Sir, something disturbing has come to light whilst looking through the case notes of the recent murders. Unfortunately, it appears that Manning could not possibly be the killer. At the time that Stella King was murdered, Manning was at the Community Centre car park stalking my sister and her friend" began Allan before he was interrupted by the DCI who had turned a puce colour.

"Disturbing! Disturbing? It's not disturbing, it's catastrophic! Do you mean to tell me that you have got it wrong, Allan? That we still have a murderer on our hands!" he exploded.

Allan took the opportunity that Clarkson, needing to take breath, afforded him.

"I'm sorry, sir, but Manning's confession to the murders together with the knowledge we have of his character led us down the wrong path. In my view, he did that on purpose to have the last laugh. I would recommend we organise another press conference and media appeal so that people, and in particular women, are on the alert".

Clarkson had calmed down.

"This is all down to you disobeying orders, Allan. If you had concentrated on the murder enquiry instead of trying to solve your sister's case as well, this state of affairs would never have been reached" he said with a smug expression, enjoying riling Allan.

"Again, I am sorry, sir, although with respect I would beg to differ on your surmise that my involvement with my sister's case had any bearing on the outcome of the case of the serial killer because Julia Szymanski was the lead in the former and not myself, until they seemingly became connected. I need to get back and together with the team we need to go over the clues that we have and crack this case fast".

"Have you any other suspects?"

"At present, no, sir. When will you be organising the press conference for?"

"As soon as possible. I will let you know, Allan, but note I am watching you. Another mistake like that and there will be consequences. Close the door on your way out" he added needlessly.

Back in the general office, Allan called his team together.

"Okay everyone, gather round. I have just notified the DCI that we are still seeking our serial killer. I'm afraid we all celebrated a little too early".

There were murmurs and glances all round.

"How come, sir?" asked Callender.

"Re-reading the case notes appertaining to the murders and comparing them with the notes concerning Manning's stalking on my sister and her friend, I noticed that at the time of Stella King's murder he was at the Community Centre car park. The timing makes it impossible for him to be the Murderer. We were misled, on purpose is my belief, into thinking he was the killer because of his implied confession. There will be another Press release and media appeal today so that people are on the alert still".

"So where do we go from here, sir?" asked García.

"Fortunately, we haven't had time to clear the incident board so I suggest we look at that together with the information on the latest victim and go back over our notes.

We know the murderer is tall and blonde which is another reason that supported Manning's confession. Clearly there is another tall and blonde man roughly thirtyish to fortyish.

Barry, go through the files and see if you can find someone with a record, fitting that description who lives in Cambridge.

Mike, find out about any rental agreements, or property purchases in the past couple of months by a man fitting the description.

Max trawl the social media platforms for anyone matching the suspect's description.

Dev, you and Sophie conduct another house-to-house in the streets where the victims lived. Establish whether they know if a tall, blonde youngish man has moved in around there recently".

Everyone nodded. There was a sombre, deflated atmosphere in the office but the team got on with the jobs in hand.

Meanwhile, Allan was staring at the incident board, Szymanski standing next to him.

"What are we not seeing, Julia?" Allan rubbed the side of his nose hard in frustration and frowning, he screwed up his face in concentration.

"The main thing linking all these murders is the way in which the victims were killed, the reference to films and that they were all holding objects" she said.

"In all cases they were tortured in the same way. They were all killed by the same method. They were all lone women. They were all strangled twice. Why? Wait a sec!"

Szymanski looked at him expectantly.

"In three of the four cases, a dog walker found the bodies and alerted us. Was it the same dog walker?" he asked rhetorically, as he marched through to his office. Leafing through the papers on his desk, he found what he was looking for.

"The first victim, Lily Anderson's body was found by a Mr Jake Parsons while walking his dog. The second victim Emily Henderson was found by a Mr Josh Finlay also walking his dog. Beginning to see a pattern, Julia?" he said excitedly.

"Yes but they are two different people, sir".

Allan was busy looking through his papers and then having read through a couple of pages of notes he looked up with an animated expression.

"Stella King's body was found by a cyclist whose name according to these notes was a Mr Horace Ingles and Kim Watson was found by another dog walker a Mr Ian Mansfield. Okay the cyclist is the odd man out but let's check the addresses of each of them".

"On it, sir" and Szymanski was already halfway to the door.

As she went out, Allan's office phone rang.

"Press conference is in an hour. Be ready Allan!" commanded Clarkson and hung up.

Allan gathered up the papers spread over his desk and put them to one side, he needed to devote his time to the next task in hand.

While he was finishing his notes for the conference, Szymanski knocked on the door.

"Sorry, Julia, give me forty-five minutes and I'll be with you" he said, not giving Szymanski time to speak.

****

Allan walked onto the platform and sat next to the DCI who made the usual announcements and handed over to Allan as quickly as possible, eager to have as little to do with what had to be explained.

"Good afternoon everyone. Today, new evidence has come to light that proves that Mr Roland Manning is not the serial killer we are seeking for the murders of Lily Anderson, Emily Henderson, Stella King and Kim Watson. He was, however, wanted in connection with a cold case and for recent potential murder. It is imperative that the public remain vigilant and report anything that appears out of the ordinary to them that could have a bearing on this case. For this reason, we called this press conference. Please be assured that we are all working extremely hard to find the killer. Any questions?"

Immediately many hands shot up and Allan pointed to one of them.

"What evidence has come to light?" asked a tall, red-haired man at the back.

"I cannot comment on that at this time other than that it is watertight evidence" and he indicated to someone else to speak.

"Do you currently have any suspects?" asked a small dark-haired reporter.

"I cannot comment at this time" he said pointing to another.

"So, is it fair to say that the police made a mistake in identifying the wrong man?" asked a tall man with a sallow, sardonic expression.

"No, strong evidence suggested that Mr Manning was our murderer but this has since been thrown out due to further evidence coming to light" answered Allan.

Allan answered several more questions until Clarkson got up.

"Thank you everyone. That'll be all for now" and he walked stiffly out, Allan close behind.

Clarkson didn't turn round but walked upstairs without a backward glance at Allan who made his way to the general office.

"Julia" he said as he walked past her desk.

Szymanski duly followed him into his office.

"Very interesting, sir" she said as she sat down.

He raised his eyebrows questioningly, sitting down at his desk.

"Three of the phone numbers given, don't exist and there is no record of three of the names given. The only one that does exist is that of Mr Jake Parsons who lives a stone's throw from Wandlebury Park, at 24 Wandlebury Park Avenue" and Szymanski smiled triumphantly.

"Right. Let's bring in our Mr Jake Parsons for questioning. Get the ARU to meet us at that address in two hours.

At six o'clock that evening the ARU were in place. Allan and Szymanski walked up the path of a neat front garden and rapped loudly on the door.

They rapped again. There was no answer.

Szymanski on Allan's order summoned the ARU. Meanwhile, Allan went round the side of the house immediately catching sight of a disappearing t-shirt and jeans over the side fence in the narrow alleyway.

"He's doing a runner!" he shouted running hard after the suspect.

Parsons was tall and lithe and about thirty years of age. Allan could hear his colleague running hard behind him. They turned the corner into another residential street narrowly escaping being run over by an oncoming vehicle. Parsons was widening the distance between him and his pursuers as he approached the park. Allan thanked the gods that he was as fit as he was. A small group of people, mothers, fathers and children were approaching, straddling the pathway as Parsons bashed into one of the adults and clipped the side of one of the children sending them sprawling to the ground. Allan wanted to stop and help but couldn't risk losing the suspect.

"Sorry!" he shouted as he raced through the little group in hot pursuit.

Reaching the other end of the park the suspect crossed the A1307 and was immediately hit by a car. The car behind managed to stop thus avoiding a pile up and multiple casualties.

Allan phoned for an ambulance. Reaching the scene of the accident he was met with a bellowing from the suspect. He was holding his arm, his leg was in a funny position and there was a nasty gash on his head. Szymanski arrived and put her hands on her knees, her head down catching her breath. A crowd assembled around the man on the ground and the driver who had knocked him down had tears running down his face.

"He just ran out. I didn't have time to stop! He just ran out! Shit, is he going to die? Is he going to die?" he said in a state of shock, running his hands through his hair.

Szymanski recovering from her run, assured him that the man was not going to die and took him over to the paramedics who had just arrived and were about to attend to Parsons. She asked for an insulated blanket and was directed where to find one in the ambulance.

Parsons was soon assessed, placed on a stretcher and put into the waiting ambulance.

Allan and Szymanski retraced their steps to their car and drove to A&E at Addenbrooke Hospital.

Three hours later a nurse informed them that Parsons was well enough to be interviewed having broken a leg and arm. He had also suffered a head wound which looked worse than it was.

"Mr Jake Parsons? Detective Inspector Allan and this is Detective Sergeant Szymanski. We'd like to ask you a few questions, if you don't mind?" Allan said sitting down on one of the chairs by the bed and without waiting for a reply he continued.

"Mr Parsons can you tell me why you did a runner earlier?"

"No comment," he answered in a better-spoken voice than the detectives had anticipated.

"Just so that you are aware. This is a murder enquiry Mr Parsons and it is a criminal offence to withhold information that may be helpful to the case. So, I ask you again, why did you run?"

"No comment".

"Okay. On three out of the four murders, you were the person who found the bodies".

"Not true" he said.

There was a silence and Parsons continued.

"I found the first one, Lily Anderson, I think they said her name was, on the News. I don't know anything about the others".

"No. Well funnily enough yours was the only name that came up as authentic. All the other names and telephone numbers don't exist. Even more strange is that each of those people seemed to have the same breed and size of dog and not only that, all the dogs had the same name! That's a bit of a coincidence, don't you think?" asked Allan calmly looking directly at Parsons.

Parsons wriggled uncomfortably in his bed.

"Remember this is a murder enquiry, Mr Parsons", interjected Szymanski.

"And right now you are our prime suspect" added Allan.

"Okay, okay. Look I go out in the early hours and take different routes and I know it seems really strange, unbelievable that I found three but I didn't find the other one. That definitely wasn't me. I vary my route regularly to avoid meeting people and to avoid any unpleasantness. I've been beaten up regularly before. It's ironic really that I have been in the wrong place at the wrong time three times. It is unbelievable, I realise that, but it is true. I just happened to find them. I have nothing to do with any of the murders. You have to believe me" he said, his eyes pleading with them.

"I'm struggling to make sense of what you are telling us, Mr Parsons. You say you avoid people; you get beaten up so you vary your dog walking locations and on top of that you ran away when you knew we were the police. I ask you again, why did you run?"

"Because I thought you were going to charge me with something I didn't do" he said miserably.

"If you are innocent then you have nothing to fear. You say you walk early to avoid being beaten up and unpleasantness. What do you mean by that?" Allan asked.

The man hung his head.

"Mr Parsons?" prompted Szymanski after a few moments.

"Alright. My name isn't Jake Parsons; it's Craig Pullen".

"Is that supposed to mean something to me?" asked Allan frowning.

"It would if you consulted your records" replied Pullen.

"Explain, please" commanded Allan.

"I changed my name by deed poll two years ago, after my release from prison. I had to or I would have wound up dead in the end. Someone recognised my name and then it was all over social media. Wherever I went they knew my name and then they knew my face so I changed my name and moved area. I like to go out when no-one is around. I like children, Detective Inspector, not grown women".

Szymanski felt her lunch churning in her stomach even though it had only been a rushed sandwich.

Allan managed to keep a composed face. He too felt the revulsion running through his veins.

"So why did you give different names to the police and why did you phone in your discoveries to the police if you wanted to keep a low profile.

Perhaps the most puzzling is why you gave your real name in the first place".

"I gave my own name first of all because I was shocked. My brain wasn't working properly. I've never seen a dead person before. It was horrible. I forgot about keeping a low profile, I suppose, and I automatically phoned the police. The second and third time it happened I felt I had to phone it into the police but I didn't want them to think I was the common factor so I invented a couple of names. I guess it never occurred to me that someone would recognise my dog".

"You do realise that we will check your story" said Allan sternly.

"Yeah" was Pullen's desultory response.

Outside the hospital, Allan took out his mobile.

"Hi Dev, can you check a name for me – Craig Pullen and phone me right back" he said.

"What's your take on him being at all three murder locations, Julia?"

"Bit of a stretch on believability unless he was involved but my gut feeling is that he is telling the truth especially as, disgusting though it is, by his own admission his interest is in children not women. I don't think he is our man" said Szymanski thoughtfully.

"No, I tend to agree with you but what I did find interesting was that he said he only discovered three of the bodies not the fourth. So, who was the man on the bike who gave a false name? We need to find out about the bike tyre tracks from forensics and find out if we can trace it".

"Dev, hi, what have you got?"

"Craig Pullen. He is a known paedophile, sir. Nothing on him of late but just over seven years ago he was convicted of being part of a ring and sentenced to five years in prison. He seems to have disappeared off the radar after that. Who is he?"

"I'll explain later, Dev. Good work. Julia and I are coming back to the station now".

"Well, that's that. His story checks out. I'm going home, Julia. It's been a long day!" said a disgruntled Allan.

"No worries, Jack! See you tomorrow!" she said.

The heaven's had opened as Allan ran to his car, holding his papers under his coat to keep them dry. Popping them on the passenger seat he slammed the door shut, walked round to the driver's side and got in.

Allan sat there thinking for a few minutes. The weather matched his mood, he thought, as he looked out at the grey skies emitting stair rods so big they were making a loud pinging sound on the roof and windscreen of his car. He felt like he was getting nowhere with this investigation. As soon as he thought he had cracked it his elation was dashed and he faced another dead end.

Heaving a huge sigh, he started the car and set off for home. On the way he remembered that Vanessa was off shift this evening. She would be home around seven thirty when he planned to have the meal ready, the wine chilling (he had remembered it had to be non-alcoholic, Vanessa wouldn't drink now she was pregnant plus he could be called by the station any time) and the candles lit. He stopped off at a florist and bought a lovely bouquet of different colour roses and tiger lilies.

He was concerned about her. She seemed ostensibly to have recovered from the awful revelation that they could have a child with Lynch Syndrome and was now pragmatic in her approach to it. She had undergone the test and they would have the results in three months. Nevertheless, when she didn't know he was looking, he had noticed a sadness about her demeanour.

When he arrived home he took the flowers in first, running indoors as fast as possible and then went back to collect his papers.

Having placed the flowers in water, Allan quickly changed into gym wear and set the timer on his rowing machine for twenty minutes. He only had time for a quick work out before preparing the meal. His workouts were becoming less and less now that Vanessa was in his life but there was no enticement that would tempt him to trade his old life for the new. Knowing that she was going to walk through the door very soon made him forget everything else in his life. She was so special; he was so lucky. He worked up a sweat getting faster and faster on the machine and then slowed gradually.

Everything was ready at seven-thirty and at that exact time, Allan heard the key in the lock. Vanessa had only just got through the door when Allan rushed over, swept her off her feet, kissing her at the same time. He twirled her round and kicked the door shut. She smiled at him, putting her arms round his neck. Putting her gently on her feet, he held her hand and led her to the dining area.

"Would madam like a chilled glass of wine?" Allan placed a tea towel over his arm and slightly bowed.

"Yes, madam would but only if it's non-alcoholic" she giggled.

"But, of course, madam. Your every wish is my command!" and Allan bowed even lower and as he stood upright he winked at her and grinned.

"After food, I'm starving and I've got something I want to talk to you about" she said looking sheepish.

"That sounds ominous" he said looking serious.

She smiled back and then went off to freshen up.

When she returned, they chinked glasses and Allan presented her with the bouquet of flowers.

"Oh, Jack, thank you so much. I adore tiger lilies! What a wonderful scent!" and having admired them, she put them down carefully. She threw her arms round him and holding his head in her hands she kissed him.

They sat down to eat Allan's carefully prepared meal.

"That was absolutely delicious, Jack, and you remembered I love Eton Mess!" said Vanessa dabbing her mouth with her serviette.

"I thought I might have overcooked the duck" commented Allan.

"No, it was all completely perfect" she replied and covered his hand with hers.

"So, what is it you wanted to talk about. I know already, of course", he said grinning.

"You do!" exclaimed Vanessa, her face full of surprise.

"I do! That's a clue!"

There was a pause and neither of them said anything.

"The wedding, of course. What else!" said Allan smiling.

"Well, no, actually! You're wrong!"

"Oh! What then?" asked Allan frowning.

"About this!" and Vanessa got up and walked over to her bag where she extracted some papers which she brought back to the table and handed to Allan.

He shuffled through them.

"What are these?" he asked puzzled.

"What do they look like?"

"They look like details for several different properties. Houses".

"And you would be correct. I've been thinking".

"Always a worry!" he smiled as he said it.

"No seriously. We are going to be parents and I don't think a flat in a warehouse on an industrial estate is ideal for bringing up a child. There's nothing wrong with it here. It's a great flat. It's quirky. I really like it and if we weren't going to be parents I wouldn't want to move. It's just that................."

"It's okay. I get it. It's just I wasn't expecting this....this.....well....this conversation. I thought we were going to leave it for a little while. Where are the properties located?".

"Most of them are in and around Grantchester. Very convenient for both of us for work. Notice I didn't choose Ely after we learnt that Mum and Dad's friends live there!!" she said encouragingly.

"Coffee, then, while we look through these?" suggested Allan.

"You're okay with us moving, then?" she asked coyly.

"Let's put it this way, it would be useless to argue wouldn't it?" he replied with a grin.

"If you really don't want to, I understand. This is your home and it's unusual, it's got character. I'm sure we can make it work" she added unconvincingly.

Allan reached for Vanessa's hand.

"It's you that is important. I want to be where you are and if you want to move, so long as you want me as part of the package, it's more than fine with me" and he squeezed her hand.

"I love you so, so much" and she bent forward to kiss him.

Chapter 21

Back to reality, the next morning, Wednesday 17th March, Allan and Szymanski, quite by chance, arrived at the station at the same time and walked into together. Allan's phone rang. He had a quick conversation and then ended the call.

"That was Barry. He'd just taken a call from a member of the public in response to the latest media appeal. He thinks he has seen our suspect wheeling a bike along the pavement near where he lives in Pemblebury Road and then entering a house, number 15 to be exact".

Allan's mobile rang. He looked at the screen. It was Vanessa. Reluctantly, he declined the call and tapped a number into his keypad.

"Hi, Melanie, it's Jack Allan".

"Hello, Jack, how are you?"

"Good, thanks. Listen; the tyre tracks of a bike at the scene of Stella King's murder. Did you establish what type of bike the tyre came from?"

"Yes, we did. Hold on a moment and I'll find the info for you".

Melanie Smith disappeared and Jack rubbed the side of his nose absent-mindedly.

"Hi, Jack, from the diameter, width and pattern it was a mountain bike and a particularly expensive one at that, maybe a Trek Mountain bike?"

"Thanks, Melanie that's really helpful".

Ending the call, he stopped by Wright's desk.

"Barry, go round to 15 Pemblebury Road and get uniform to follow in a van. Do the usual, helping the police with their enquiries, it would be most appreciated and helpful if he could come down to the station and allow his bike to be taken in the van to be eliminated from our enquiries, etcetera etcetera".

"On it, sir".

Allan then rang Melanie back and alerted her to the need for a quick examination of the bike in half an hour or so.

Szymanski returned to her desk while Allan studied the incident board.

Percy Parker was still a suspect if they could break Melvyn Stott's alibi for him making it impossible for him to have committed the first murder. Other than that, and the possibility that the murderer was the cyclist that had been spotted in Pemblebury Road, they had no suspects.

An hour later, Barry popped his head round Allan's office door just as his mobile rang. It was Vanessa again. He hesitated and then declined the call.

"Mr Ingles is in Interview Room 4, sir, and the bike has been taken to forensics" Wright informed him.

"Come in, Barry. How did he seem to you when you applied to his better nature to cooperate?" said Allan tapping his pencil on the desk in front of him.

"He didn't seem at all perturbed to be honest, sir. He was very helpful and didn't mind if we took his bike".

"What did he look like – his appearance I mean?"

"He is tall, fair hair, athletic about thirtyish. I understand completely why someone felt it prudent to ring us. In looks, he fits the bill but either he is the coolest criminal liar that I have ever known or he is not the murderer".

"Hmmm. Did the bike look expensive to you?"

"Yes, it looked a pretty impressive piece of kit".

"Okay. Let's see what he has to say. Julia, with me" he called as he passed by Szymanski's desk.

"Good morning, Mr Ingles. My name is Detective Inspector Allan and this is Detective Sergeant Szymanski. First of all, I would like to thank you for coming into the station and allowing your bike to be examined. Hopefully, you will have this returned very quickly. I would like to ask you a few questions, if I may?" Allan began politely.

The man who said he was Horace Ingles nodded and smiled.

"Firstly, Horace Ingles isn't your real name is it?" asked Allan.

"Yes, of course it is!"

"This is a murder enquiry, sir, so we would strongly advise that you tell us the truth" said Szymanski with a stern expression.

"Okay, so I don't like giving my real name to the police. I don't really want to get involved. I guessed it was a murder. I like a peaceful life" he said after a few seconds hesitation.

"So, what is your real name, sir?" asked Szymanski.

"Finlay Farrow".

"Where were you between midnight on 3rd March and two o'clock am on 4th March, Mr Ingles?" asked Allan.

"Wednesday 3rd March from midnight to eight o'clock am on Thursday 4th March I was on shift" he answered promptly without any hesitation.

"We will check that with your employer, Mr Farrow, you do realise that?" said Szymanski.

"Yes, sure, no worries" sitting back in his chair, now ostensibly very relaxed.

Allan continued his interrogation but he had a negative feeling about the suspect's guilt.

"And where were you between five o'clock and nine o'clock on 5th March?" asked Allan.

"5th March. Erm. Let me think. It was a Friday so I cycled over to my sister's and arrived at about eight o'clock, stayed for dinner and left about eleven o'clock. Cycled back to my place and arrived at eleven thirty. Went to bed shortly afterwards. That's it".

"So, no-one can vouch for you from eleven o'clock until the six o'clock the next morning?" asked Szymanski.

"No, 'fraid not. I live alone," he replied.

"And you say you discovered the body of Stella King whilst on a cycle ride in the late evening on 10th March. Bit of a strange time to be cycling," remarked Allan.

"I went cycling down by the river and over to Grantchester Meadows and yes, I was the one to discover the unfortunate young lady who had been murdered. That was terrible, terrible" he said shaking his head and looking visibly upset.

"Two things strike me as odd about that, Mr Farrow. Firstly, you made no mention of that to the detective who came to see you today. It would have been quite understandable if you assumed we had come about your statement to us concerning the discovery of the body?" Allan asked.

Finlay Farrow folded his arms and shrugged.

"I just didn't want to be involved and I certainly didn't want to appear in court if there was a prosecution. In answer to your first question that is why I didn't mention it to the police officer. I didn't realise that you knew it was me".

"As it happens we didn't, we suspected because someone noticed your description and matched the description of the man we want to interview in connection to the murders".

Allan ended the recording.

"One moment, Mr Farrow" he said. He and Szymanski left the room and walked back to the general office.

"Barry, contact Farrow's alibis. Farrow has admitted he was there as a witness and has given the reason for him giving a false name. If the alibis check out, release him".

"Will do, sir" replied Wright taking the contact information written on a leaf of Allan's notebook from his boss.

"Julia, I'd be very surprised if Farrow was our killer. I think we should investigate Percy Parker again. Melvyn Stott gave him an alibi but I'm not convinced that he isn't lying" he said turning to Szymanski.

"Dev, get Melvyn Stott back in to help us with our enquiries. We need to chuck 'the full force of the law threat' at him".

"Will do, sir".

An hour later, a disgruntled Stott sat opposite Allan and Szymanski.

"Good afternoon, Mr Stott" said Allan.

Stott didn't answer but just glared at him.

"We've asked you back to go through the alibi you gave us for Mr Percy Parker for the night of Wednesday 3rd March and early morning of Thursday 4th March, where you say that Mr Parker left you around 2.15 am on 4th March. Is that correct?"

"That's wot I said. Why would it have changed?"

"Oh, I'm sure it hasn't changed. I'm just not sure that he left at that time in the first place or indeed, that he was at your place at all. I would remind you Mr Stott that it is a criminal offence to lie to the police concerning a murder investigation" Allan said sternly, frowning and looking unnervingly at him.

"The difficulty we are having is that Mr Parker's car doesn't come up on any of the cameras on the way to or from your house on that night and it is too far for him to have walked. He has not been picked up on CCTV catching a bus and no taxi firm remembers him hiring a cab on that evening or early next morning. So, you see our problem. How did he get to and from your house that evening?" Szymanski asked.

A smug expression crossed Stott's face.

"Not a problem, detective. I picked Percy up and dropped him off".

"Well, I don't buy that Mr Stott because you have already stated that Mr Parker left you around 2.15 am and not that you drove him home. So, stop lying to me and tell me the truth, Mr Stott" and Allan brought his hand down so heavily that the table shook and Stott and Szymanski both visibly jumped.

Stott glared at Allan with a sulky expression.

Allan's phone rang. Without looking at it, he declined the call.

"Well?" he demanded looking directly at Stott.

"If you look at the CCTV you will find my car on the road between our houses at the times I have said. The reason I didn't tell you in the first place is that as far as I know there is a drink driving penalty in this country and I was well over the limit. That being the case, it would mean that I would lose my licence this time".

"You do realise we will check all of that, Mr Stott?".

"Yeah, check all you like!" Stott replied folding his arms across his chest and slouching back in his chair with a nonchalant expression.

****

While Allan was engaged in seeking the serial killer, Vanessa had had a phone call from her father who had left a message on her voicemail to call him when she was able.

On a break she returned his call.

"Hello, Dad, Vanessa. You rang. I haven't got long. I'm at work. Is everything okay?".

"Fine, fine, dear. Actually, no, it's not fine. It's your mother".

"What! Is she okay, Dad? What's happened?" she asked suddenly alert, her whole body becoming taught.

"Yes and no. I need ……………we need you to come over. I can't speak over the phone. When can you come?"

Her father didn't sound like his normal ebullient self. It seemed as though all the stuffing had been knocked out of him. His daughter knew that he wouldn't ask her to take time off from her work if there wasn't a very good reason.

"I'll ask for tomorrow off. No better than that, my shift stops at lunchtime today, so I should be with you at two o'clock latest. Okay Dad?" she asked.

"Yes, much appreciated, Vanessa. We'll see you then" and he hung up.

Vanessa tried ringing Allan to let him know about her concerns and that she might be late home. It was one of their few evenings together. She didn't leave a voicemail but decided to call him again later.

Somehow she managed to get through the rest of her shift by shutting her mind off from her personal worries and concentrating fully on her patients.

At one-fifteen she got in her car and arrived at her parents' house thirty minutes later. Parking her car on the gravel drive she walked up to the front door and rang the bell. Her father answered the door.

"Come in, come in" he said in a far less confident voice than she had ever known. She walked into the lounge in front of her father.

"Would you like some tea, Vanessa?" he asked.

"No thanks, Dad. Where's Mum? And what is this all about?" she demanded with a serious expression.

"Sit down, sit down. I'll get your mother and I will make some tea" he said and left without another word.

Vanessa sighed and pulled out her mobile and rang Allan's number. It went to voicemail and again, she didn't leave a message.

She looked at her watch. She had been waiting for fifteen minutes now. Surely it didn't take that long for her father to make the tea. She got up and went in search of her parents.

The door of the kitchen was slightly ajar and she was about to enter when she heard her mother speaking in a heated whisper.

"I don't want her to know the reason we did it, dear. We have to make up something else. It's not fair to put a dampener on the wedding. I want it to be the happiest day of her life".

Vanessa opened the door and stood there for a moment. Her parents turned to her with guilty expressions. Her mother made the first move towards Vanessa.

"Hello, darling. How lovely to see you. Is Jack with you?"

"No, mum. You didn't want me to know the reason you did it. Did what exactly?"

"I've made us all tea. Let's go and sit in the lounge and we can talk there in comfort" her father suggested.

The three of them walked into the lounge and sat down. Edward poured and handed round the cups of tea.

"So? Please answer my question one of you", said Vanessa breaking the awkward silence and looking from one to the other.

"Darling, you remember we know the vicar of our local church very well?" Felicity asked sheepishly.

"Yes, what of it?"

"He is always very understanding I find. He's well thought of you know by all the villagers. Whenever anyone has a problem they always feel he will listen and give good advice and….."

"Mum, can you please answer my question" said Vanessa putting her cup and saucer down on the coffee table.

"Yes dear, of course. Well, you see, it all happened so suddenly" she started.

"What happened, mum? You aren't making any sense". Vanessa was becoming exasperated.

"Dad, can you please tell me what is going on?"

Her father had been sitting bolt upright, his hands balled in fists resting on the sofa either side of him. His knuckles white. His pallor was a ghostly white and his eyes lowered.

Vanessa got up, walked across to the settee where her dad was sitting and sat down beside him. She put his arm around his neck, something that she wouldn't normally naturally do. Her father was very much the colonel type; not the sort of man who enjoyed displays of emotion or affection but on this occasion he made no effort to pull away from his daughter.

"Vanessa, we have booked the church for your wedding for three weeks' time. We've managed to get most of the guests on the list to attend and….." Vanessa pulled away from him, a look of horror and anger on her face.

"I can't believe I'm hearing this. How could you! I said we were booking it! What is the rush? Anyway, you said it would take more than a year before the date of the wedding to book the church and......" Vanessa stopped as Edward got up from the settee and crossed over to where his wife was sitting with a set face, her chin up. He took hold of Felicity's hand and then looked across at this daughter.

"Your mother has terminal cancer, Vanessa. She has no more than two months at most".

Vanessa froze. She felt totally numb with shock. She couldn't move for a few seconds and then she knelt down in front of her mother and took both her hands in hers.

"Oh, mum! When did you find out? Are you having a second opinion?" she asked knowing as a doctor, that it was rare for a consultant to make a mistake.

"Just after your visit here with Jack. I went to our local GP who referred me. I saw a consultant, Mr Adam Catterell, privately the next day. The chest Xray was enough but a scan was done as well. There is no doubt" said her mother in a matter-of-fact voice.

Vanessa got up and sat down next to her mother, giving her a humungous hug which Felicity didn't resist. When Vanessa released her, her mother's face had crumpled and tears were falling down her cheeks.

All three of them sat squashed together, arms round each other for some time and then everyone wiped away their tears.

"Your mother's dearest wish is to see you and Jack married in church. A white wedding with an abundance of flowers and all our friends and family attending to celebrate. We thought a marquee here in our garden for the reception. Obviously, the colour scheme would be up to you and the design of the dress. When we explained the situation to the vicar he said he would juggle things and make the booking. He felt sure you would understand the need to bring the wedding forward" said Edward.

Inside, Vanessa felt some remorse for lying to her parents about making arrangements for a white wedding which she and Jack knew they had no intention of doing. Suddenly, it didn't matter to her whether they had a very small wedding or not. The most important thing was that she married Jack and now the next most important thing was to grant her mother her dearest wish.

"I think that we should make this the happiest day for all of us. For Jack and me and for you and mum. I'll have to get my skates on to choose a dress but where there's a will there's a way, the saying goes. You should have told me straightaway though, when you found out" and tears started to stream down her cheeks again, as she spoke.

"Your mother didn't want you to know. She felt it might spoil your special day and I felt that if we didn't tell you the reason why we had taken matters into our own hands that you would, quite understandably, be angry. It turns out that I was correct".

Vanessa managed a laugh.

"Now, mum, I know Adam Catterell is an excellent consultant so I'm sure he has explained to you what is ahead?"

"Yes, darling".

"I'm guessing that you have lung cancer, is that correct?" she asked knowing that Mr Catterell was a consultant in that area.

Her mother gave a short nod.

Vanessa remembered her parents both smoking until she was about eight years old and an overwhelming sorrow rose up inside her for all those who had been sucked into a deadly fashionable habit.

On her way home she rang Jack again, and this time he picked up. Stott was still in the interview room while his story was being checked out by Szymanski.

"Hi, darling. I'm sorry I didn't pick up but you know what it's like!" he stopped as he heard Vanessa's snuffles.

"What's wrong? You sound as though you are crying?" he stopped in the corridor and turned to a window staring at nothing in particular.

"It's mum! Oh Jack. I feel so horrid now" and she pulled into a layby unable to concentrate on her driving. She let the shock consume her as she pulled out a tissue from her pocket. She blew her nose and wiped her cheeks, although more unstoppable tears were gushing down her face.

"Vanessa, darling, you aren't making much sense. What about your mum? What is making you feel bad?" he asked.

Vanessa drew several deep breaths and swallowed hard.

"I had a call earlier today from dad who wanted me to visit them urgently. It was nearly the end of my shift so I was able to go. Oh, Jack! I really didn't see this coming! Mum went to see a consultant because she had been having shortness of breath and pains in her upper back. She had a chest Xray and a scan so there isn't any doubt" she faltered and Jack waited patiently for her to continue.

"Jack, she has terminal cancer. She has weeks to live" her voice sounded strangled.

Jack was stunned. He felt inadequate for this situation. He didn't know what to say. What could he say, yet he rallied himself and broke the silence that had engulfed them after facing the enormity of Vanessa's words.

"I'm so, so sorry, Vanessa. What a terrible shock for all of you. Poor Felicity. I take it your mum has had a second opinion?" he said finally.

"There is no need for that. I know the consultant, well, I know of him. He is the best there is. If I thought there was the slightest doubt, believe me, she would be having another test tomorrow!" and a sob escaped as she spoke.

"How is Edward taking it? Sorry, that's a stupid question" said Jack putting his head down and rubbing his forehead.

"No, it isn't, Jack. He is bearing up in front of mum but when he speaks to me he lets his guard down and it is obvious that he is shattered. They both seemed so small and vulnerable today. Dad is usually, as you know, ebullient and definite, commanding even and mum is normally positive not to say bossy. I admit their attitudes have irritated me in the past but this afternoon I found myself wishing so much that they were their usual selves, that this was just a nightmare and I would wake up shortly".

"Vanessa do you feel able to drive home or would you like me to come and pick you up?"

"I'm alright but thanks, darling. I'd really appreciate it though if you could come home early this evening. I don't want to be alone at the moment, and I do have something important to discuss with you".

"I'm on my way now! Drive carefully and if you feel too overwhelmed just call me and I'll come and get you. Okay?"

"Yes, thanks, Jack. See you at home. Love you".

"I love you too, so much".

Allan walked down the corridor, up the stairs and back into the general office.

"Julia, I need to go home straightaway. I'll pick up with you tomorrow".

"Something wrong, sir? At home, I mean?"

"I just need to be with Vanessa this evening. Did Stott's story check out?"

"Yep. Just confirmed".

"Okay. Let him go then. Another dead end. Parker and Stott have nothing to do with this. I'll be in early tomorrow and we need to go back to the drawing board. There is something we have missed and we are going to find out what in the morning" he said and Szymanski nodded her head, her mouth in a grim straight line.

Forty-five minutes later he had his key in the latch and opening the door he faced the tear-stained cheeks and red-rimmed eyes of the woman he loved.

They kissed and cuddled, neither speaking for half an hour or so and then still nestling into Jack's arm, Vanessa spoke.

"The reason I felt and still do feel guilty about things is that we were going to deceive them both about the wedding plans. I know it's absurd because it is our wedding but somehow when dad spoke to me, it got to me about how much a white wedding for their only daughter means to them" she said.

"What are you saying, darling? You now want a white wedding?"

"They have gone ahead and booked it for three weeks' time" and she explained what her parents had done.

Jack sat for some minutes without speaking.

"Normally, I have to admit I would be furious but under the circumstances I think we should forget about our wishes and think about your mum. However, what are you going to do about organisation at such a late stage. You haven't the time and I certainly haven't!"

"Apparently, they want to organise the whole thing. I have to choose my dress; you will have to go for a suit fitting and we need to decide a colour scheme. Apart from that we just need to turn up!" she said tilting her head upwards.

"Okay! Have you already told them that we are agreed?"

"No! I said I needed to talk to you about it and that they shouldn't have just gone ahead without consulting us!"

"Ring them and tell them that we are agreed and find out what the exact date is so that we can put our friends and colleagues on the guest list!"

"Jack, I am the luckiest woman in the world. Oh, and my mum had a request to make".

"What was that?"

"She said she wants us to go on as if she wasn't leaving us. She wants us to be happy for the last few weeks that she is around and that will make her happy. It will be terribly difficult but I think we should try to carry on as normal for her".

"Agreed. Definitely!"

"I love you so much, Jack!".

Jack smiled as he disengaged himself from her and then taking her face in his hands, gently pushing away the strands of hair that were across her face and looking into her eyes he gently kissed her lips.

Later that evening, they had just finished eating when Allan's mobile rang.

"Hi, Jack" said Jane's familiar voice.

"Jane! How are you both and how's my little fighter doing?"

"We're all well and happy to be safe and sound. Glad that horrible guy is never going to bother us again! Listen I'm ringing about the wedding. What's happening? I did wonder if you were going for a quiet one, although Vanessa's parents wouldn't be very pleased! Anyway, have you now fixed a date? What is Vanessa wearing? I need to know because I don't want to be overdressed but I don't want to be underdressed either!" Jane would have undoubtedly gone on with questions except she ran out of breath which allowed Jack, who had wandered into the hallway out of Vanessa's hearing, to jump in and explain the sad news about his future mother-in-law, since they last spoke.

"Oh, how terrible! What an awful thing to happen. I'm so sorry! How is Vanessa? Stupid question. She must be devastated".

"Yes she's pretty shaken up over it and you're right we were going for a small affair but not now.

Vanessa, understandably wants to adhere to her mother's wishes and go for the full white wedding. Her parents have managed to book the church and they have spoken to friends and extended family about the situation and almost everyone, I understand, is changing their plans to attend the wedding in three weeks' time".

"Three weeks! How on earth is Vanessa going to find a dress in that time?"

"Search me but she is! So, you'd better get your skates on with finding a hat and suitable dress! Phil will have to attend a fitting for a suit as he will still be the best man, of course. Edward and Felicity will be in touch about the exact date. Anyway, sis, I have to go now. I need to be with Vanessa but I'll be in touch".

"Well, hearing's believing! Quite understand though, and give her our love won't you! Our thoughts are with her" she said.

"Will do! Bye!" replied Allan and hung up.

Chapter 22

It was six o'clock in the morning on Thursday 18th March and, apart from Allan and Szymansky, none of the rest of the team were in as yet. The only sound was the constant hum of the machinery.

"Morning, Julia. When you're ready, let's look at the incident board again and see what we've missed", said Allan.

Szymanski got up immediately and perched on the side of a desk next to where Allan was standing, one finger stroking the side of his nose.

"So, to recap. We have four murders. In each case the victim was a woman. In each case the women were dressed and/or had clues on their person suggesting a film. The films first showed on screen a decade apart. 1951, 1961, 1971 and 1981. In each case the women lived alone and had virtually no friends or relations. They all lived in the same area. They were all killed in exactly the same way having been tortured first. Why films and why a decade apart?" Allan was staring at the board, his hands either side of him gripping the desk he was propped against.

"It's weird to say the least. We could, perhaps, get Roger Quinn back but I'm not sure what more he could add. We would seem to be looking for the same type of individual. Nothing has changed there. At least we know what sort of person we are looking for but apart from a physical description, which could be altered anyway, I don't see we have much to go on at the moment, do we, sir?"

Allan was engrossed in his own thoughts. Suddenly, he leapt up.

"What were the addresses of the victims?" he muttered rhetorically, running into his office and leafing through the papers on his desk. Sitting down he examined the reports on each incident.

"Yes, yes, that's it. The years don't you see?" he said excitedly, looking up at Szymanski who had a blank expression on her face.

"No, I'm sorry, sir, I don't really see" she said apologetically.

"Look, take 1951, the date of the film relating to the first murder. If you add 1+9 that equals 10 and then drop the 1 at the end you have 105!"

"But you could just as easily add the 5 and the 1 and make 6 which would make it 106. I'm not sure

I follow. So, what if it makes 105?" countered Szymanski.

"Because, Julia, the first murder was 105 Avon Street. Take the next murder. The film was first shown in 1961. The killer struck at 106 Beacon Street. The third murder was at 107 Carson Drive and finally the fourth murder was at 108 Denby Road!"

"Okay, sir. I see what you are driving at. Yes it is possible, I suppose. Why would the killer leave such an elaborate clue though" said Szymanski with a doubtful look on her face.

"At a guess I would say for one of two reasons. Either he thinks he is far more intelligent than the police, in effect he is playing with us, or he wants to be caught".

"So where does all this get us, sir?"

"It tells us where he is likely to strike next".

Szymanski put her head on one side questioningly and looked directly at her boss.

"All these streets, Avon, Beacon, Carson and Denby are close to each other and are in alphabetical order. We need to look for any nearby streets beginning with the letter E and with a house number 109 in it. Then we need to establish which of the houses in those streets have women occupants who live alone and have few, if any friends, and virtually no relations. Hopefully, there won't be too many and we can then watch and wait. I have no doubt that he will strike again within the next few days".

"Morning, sir" said Patel and García who walked in at the same time.

"Morning" replied Allan and Szymanski simultaneously.

The rest of the team came in shortly after and when they were all present, Allan called them to attention.

"Good morning, everyone. Hope you all had a good lie in this morning!"

Everyone smiled and grunted with the exception of Max.

"It is only seven o'clock, sir" she said, a serious expression on her face.

The rest of the team groaned and raised their eyes to the skies, shaking their heads and folding their arms. Max was a great cop but had little or no sense of humour.

"Joking aside, Julia and I have been reassessing the incident board and made some inroads" he said and proceeded to explain their deductions.

"So, the first thing is to establish how many roads begin with the letter E within a radius of two miles around the four streets where the victims lived. Once we have the roads we can find out which ones have the number 109 and then which of those have a woman occupant. We need to contact those women and find out if any of them are more or less socially isolated. We are nearly there! I believe we are on the cusp of catching this bastard" Allan finished.

While Allan was speaking, Patel had been quietly tapping keys and looking at his laptop.

"Sir, there are four streets beginning with E within that radius and all have the number 109 in them. There is Everton Street, Eagle Drive, Emsley Road and Eaton Crescent".

"Well done, Dev! For the sake of speed, we all need to take a location and interview the occupants. Dev, you and Sophie take Everton, Barry, take a WPC with you to Eagle, Mike, you and Max take Emsley and Julia and I will take Eaton. Peter, you stay here as point of contact. I suggest we go now and we should catch them before they go out. It's still breakfast time!"

Everyone, except Peter, scurried off to collect keys and jackets.

Twenty minutes later doors were knocked on and opened.

At 109 Eaton Crescent, a young blonde woman answered the door.

"Good morning, madam. I'm sorry to trouble you so early in the morning but we need to ask you a couple of questions. I'm Detective Inspector Allan and this is Detective Sergeant Szymanski" Allan said and both detectives held out their warrant cards for inspection.

The young woman peered at their credentials and nodded. She opened the door wider and they followed her into an ultra-modern lounge all glass and tubular steel which didn't really compliment the Victorian exterior façade.

"Please sit down" she said.

"Could I ask your name?" Szymanski enquired.

"Sure, it's Daisy, Daisy Phillips" she replied.

"May we call you Daisy?"

"Sure" she replied.

"Daisy, do you live here alone?"

"Yes, why?"

"Do you have any relations and if so, do any live near here?"

"No, I don't as it happens. I'm an only child and my parents died three years ago. They were only children too. Can I ask what this is about?"

"Do you have a lot of friends, boyfriend?"

"What is this about, please?" she asked, unable to hide the irritation in her voice.

"Please, just answer our questions, Daisy" said Szymanski in an encouraging tone and smiling at her.

"Okay, yes I do have a boyfriend who stays here regularly and we belong to a health club. We play tennis with friends as often as possible. We also belong to a hiking group and we meet regularly with them. Sometimes I go out with the girls from the office of a Friday night. So, yes, I have a lot of friends, a boyfriend and a good social life" she said and sat back her arms folded.

Allan and Szymanski got up at the same time.

"Thank you very much for your time, Daisy. It is much appreciated" and they went towards the door when Allan turned back.

"One thing, it is important that you don't mention to anyone that we have been here. Can you do that?"

She looked at him blankly.

"Yes I suppose so but can you answer my question, please. What is this all about?"

"I'm sorry, Daisy, we are not at liberty to tell you that but thank you again for your cooperation" said Allan firmly, and he and Szymanski left, leaving Daisy with a puzzled and irritated expression on her face.

"Well, that would seem to be one crossed off the list" said Allan darkly.

At the same time as Allan and Szymanski were questioning Daisy, Townsend and García were at 109 Emsley Road.

When they knocked on the door there was no answer. They tried several times to no avail. Townsend peered through the front window into an empty sitting room. García walked round to the back and shaded her eyes against the kitchen window. It all seemed immaculate. She looked up at the upstairs windows. All the curtains were open. Walking back round to the front, Townsend was also looking at the upstairs windows where again, the curtains were all open. At that moment, an elderly gentleman walked over to where his refuse bins were and emptied some rubbish from a small house bin. He looked up as Townsend and García walked over to him.

"Good morning, sir" said Townsend and they both showed their identification.

"Hello" the man replied.

"Can you tell us who lives here?" García asked.

"Yes, a young couple. No idea what they do but they are away a lot. Haven't seen them in, let's see now, must be a couple of months. I don't really know them. They haven't got time for the likes of me. They probably think I am a doddery old fool and not worth the time of day!"

"I'm sure they don't, sir! They are probably just busy!" said Townsend kindly.

"Thank you for your time, sir" said García.

"Yes and have a good day!" added Townsend.

"Not Elmsley Road then!" said García as they went back to their car.

"No, let's hope one of the other addresses turns up our potential victim!"

"Yes, indeed, otherwise the boss hasn't cracked it with his theory on the numbers clue. If it is a clue!" said García bluntly, raising her eyebrows.

Patel and Callender arrived at 109 Everton Street and immediately knew that this was not the next killer location. There were a number of plastic toys in the front garden, a sit-on fire engine and a doll's pram. In the porch was a double buggy. They looked at each other whilst still sitting in the car.

"No point in knocking on the door, is there?" Callender ventured.

"None at all" replied Patel.

Meanwhile, Barry and WPC Karen Lane had arrived at 109 Eagle Drive.

"Good morning, madam. Detective Sergeant Wright and my colleague here WPC Lane would like a few moments of your time, if that's okay" said Wright as he and Lane showed their identification.

The door was barely open and on a security chain. A hand reached round the door and the two detectives allowed their badges to be taken and examined. At length, the chain was removed and a diminutive figure stood before them. She had grey hair put up into a bun at the back and a tip-tilt nose. Her age was anything between sixty-five and seventy-five. Wright and Lane glanced at each other, Lane's mouth in a grimace.

"Sorry, you wanted to ask me a few questions?" asked the woman with a puzzled expression.

"Yes, madam. May we come in. It will only take a few minutes" Wright said.

The door opened wider, the two detectives walked in and were guided to a large kitchen/diner at the back of the house.

"Would you like a tea or a coffee?" the woman asked.

"No............." began Wright.

"Yes that would be lovely. Thank you" interrupted Lane.

Wright shot her a look and she shrugged her shoulders.

A few minutes later, the kettle boiled and the tea was made. The old lady brought over a tray loaded with a teapot, cups and saucers, a jug of milk and three large pieces of homemade cake and put it down on the kitchen table. The three sat down and the old lady offered Wright and Lane a slice of cake. The former passed and the latter accepted with a smile.

"Can I begin by asking your name, madam?" asked Wright.

"Of course, officer. Marjorie Maidman" she replied pouring the tea, carefully holding the lid in place.

"May we call you Marjorie?" asked Wright politely.

"Yes, you may" she said looking over her specs.

"Thank you, Marjorie" Wright replied taking the proffered cup and saucer from her and helping himself to a splash of milk.

"Marjorie, can I ask, do you live here on your own?"

"Yes I do" she replied, sipping her tea.

"This may sound a little intrusive, Marjorie, but do you have many relations?" asked Lane.

"No, unfortunately, not. My parents sadly died a long time ago. I had a brother but he died of cancer a couple of years hence. I do have an aunt who lives in Australia, Sydney, I think" she paused with a faraway look and then continued "Yes, yes in Sydney but we aren't in contact. Can I ask why you want to know all this?" she said looking at Lane.

Lane looked at Wright.

"So do you have many friends, belong to many clubs?" asked Wright, completely ignoring her question.

"No, not really. I like my own company most of the time and I'm lucky enough to have a small private income which allowed me to retire early".

"You've been very helpful, Marjorie. Just one final question. Have you seen or been approached recently by a tall, blonde young man in his thirties or early forties?" Wright asked.

"No, I can't say as I have" she said screwing up her eyes and shaking her head.

"Is this what your visit is all about? Is this the man you are currently seeking? It was on the television. There was an appeal to the public with a description of a man connected to the murder of those poor women?" asked Marjorie looking at Wright intently with shrewd blue eyes.

"I'm sorry, Marjorie, I'm not at liberty to say at the moment, but thank you very much for your time. You have been most helpful", said Wright getting up and walking towards the door. Lane followed him and then turned.

"We'll let ourselves out, Marjorie, and thank you for the tea and the cake was delicious. They were most welcome" she said.

An hour later, the team were all assembled back at the station and exchanged notes.

"Great work everyone. Marjorie Maidman is the only one that fits the bill" began Allan.

"Isn't she a bit old. All the others were young women" commented Callender.

"True but if we are to accept that the years that the films were produced correspond to door numbers and that he is working through the alphabet regarding street names, the fact that this lady has no friends, relations and is lonely fits the other victims' circumstances. Given that our killer is attacking at various times of the day, we need to stake out 109 Eagle Drive 24/7. Dev, organise an armed response unit to be in a ready situation if we need them. We need the back entrance covered by yourself and Mike. The rest of us will also be in unmarked cars on the opposite side of the street," Allan said turning to Patel.

"On it, sir" replied Patel.

Allan was about to continue but he was interrupted by García who had picked up a call.

"The DCI wants a word, sir" she said putting down the receiver.

Allan excused himself saying that he would return shortly to finish the team meeting.

Seated in front of Tom Clarkson, Allan sat quietly waiting while his boss made a show of being too busy to speak to him. After a few minutes, Clarkson put his pen down and sat back in his chair, his fingers steepled.

"I hope you are going to make an imminent arrest, Allan. I have the Super breathing down my neck and the Press are having a field day accusing us of being slow and incompetent. I am bound to say I tend to agree with them".

"My team have been working hard to find the killer, sir, and I have every confidence that we are close to an arrest. We believe that we have pinpointed the next victim's location and DC Patel is, at this very moment, organising an ARU to join us at that location when needed" said Allan steadily, looking the DCI straight in the eye.

"When will this take place?" demanded Clarkson.

"There will be a stake out 24/7, sir. I believe the killer will strike imminently".

"So, by tomorrow night then, the murderer will be in custody. Is that correct?"

"That is what we are aiming for, sir".

"I don't want to hear words like 'aiming', Allan, I want a definitive answer from you!" said Clarkson his face flushing red.

"Yes, sir".

"I can't delay a press conference for long and when we do have that conference, I want to relay a positive message. In other words, Allan, I want results. I will hold you personally responsible if anything goes wrong! Do you understand?"

"Completely, sir. Was there anything else, sir?" Allan asked with his most innocent expression.

Clarkson couldn't make out whether he was being mocked or not.

"That'll be all, Allan and close the door on your way out" he ordered, already feigning interest in the papers on his desk.

Allan shut the door quietly behind him.

Back in his office, Allan called in Callender and García.

"I am going to ask if one of you would be comfortable in taking the place of Marjorie Maidman. If we have worked it out correctly, the killer is going to strike very soon. We can't risk the life of an unsuspecting civilian. If you don't want to take that risk, you don't have to. It won't reflect on you adversely if you say no, but it goes without saying that it would be greatly appreciated if one of you could help with this" he said looking at each of them earnestly.

"I am very happy to do it, sir. Just give me my instructions" said Callender before García could speak.

"That's great! Thanks Sophie! You will be told everything you need to know shortly" said Allan beaming at her.

Callender and García left the office and Allan followed, grabbing his coat and keys, before collecting Szymanski.

"Where are we going?" she asked.

"Paying a visit to Marjorie Maidman. We need to get her out of there so that Sophie can take her place.

It was mid-afternoon and the weather had remained fine and clear. The unmarked police cars were in place and Eagle Drive was quiet, it not being a through road.

"So, how are things at home, Julia?" asked Allan. They were sitting in Allan's car and had taken the opportunity of eating their baguettes while watching 109 across the street for any movement.

"Good thanks, Jack. Sylas has finally moved out!" she said taking a bite into her cheese and salami baguette while keeping her eyes peeled on the target house.

"You must be relieved. Did he go back to Poland?" asked Allan munching his prawn and avocado baguette.

"Not sure! We woke up this morning and he had gone. His bag and what little stuff he had with him had disappeared. What was weird though, he didn't leave a note. Nothing. It was as though he had never been there!"

"Did you find out what was troubling him?" asked Allan with a sideways glance at his colleague.

"No, we didn't. We both tried to encourage him to open up but he just wouldn't. Maybe he had got over being dumped. That's what Sally and I think, anyway. Perhaps he'll contact us again and explain. You never know!" replied Szymanski screwing up her paper bag and brushing the crumbs off her trousers.

"Thanks, Julia, this car has just had a valet!" Allan remonstrated.

"Sorry, Jack" she said without any hint of remorse and a twinkle in her eye.

Allan finished his baguette and put the bag into the glove compartment to be disposed of later.

"What was that?" Szymanski sat upright, staring intently towards 109.

Allan lifted his binoculars and scrutinized the area. Using his walkie talkie, he spoke to Wright and García, who were parked a little way up, on the other side of the house but the same side of the street as them.

"Did you see a shadow moving near the house?" he asked.

"Yes, possibly. Do we wait?" asked Wright.

Allan looked up at the first-floor top window which, up until now, had been in darkness. Callender had been told to switch the light off and on three times if she heard an intruder in the house. There was no light and the window remained dark.

"No move yet!" he said and immediately alerted the ARU to join them. Within minutes they had arrived and were in place.

Ten further minutes passed and all eyes were still glued to the house. Suddenly, the lights flashed three times in the window.

Allan was on the walkie talkie.

"All units move in, I repeat, all units move in. We have a go situation!" he barked as he got out of the car and raced across the road closely followed by Szymanski.

The armed police shouted their entrance and moved in single file into each downstairs room. Others filed upstairs. They checked on Callender in the main bedroom and filed into each of the bedrooms. As each room was checked they shouted that it was clear.

Downstairs, it was the same.

"Clear, there's no-one here, sir, but a pane of glass in the kitchen window has been broken, so unless it was already like that, my guess is that someone did break in but decided not to go any further. Probably ran off down the back alley" said the leader of the ARU.

"But if they had, sir, surely they would have been caught by Dev or Mike at either end of the alley?" exclaimed Szymanski.

Allan was already speaking to Patel and Townsend on the walkie talkie.

"Nothing, sir. There was no movement here. No sign of anyone" replied Patel to his boss' question.

"Same here, sir. Nothing stirred," said Townsend.

"So how the hell did he get past you and why did he break the glass and not go any further? Most important, where is he now?" Allan stamped his foot and ran his fingers through his hair, one arm on his hip.

Callender joined them.

"What exactly did you hear, Sophie?" asked Allan.

"Breaking glass, sir".

"And then?"

"I thought I heard someone come up the stairs and there was a scraping noise. I can't place what it was but, in any case, I must have been mistaken because there is no-one here".

"Okay, thanks, everyone. I'll get forensics to do their work on the back door, stairs etcetera to see if this bastard has left us any identity clues. Otherwise, I'll see everyone back at the station first thing tomorrow" said Allan.

Twenty minutes later, the house was silent. The police presence had gone apart from a police cordon around the house and Allan sat deep in thought in his car, Szymanski in the passenger seat.

"Penny for them, sir" she said putting her seat belt on.

"If there was no way that the killer, and he was definitely there, the broken windowpane in the kitchen door proved that, could have escaped either from the back or the front of the house then……."

"Then he must be still in the house!" said Szymanski finishing Allan's sentence.

They were both out of the car in seconds. Running over the road, they entered the house through the front door.

While Allan and Szymanski were talking in the car, upstairs in the house there was a scraping noise and the loft hatch was moved back. Two legs swung down on the banister of the landing and the figure dressed all in black, after replacing the hatch, made its way down the stairs, out of the back door and into the garden.

"Police, stop right there!" shouted Allan as the dark clothed hooded figure continued running up to the fence and vaulting over the top.

Szymanski was already out of the side gate and into the alleyway running hard after the suspect. Allan was close on her heels and soon overtook her. The suspect was fit and darted into the side street running over the road and down another alley. Allan signalled to Szymanski to try to cut the culprit off while he continued to chase behind. The suspect was light of foot and very fast, managing to get to the alley exit with time to spare, avoiding being caught by Szymanski. Suddenly, the figure stopped for a fraction of a second and fired a shot. Both Allan and Szymanski managed to avoid the bullet but the escapee gained more ground between them and their pursuers. The figure stopped again and fired two more shots and raced on. One bullet had grazed Allan's cheek.

"Jack are you okay?" asked a breathless and concerned Szymanski.

"Yes. It's a scratch. C'mon. We need to catch this guy" he said calling across his shoulder as he ran.

The suspect had gone into a building site and started to climb up the scaffolding on one side of a partly renovated five-storey office block. Allan and Szymanski climbed up behind him. The suspect reached the roof and fired shots down the ladder. The shots went wide of their mark and fortunately neither pursuer was injured. They pressed on upwards and climbed onto the roof. All was eerily silent and Allan and Szymanski stood completely still for a few moments, both catching their breath. They bent over with their hands on their knees but scouring the roof with their eyes. Then a shot rang out, giving away the rough location of the suspect. They both surged forward in the direction of the shot. Then they saw their culprit. He was standing on the edge of the flat roof. They were facing him but his face was in shadow and he was hooded so neither detective could get a good look at their suspect.

"Stay away! Any closer and I'll jump!" said a man's voice.

"It can't be! No, it can't be" said Szymanski in a whisper, her voice full of horror and denial.

"What? What do you mean?" hissed Allan.

Szymanski didn't answer but walked slowly towards the figure.

"I said don't come any nearer!" the voice said.

"It's Julia, Sylas, it's Julia. It's over. Come down from there, please" she said in a steady, encouraging voice.

Allan stayed still.

"What? Julia! What are you doing here?"

"You know I'm a police officer, Sylas. That is what I am doing here. Now, please come down. We can work it out. Whatever you have done, I will help you, Sylas," pleaded Szymanski, an icy chill creeping down her spine as the awful realisation hit her that her old friend, Sylas Bukoski, was almost certainly the serial killer.

"No, no-one can help me. I have done terrible things. I'm going to jump".

"You aren't going to jump Sylas, if you were, then you would have done by now! Here, give me your hand and we'll go to the station together" and Szymanski walked closer and extended her hand.

"You are going to put me away, aren't you? I will go to prison, won't I? I'm going to jump!".

Meanwhile, Allan was quietly walking along the scaffolding towards where Bukoski was standing. It all happened in a few seconds. Just as Bukoski was turning to jump Allan came along behind him and give him a tremendous shove so that he fell on the roof at Szymanski's feet.

She cuffed Bukoski and then helped him stand up. Allan pulled off Bukoski's balaclava and revealed a mop of blonde hair.

Allan read him his rights.

Back at the station, Bukoski was put in a cell for the night.

Allan and Szymanski made their way to Allan's office.

"We need to nail Bukoski. We can't have any reason to let him go. The times of the murders, could he give you as an alibi? You need to check asap. Szymanski nodded.

"I should have put two and two together, sir. I would have to ask Sally to confirm about times in the day and I will check on the relevant times at night but, as he had a key, he could have come and gone at night without us knowing. I said that he did wander about at night, he said because something was troubling him. We now know what that was. I should have realised. I'm sorry, sir!" she said bitterly. Szymanski reverted to addressing Allan formally even though there was no-one around. Her face was abject misery.

"What two and two is that then?" asked Allan. The two were sitting in his office.

"Sylas is tall, blonde, the right age and as I said, he was acting strangely".

"Well, perhaps, *I* should have picked up when you told me of someone you don't know very well now, about the right age and acting strangely!"

"No, sir, you didn't have the full picture. I told you he was acting a bit odd but I didn't describe him to you. He is blonde, tall and ...."

"Listen, Julia, don't beat yourself up. Everyone knows if something or someone is too close you can't see the wood for the trees. He was a friend. It is natural not to suspect a friend. The important thing is, we have caught him!"

"Thank you, sir".

"And another thing, can you please stop calling me 'sir' it's driving me nuts!"

"Yes, sir, I mean Jack" she said smiling.

"Well, I don't know about you but I've got a home to go to! Good work today, Julia; but for you, he could have jumped!".

Chapter 23

The next morning, Friday 19th March, Allan strode purposefully into the general office area.

When he reached the incident board outside his office he turned to face the expectant and excited faces of his team.

"Okay everyone. First off, great work, all of you. I'm pretty certain we now have our serial killer in custody. Dev and I are going to interview him now and with any luck an uncomfortable night in one of our cells will slacken his guard".

Szymanski looked questioningly at him.

"Sorry, Julia, obviously normally you would be present at the interview but in this case, I'm sure I don't have to remind you that as the suspect is a friend of yours, you can't take part".

Szymanski was about to say something but then thought better of it and just nodded that she understood. Allan guessed she was feeling that telling her she could not participate was a bit rich considering she had asked Allan if he should think about stepping aside when Szymanski was briefly under suspicion of being involved in a recent crime concerning the spread of a virus. He felt sure she would say something privately to him later but he would face that when it happened.

In the meantime, Allan gathered his papers together and signalled to Patel to follow him as he went past. They made their way to the interview room. As they approached the door, Allan stopped.

"It is of the utmost importance that we do not let this bastard slip through our fingers. I would suggest that we employ the good cop, bad cop technique. You start by being sympathetic, I'll follow on and so on" Allan said looking at Patel, who nodded his agreement.

"Good morning, Mr Bukoski, I hope you slept well?" asked Patel in a kind voice.

Sylas Bukoski just stared at him.

"Let me order some fresh coffee for you" and he left the room. Allan sat and looked at his papers, not taking any notice of the suspect.

After a few moments Patel walked back in with three coffees in a cardboard tray. He carefully placed one on the desk for each person and then sat down.

"So, Mr Bukoski, we would like to ask you some questions, if we may" said Patel without indicating that the suspect needed to answer.

"I want a lawyer; I know my rights" Bukoski said gruffly.

"Of course you have the right to a lawyer, Mr Bukoski. Do you have a lawyer that you can call or shall we provide one?" Patel asked calmly.

"Provide one" said Bukoski.

Thirty minutes later the legal aid solicitor arrived and asked for some time with the accused.

Twenty minutes later the legal aid solicitor emerged and shook his head.

"Apparently, he has changed his mind and says he doesn't want me to attend. Bizarre!" he announced as he left.

"So, Mr Bukoski, we understand that it is your wish not to have a lawyer present. Is that correct?"

Bukoski nodded.

"For the tape can you speak please" asked Patel politely but firmly.

"No, I don't want a lawyer".

"Not a problem, Mr Bukoski. Now, as I said, a few questions. Why were you hiding in the loft of 109 Eagle Drive?"

"No comment".

"Why did you run away from the police last night?"

"No comment".

"Where were you between the hours of midnight on 3rd March and two o'clock in the morning of 4th March?"

"No comment".

Allan got up and walked swiftly round to where Bukoski was sitting. He slammed his right hand down on the desk in front of Bukoski with such force that the table shook and the suspect visibly jumped. It was the first time that the suspect had shown any emotion. Now his eyes were darting in all directions. Allan placed his face immediately in front of Bukoski's and spat his words out.

"I'm tired of playing games, Mr Bukoski, and when I get tired, I start to lose my temper. Are you following me?"

The suspect nodded but remained silent.

"Okay. Good. So, answer the nice policeman's questions. NOW!" he shouted at the end of his calm comments.

Bukoski visibly shook again.

"I was approached by a man in a pub who asked me to do him a favour. He told me that the lady who lived there was his sister and they had had a row. He needed me to get into the house to retrieve some papers that she wouldn't give to him and……"

"Don't piss me about! The truth…. NOW!" shouted Allan.

Bukosky shook again.

"Okay, I was burgling. Alright. I was there to do her place over. Satisfied?" asked Bukosky aggressively.

Allan went and sat down. Patel began his questioning again in a placatory manner.

"We still need to ask you some questions, Mr Bukoski. So, where were you between the hours of midnight on 3rd March and two o'clock in the morning of 4th March?"

"I was at a friend's house. I've been staying there while I've been in Britain. I came over from Poland a couple of weeks ago. She's a police officer here. She was there on the roof, last night. She'll tell you." he said sulkily.

"We've already asked her and she can't provide you with an alibi for any of the times and dates of the four murders. So, first off, I'll repeat, do you have an alibi for between the hours of midnight on 3rd March and two o'clock in the morning of 4th March?"

"I don't know. I've had some problems lately. I was probably out walking. I find that helps".

"What problems have you been dealing with?" asked Patel in a sympathetic voice.

"It's none of your business", the suspect snapped.

"Yes it is, when there is a murder enquiry" said Allan impatiently.

"Okay if you must know, I split up with a girlfriend recently" he replied.

"I'm sorry to hear that, Mr Bukoski. So, if I understand correctly you have been walking out at night but not with anyone and therefore you have no alibi for that night. If I were to ask you for an alibi for between five o'clock and nine o'clock on 5th March would you be able to help us there?" asked Patel.

"No. I can't help you with any alibis. I was probably walking. Now can I go?".

"I'm afraid not, Mr Bukoski, because you cannot provide alibis for any of the dates and times in question. Together with apprehending you in the house of a lady that we suspected was your fifth target, I think you are looking at a very long stretch in jail," Allan said, now assuming a calm and authoritative air.

Allan ended the interview and the two detectives left the room.

"It's all circumstantial at the moment though isn't it, sir" said Patel looking despondently at his boss as they walked back to the office.

"Yes, agreed, but we have a card up our sleeve. We have the Emily Henderson witness who spotted a tall man with blonde hair and the man who rented out films remembers a tall, blonde man. We'll get them in and see if they can identify Bukosky".

Allan's mobile rang.

"Allan" he barked.

"You're going to like this" said the familiar voice of Strange.

"I hope so, Stew, I need a break".

"We have tweezered a minute piece of cotton thread from the nail of Kim Watson. It doesn't match anything she was wearing. I have sent it to the lab to extract any DNA!"

"That I like! We have a suspect in custody. Can you arrange for his DNA to be taken preferably like yesterday?"

"I'll pop over myself now".

"Great. See you in a bit!"

Allan hung up.

"Now we are getting somewhere, Dev. Organise that identification line up as quick as you can" Allan said.

"On it, sir".

A little while later, Strange was led to the interview room where Bukosky was being held.

"What if I don't want my DNA taken!" said the suspect in response to Strange's request for him to open his mouth wide.

"Then that would be tantamount to an admission of guilt. After all, why would you mind if you have nothing to hide?" said Allan standing at the other side of the room with his arms folded.

Bukosky reluctantly opened his mouth and the swab was taken.

It seemed an age before Allan's mobile rang but it was in fact no more than an hour. He was back in his office and stopped drumming his fingers, taking the call immediately on the first ring.

"It's a match!" was all Strange said.

"Brilliant!" replied Allan and hung up.

He moved across the office in two strides and walked over to Patel.

"We've got him! Have you organised the identification parade?"

"Fantastic, sir. Yes, it will take place in a couple of hours' time. It would be great if one or both recognise him".

"The icing on the cake!"

It was late afternoon. Allan and Patel entered the interview room and Allan turned on the tape.

"We now have enough evidence to charge you with the four murders and attempted murder of a fifth victim. Your DNA is a match on one of the victims and two people have positively identified you as being at the scene of one murder and purchasing a relevant film. Together with the fact that you have no alibis for the nights in question, I am charging you with the murder of Lily Anderson, Emily Henderson, Stella King and Kim Watson and the attempted murder of Marjorie Maidman. You do not have to say anything but it may harm your defence if you do not mention when questioned something which you later rely on in court. Anything you do say may be given in evidence", said Allan.

"Are you sure you don't want a lawyer now?" asked Patel.

"No".

"Why did you commit these heinous crimes, Mr Bukoski?" asked Allan severely.

"I hate them!" he spat.

"Who do you hate?" asked Allan.

"Women. I hate women. You have no idea! You don't know anything about me! My mother, my birth mother, she went to the cinema and left me there. My first victim wasn't blonde so I had to put a wig on her. She had to be blonde because then she was my mother. I was brought up in a home and then by foster parents. Then I met a woman. I fell in love with her. We both loved old films. Had a passion for them. She was my world and then she broke up with me. The bitch. Anyway, good riddance, I thought in the end. Better off without her. Then I met another woman, a British woman, here in Britain. I thought this was it. Happiness at last! We went to see a film and she told me she had met someone else. That she was sorry but we weren't meant to be. That's when I vowed revenge. That's when I killed those women and I would have killed that other bitch if you hadn't mucked up my plans!" he ranted aggressively.

"You inflicted all your pent-up rage on four perfectly innocent victims?" exclaimed Patel.

"Yes. It amused me to dress them in the costume of a particular film and the dates of the films were the numbers of the houses where the victims lived. I researched well into that. I was lucky that my riddle worked and that suitable victims lived at suitable numbered addresses".

"We figured that out" said Allan grimly.

"Yes I thought you might but I hoped it would go on longer before you did" he said ruefully.

"Did you torture them before they died?" asked Allan levelly.

"Sure, I did. I crushed fragments of glass in a bowl. Then I cut their hands and feet and rubbed the glass into them very slowly with a scouring pad. You should have heard them scream. It was very satisfying. Then I strangled them to an inch of dying. They choked and spluttered, gasping for air, trying to survive. There was a look of terror in their eyes. It was gratifying. I was in control. I was in control of whether they lived or died. But, of course, they knew and I knew that living wasn't an option, that wasn't going to happen. Then I killed them".

"Where did you take your victims to torture and kill them?" asked Allan after a few moments.

"No comment" was the sullen reply.

"You have admitted killing and torturing these women. There is no reason to hold back where you carried out these crimes" said Patel.

"If I tell you, what's in it for me? I want to cut a deal" Bukosky said aggressively.

"You are in no position to bargain" replied Patel.

Bukosky just stared at them with a soulless expression.

"We can't make a deal with you; we don't do deals. However, if you cooperate with us when the judge hands out your sentence they may be more lenient than if you don't. Now I ask you again where did you carry out these crimes?"

"Okay. There is a lock-up at the back of Grove Street, that's where" he said reluctantly.

"You have the keys?" asked Patel.

"Yeah. They are in my wallet in the tray where the officer put my personal belongings. How do I know, now I have cooperated, that the judge will hand out a more lenient sentence?"

"You don't. Take him down" ordered Allan to the uniforms standing either side of the interview room door.

Both men sat at the table for some moments when the suspect had been escorted out of the room.

"Well, that was one of the most chilling admissions of guilt, I've heard in a long time!" said Allan.

"Yes, sir, horrific. Totally out of his mind" agreed Patel.

"Or just plain evil! Get forensics to meet us at this lock up as soon as and get the key from the duty sergeant".

"Yes, sir" said Patel who made his way back to his desk while Allan walked up the stairs to the DCI's office and knocked on the door.

"Come in!" said Tom Clarkson.

"Good afternoon, sir" said Allan as he closed the door behind him.

"Sit down, Allan. I hope you have some good news for me" he said with a hint of sarcasm and steepling his fingers.

"Indeed, I do, sir. We have the serial killer in custody. His name is Sylas Bukoski. He is a British citizen although he has been living in Poland for a while. He has confessed to all four murders and the potential murder of a fifth victim. We are shortly to examine the lock-up where he has told us he carried out the torture and murder of the victims. Forensics will, without doubt, be able to build up evidence of his DNA and those of his victims in the event that Bukoski tries to retract his confession".

"Why did he confess? You are sure that it is this man? After all you made a mistake before, Allan. You thought Manning was the killer and it turned out he wasn't. I hope, for the sake of your career, that you haven't made another unfortunate mistake!" Clarkson's tone was one of nasty satisfaction.

"He confessed because we told him we had evidence of his DNA found on one of his victims and he had no alibis for any of the dates and times when the murders were committed. Now that we also have the location where the murders took place, a lock-up in the grounds of a derelict factory, we will also have further forensic evidence. The case is watertight, I can assure you, sir" Allan replied.

"Well, I hope so, Allan, because I don't need to tell you what will happen if we hold another Press conference to the effect that we have apprehended the serial killer and subsequently it is found that *you* have made another mistake!"

"Will you be holding the Press conference this evening, sir?" asked Allan, ignoring Clarkson's threats.

"I will contact you when I have arranged it and be ready, Allan. Close the door on your way out" the DCI said dismissively while Allan privately wished his old boss, Jim Hopkins, would miraculously come out of retirement and take back the post of DCI from Clarkson.

As Allan entered the general office, Patel greeted him.

"All arranged with forensics, sir. They should have arrived at the lock-up as we speak".

"Well done, Dev. Let's go!"

The drive was a little less than twenty minutes. Strange was already there, as Patel had correctly guessed.

"Pretty gruesome, Jack" Strange grimaced as the two detectives walked into the lock up.

"That's an understatement!" muttered Allan.

A large table to the side was littered with large and small fragments of broken glass, a pestle and mortar and abrasive pads. There were knives of various sizes hanging from the wall above the table. A chair had been placed in the centre of the room raised on some sort of wooden dais. There were ankle cuffs attached to the front legs, handcuffs attached to the sides and chains around the back of the seat. Against the wall opposite was a long table with chains attached and above the table were various ropes, some covered with plastic, some not.

"Bukosky was one evil guy but at least he saved us the trouble of trying to locate this place. The forensic evidence from here ensures a conviction" said Allan grimly looking around.

"Do you think his sentence will be more lenient because he cooperated, sir?" asked Patel.

Allan shook his head.

"I doubt it! In my view, Bukosky should and will go down for several life sentences".

Allan's mobile rang.

"Sir, the DCI said the Press conference is taking place in one hour and he expects you back, in his office in thirty minutes to finalise the police report on the situation. He wants you to take the lead apparently" said Szymanski with a hint of sarcasm in her voice.

"Okay, thanks Julia, on my way now" Allan replied.

He immediately went to the DCI's office when he returned and made it with one minute to spare.

"I've just been to see the location of the murders, sir, and there is no doubt we have caught the killer" said Allan.

Clarkson gave one of his most insincere smiles.

"Good! I think, on reflection, I will take the lead on this one, Allan and you can sit and observe. Be my back-up but I'll do the talking. I don't need to discuss what should be said just leave this one to me" he said.

Half an hour later they were seated in front of the usual crowd of Press and photographers.

"Good evening, ladies and gentlemen, and thank you for coming today. As you probably all know my name is DCI Tom Clarkson and accompanying me is DI Jack Allan. Today we arrested and charged the man responsible for the recent spate of murders in Cambridge. A mistake was made in the first instance, the wrong conclusion was jumped to but there is no shadow of doubt this time. The location of the murders was examined this afternoon by the lead officer and forensics have ample evidence for a certain conviction. The streets of Cambridge will be safer tonight and this outcome, I hope, will be of some solace to the victims' families and friends. Now I am open to questions".

"Yes, you mentioned giving solace to the victims' families and friends, but I thought it was understood that none of the victims had family or friends?" asked a tall, dark-haired female reporter standing at the back of the crowd.

The DCI feigned an embarrassed cough.

"That is correct".

A few sniggers could be heard. The DCI was not a popular figure with the Press.

"So, where was the location and what were the details?" asked a short, fair-haired man dressed in a loud check jacket.

"Erm, that will all be explained later" said Clarkson who then tried to move on by pointing to another reporter.

"No, just a minute, I would like those details now. Can we hear from your colleague, Detective Inspector Allan? I believe he was the lead investigator. Perhaps he is more aware of the details of the case!"

More sniggering from the reporters.

"Detective Inspector Allan would you oblige with the details, please" said Clarkson as graciously as he could, displaying a wooden smile.

Allan proceeded to give the details that he had, if he was honest, held back in his earlier conversation with Clarkson. When he had finished, Clarkson took over once more and pointed to another reporter.

"What was the motive behind these killings?"

"A motive has been established but the details will be revealed during his trial".

Two more questions were answered by Clarkson after which he got up, raised his hand signalling the end of the conference. He walked out and straight up the stairs to his office.

When Allan reached the general office he was met by an excited buzz which stopped as he walked in.

"Well done everyone!" he said as he reached the incident board.

Everyone clapped and cheered.

Allan held up his hand.

"The Press are aware of our success in capturing this bastard who will hopefully rot in jail for the rest of his evil life!"

"Are drinks on you, sir, tonight?" asked Wright.

Allan grinned.

"Cheeky bugger! Yes, they are! Let's hit the Dog and Mouse!"

There was a scraping sound as the team pushed their chairs under desks and collecting their belongings, left for the pub. All that is, but Allan and Szymanski.

"Sorry, you couldn't be in at the end, Julia, but you knew the offender. It was tough but necessary that you couldn't be involved" Allan said as he started to take bits of paper off the incident board.

Julia bit her lip and remained silent, standing awkwardly by her desk.

"I know, I know, that's rich coming from me. Me who wouldn't back off the last case even though my girlfriend may have been involved. Will you ever forgive me? I was trying to……."

"It's not that, Jack. It's the fact that I didn't twig it was him. I should have done. I know you said that I shouldn't beat myself up about it but it doesn't say much for my judgement of character, does it? That's important in our job, isn't it?" said a forlorn Szymanski.

"Listen, Julia, look at me, please".

Szymanski turned to look at her boss.

"You are one of the best detectives I know. One day you will be the same rank as me and you will probably go higher than my rank. So, I don't want to hear any more of this self-reproach. Everyone knows that on a personal level we can all be blind, hoodwinked. Let's go and join the others at the pub. I won't be forgiven if I don't appear soon! The drinks are on me!"

Szymanski managed a smile.

"Thank you, sir, I mean Jack" she said.

Allan returned her smile and turning the lights off, they both left to join their colleagues.

Just as they got to the door, Allan's mobile rang.

"Hi darling" he waved to Julia to go on and he would join soon.

"Everything okay. I'm just going for celebratory drinks at the Dog and Mouse. Did you want to join?"

"No, no, you enjoy! Listen, they've accepted - 18 Wildflower Close – they've accepted! I'm so excited, I couldn't wait to tell you! I'm going to ring mum now. I think she will be thrilled for us; she did tell us to get on with living!".

"She did indeed and that's the best news! Now for the nail-biting bit!"

"Yes the chain could break, they could withdraw, all of that! But for now, life's wonderful isn't it?" she laughed.

"Yes, indeed! I'd better go! I won't stay long! See you soon! Oh, and, by the way, I love you!"

"Love you too! Bye!"

Allan was grinning all the way to the pub. Things were definitely looking up.

It was heaving with people drinking and chatting when he arrived at the Dog and Mouse. He pushed his way through and spied his colleagues in a corner at the far end of the pub.

"Sir, sir, over here!" Patel shouted above the din.

He waved and smiled, finally reaching the merry little group. Strange and one or two others who had been involved in the case had come along to join in the celebrations.

"What are you having, Julia" asked Allan bending down so as to speak closer to her ear.

"Spritzer, please, sir, thanks".

"Anyone else for drinks or are you all okay at the moment?" Allan shouted.

There were thumbs up from the team.

"We told the barman that you would be good for the drinks, sir" said Wright grinning.

"Good. I'm going to the bar. Back in a minute", Allan replied.

He pushed his way through to the bar.

"Hello, Jack" said the barman.

"Hi Pete, here's my card, just put the drinks for my team on that. Think Barry told you I'm good for the tab?"

"Yeah, no problem. I hear congratulations are in order?" Pete said with a wink.

"Thanks. We were too early patting ourselves on the back a few days ago but today there is definitely cause for celebration".

"Never doubted a successful conclusion – not where you are in charge, Jack!"

"Thanks for the compliment but it's a team win not just mine!"

"Nevertheless, you're like a dog with a bone; you don't let a case go until you are happy that it is well and truly solved! Now what are you having?"

"A pint of your best and a spritzer. They're not both for me by the way!"

The barman grinned.

Allan managed to make his way back to his team without spilling a drop. Handing Szymanski her glass, who nodded and smiled as she took it, he left her talking to García and sipping his drink he turned to find Strange behind him.

"First of all, Jack, I'm not scrounging a team drink. I'll be paying for this!" said Strange raising his glass of white wine and smiling.

"You'd better not, Stew. Consider it a thank you for all your speedy and thorough work" and he clinked Strange's glass.

They both savoured a mouthful of their drink.

"Must rank as one of the most horrifying series of murders that I have come across" said Strange, staring into his drink.

"I won't argue with that comment. It all began in his childhood. His mother abandoned him and then twice the women he loved went off with someone else" replied Allan swishing his beer around the glass.

"Seems like a poor excuse to murder four women and nearly kill a fifth" said Strange looking up from his wine.

"Oh, I'm not saying I understand it, I'm just saying what the suspect said was the reason. Let's hope there's not too many like him out there!"

"Indeed! Well, Jack, you have managed to solve the mystery of a cold case, rid the world of Manning alias Qiáng, a dangerous psychopath, and catch a serial killer, Bukosky. I'd say that's Game, Set, Match!" and he raised his glass again.

The corners of Allan's mouth twitched into a slight smile as he inclined his head.

THE END

Epilogue

Two weeks later it was a beautiful day in April. Sunny and warm with little puffy white clouds in a powder blue sky. The village church lychgate was adorned with shell pink, cerise and white roses. Some of the wedding guests were already in the church and more were walking up the path admiring the beauty of the setting. At last, everyone was inside and the sound of hooves on the road could be heard.

The open carriage came to a standstill and the father of the bride alighted, turning to help his daughter out. She carefully lifted the folds of her skirt and as she stepped down, her two bridesmaids quickly took hold of the train to avoid it dropping on the ground.

The skirt of the dress and train were pure white silk, the train being edged with lace to match the fitted bodice. Her veil, which was held in place by a sparkling tiara, was also edged with the lace. Her hair was piled up at the back of her head with tiny flowers showing here and there.

The foursome made their way into the church and the traditional sound of 'Here comes the bride' could be heard.

Heads turned and little gasps of admiration could be heard as Vanessa walked up the aisle.

She handed her bouquet to one of the little bridesmaids as she came to stand beside her fiancé.

"You look amazing, darling" he whispered looking at her adoringly.

"You don't look bad yourself" she said her eyes sparkling with happiness.

They both smiled and then took their vows.

"I now pronounce you man and wife. You may now kiss the bride" said the vicar warmly.

They turned to each other and kissed a long time. There were tears in the guests' eyes and someone said how emotional they felt. Others nearby nodded their agreement.

"I love you so much Mrs Allan".

"I love *you* with all my heart, Jack" replied Vanessa.

The bride and groom walked back down the aisle, the smile on Jack's face and the radiance on Vanessa's telling the world how very much in love they were.

Thank you for reading the second book in the DI Jack Allan series. I hope you enjoyed it!

I'd love for you to put a rating or review on the platform of your choosing, maybe Amazon, Goodreads and/or Waterstones.

Watch out for the next book in the series!

Printed in Great Britain
by Amazon